This Is Home

Also by Lisa Duffy

The Salt House

This Is Home

~ a novel ~

Lisa Duffy

ATRIA PAPERBACK

New York London Toronto Sydney New Delhi

ATRIA
PAPERBACK

An Imprint of Simon & Schuster, Inc.
1230 Avenue of the Americas
New York, NY 10020

First Atria Paperback edition June 2019

For information about special discounts for bulk purchases, please contact Simon & Schuster Special Sales at 1-866-506-1949 or business@simonandschuster.com.

The Simon & Schuster Speakers Bureau can bring authors to your live event. For more information, or to book an event, contact the Simon & Schuster Speakers Bureau at 1-866-248-3049 or visit our website at www.simonspeakers.com.

Manufactured in the United States of America

10 9 8 7 6 5 4 3 2 1

Library of Congress Cataloging-in-Publication Data

Names: Duffy, Lisa, 1970– author.
Title: This is home / Lisa Duffy.
Description: New York : Atria, 2019. |
Identifiers: LCCN 2018038412 (print) | LCCN 2018040360 (ebook) |
ISBN 9781501189265 (eBook) | ISBN 9781501189258 (pbk.) | ISBN 9781982115753 (library hardcover)
Classification: LCC PS3604.U3784 (ebook) | LCC PS3604.U3784 T48 2019 (print) |
DDC 813/.6—dc23
LC record available at https://lccn.loc.gov/2018038412

ISBN 978-1-5011-8925-8
ISBN 978-1-5011-8926-5 (ebook)

For my children, Samantha, Matthew, and Mia.
What is best in me I owe to you.

My lifetime
listens to yours.

—MURIEL RUKEYSER

This Is Home

Prologue

After John left, Quinn would lie awake at night and picture the look of shock on his face. The way he had woken up from the nightmare and stared at her as if she were a stranger in the bed next to him instead of his wife. The woman he'd known since they were kids. Teenagers with dreams and hopes. Wants and desires.

Perhaps her look mirrored John's. He'd come home from the war a different person. A stranger to her. Someone she moved around carefully, gently, as if he were a bomb, ready to explode.

Of course, there was the PTSD. A medical explanation for what Quinn thought of in simpler terms: an imaginary switch inside John's body that flipped suddenly and without warning and lit up the spaces inside of him that were dark and wounded and afraid.

Quinn thinks of the days when they were first married and she was pregnant with twins.

She'd picked out names, even though she was only in her first trimester. Matthew and Michael Ellis for boys. Michelle and Melissa Ellis for girls—she'd choose somehow if they got one of each. But only the *M* mattered. *Me* and *Me* is what they'd call each other. Their initials. They'd think it was a coincidence. But she had planned it. Dreamed it.

Imagine coming into the world with someone who looks like you? Someone who fills the space next to you as you grow.

When Quinn miscarried in the eleventh week, she told John she couldn't imagine anything more devastating in this life.

Looking back now, she thinks of how naive she'd been.

How wrong.

The sound of a trumpet fills the air around her. A folded flag is handed to her by a man dressed in a uniform, but under his cap, she sees the smooth skin of his face, the wisp of hair on his upper lip, and she realizes he is just a boy.

A boy just like John had been.

She wants to take off his cap, loosen his tie, and smooth the hair back from his forehead. She wants to tell him to take off that uniform.

To give her that damn gun.

She wants to lean forward and whisper in his ear:

Run.

Instead, she takes the flag and presses it against her chest to keep her heart from slipping out.

~ 1 ~

Libby

The year I turned ten, my father shot the aboveground pool in our backyard with his police-issued pistol.

I don't remember it, but I hear about it all the time. My father likes to tell the story at the bowling alley bar, when all eyes are on him. There's usually Wild Turkey over ice in the glass in front of him, or maybe a bottle of beer. Sometimes both. The story gaining speed with every sip. The guys egging him on, all of them off-duty cops, remembering the fall cookout in my backyard.

My mother in the kitchen with the other girlfriends and wives and the men outside in rusty lawn chairs watching my father scowl at the eyesore of a pool taking up space on his newly purchased property. Stagnant water the color of tree bark sat high against the rim, and the entire structure leaned off center, and someone called out: *Jesus Christ, that thing's a damn cesspool Tower of Pisa.*

The scum-filled pool had come with the house, and my father hated it. None of the guys remember who first joked about pumping it full of bullets to empty the water, but they all remember my father standing up, taking two steps forward, and drawing his weapon.

They say he shot that gun as if he were a cowboy in an old Western film, quick draw and from the hip, firing until he ran out of bullets and the pool was a wheel of Swiss cheese, dirty water spurting from every hole.

The story always ended the same.

The telling of it might veer in different directions, but the ending always looped back to my father saying: *Who was going to stop me? I'm in the biggest gang in town.*

The year my father shot the pool, I got out of bed most nights at midnight to sit with him when he got off work. That was six years ago, and my mother always said I was too young to be up that late.

But my father never sent me back to bed. He'd drink a beer, eat a turkey sandwich. Lettuce, tomato, mayo. Potato chips smashed between the bread. His gun belt on the table between us.

My night owl, he'd say as I slid into the chair across from him. *Just like me.*

Back then, you could slice our family crosswise like a sandwich. My mother on one side: Olive skinned. Quiet and distant. My father and I: Fair skinned. Restless and temperamental.

Then half of that sandwich disappeared. Cancer took my mother away pound by pound and then breath by breath.

Then the medical bills piled up, and our house went up for sale.

We moved into the middle apartment in Aunt Lucy's triple-decker after that. When we had no place to live.

Now it's just me and Rooster Cogburn and my father, Bentley, who everyone calls Bent, even me, which suits him.

We got Rooster Cogburn from the shelter. He ended up there after the police were called to his house for a domestic dispute. Bent was the one who showed up and dealt with the mess and then brought him to the shelter. When months went by and no one wanted Rooster, Bent took him home because he was a guard dog if he had ever seen one.

The vet said she'd never seen a lazier dog, but Bent ignored her, and now we have a ninety-seven-pound mutt who never gets off the couch. He sleeps on his back, with his legs in the air, like he's been shot.

He's no guard dog either. I've heard him bark a handful of times, and even then it sounds like a bored half-yawn type of thing.

Rooster and I go for a walk a couple of times a day, and we make it half a block before he sits down and stares at me. Looks at the bag in my hand, full of his stinking poop, and eyes me again. Like, *What? Deal's done. Let's go home.*

Me and Bent and Rooster don't live far away from anything.

If I lean out my bedroom window far enough, the tips of my fingers touch the dirty siding on the house next door.

Paradise is like that, though: everything stuffed in tight.

On the other side of town there's a four-lane highway that runs straight through to the city. There are stores and houses and restaurants up and down both sides. Like the folks who first came here couldn't decide if Paradise was a town or a city or an interstate, so they threw up their hands and made it all three.

Bent calls Paradise the groin of Boston. He used to call it the armpit, but then everyone argued with him and said, *No, no, no, the armpit is Allston*, which made sense because it's tucked in close to Boston, and Paradise is farther out. Bent changed it to groin, and whenever he says it, folks get riled up, especially at the bowling alley with all the locals standing around. They'll whip their heads around and mutter things like *Whoa!* or *What did you just say?* even though they heard exactly what he just said.

Me and Desiree just look at each other and shake our heads because it goes the same every time, and Desiree swears Bent says it just for the reaction.

Plus, it doesn't make any sense because Paradise is north of

Boston and out by the ocean, so technically if this town is a body part, and Boston's the heart, then we're something like the left eyebrow.

Maybe an earlobe.

Aunt Desiree lives in the apartment above us with Aunt Lucy, and even though they're sisters, they look nothing alike. Mostly because Desiree is several shades darker than Lucy even in the dead of winter because she's in the tanning booth twice a week. Desiree's a former fitness model who bartends at the bowling alley.

She moved in last month after she broke up with her boyfriend. It was only temporary, she told me while I helped her carry boxes into the back bedroom. I didn't mention that me and Bent living here was only supposed to be temporary too.

You have to be careful with Desiree—she has a way of taking things the wrong way. Not with me, because I keep my mouth shut about most things.

Bent and Lucy never do, though.

Just yesterday, Desiree said she was so hungry she could eat a horse and Bent said, "Well, what's new?," and Desiree put her hands on her hips and snapped, "Is that some sort of fat joke?"

I knew all he meant was that she's always hungry because she never eats. Bent just shook his head and walked away. Which is pretty much his standard response when Desiree gives him her attitude.

I don't blame him. Desiree has fingernails that could gouge your eyes out—bright red and long and sharp—and an edge to her that rubs people the wrong way. Nobody messes with her. Like ever.

Bent's a policeman in Paradise, and even though he's the worst bowler in the police league, he always gets a spot on the team. Desiree thinks it's because he always buys the first round of beers, but I think it's because he came up with the name Ball Breakers and had all the shirts made with last names printed on the back, and now they can't kick him off without feeling bad about it.

Lucy's the only woman on the team, and she always gives Bent a look when I tag along. The first night I showed up with him, she walked right up to us and pointed to the clock on the wall.

"Nine o'clock, Bent. She has school tomorrow. She should be home doing homework or taking a shower. Doing teenager things. Not sitting in a crappy bowling alley."

"It's not crappy in here," Bent answered, sounding offended from the tone of his voice. "And stop overreacting. You know Lib's not your typical teenager."

"Well, maybe she wants to be," Lucy snapped. "Did you ever think of that?"

"Well, maybe I want to be Cinderella," Bent said, and went to the bar to order drinks for the team.

Lucy narrowed her eyes but let it drop. Probably because how do you argue with that kind of logic?

Bent Logic, me and Desiree call it.

The kind that makes no sense.

Lucy just put her arm around my shoulders and brought me over to the team, fussing over me and bringing me more snacks and water than I could consume in a week's time.

For the most part, Lucy, Bent, and Desiree all get along, but living in a house together isn't always easy, and even though they're all adults in their thirties, they play their parts perfectly.

Lucy's the bossy oldest, Bent's the free-spirited middle child, and Desiree, the baby, doesn't listen to a word either of them says.

In this case, though, with me showing up at the bowling alley on a school night, Bent wasn't altogether wrong telling Lucy she was overreacting. I'm at the pediatrician every single time Lucy gets involved.

A small splinter is relayed to Bent as a tree limb wedged in my hand.

A low-grade fever means I'm on the verge of a seizure.

And forget about the time I tumbled in the waves at the beach and couldn't figure out which way was up or down, so by the time I surfaced, I was gasping and blue lipped. We went straight to the emergency room for that because Lucy was convinced I was drowning from the leftover water in my lungs. She kept shaking my shoulders on the ride to the hospital, while Bent gritted his teeth and stared straight ahead, telling her to calm down every time she shouted *Libby, stop closing your eyes! Don't fall asleep because you WON'T WAKE UP*.

That was the last straw for Bent. They got in a big fight over that when we got home, and Lucy said if Bent thought he could raise me better all by himself, then he should go ahead and *do just that and she'd mind her own business.*

Which really meant she took her extra toothbrush out of our bathroom, stomped upstairs, and then texted me: *supper here when ur ready unless u want chef boy-r-d at ur place.*

When Bent says I'm not your typical teenager, what he means is we're not your typical family.

Bent keeps the craziest hours because he's a cop and a workaholic. If he's not working the night shift, he's picking up a detail. Most nights, Lucy or Desiree sleep in the spare bedroom.

And now some creepy lady lives downstairs. She moved in a couple of days ago, but she hasn't left the apartment yet.

Like at *all*. Well, that's not true. I saw her leave in the middle of the night dressed all in black. Pants and a huge sweatshirt with the hood up, even though it's a million degrees outside.

I've decided she's a serial killer.

Which is what I've been explaining to Bent for the last ten minutes.

It's Wednesday. The first one in August.

The heat is making Rooster Cogburn hang his tongue out and pant, even though he hasn't moved since I took him out for a walk an hour ago.

Bent is still in his uniform, and there's a crease in his forehead. He keeps looking over at his bedroom, and I know he'd rather be sleeping than listening to me. He's just coming off a double, and he's working a detail in six hours, so I have to talk to him before he goes to bed. He knows this, so he's doing his best to stay awake and listen to me.

"You said we were going to move to a real house," I tell him. "Just us. No people upstairs or downstairs."

"Those *people* are your aunts. And they help me with you. I can't be at work and home, Libby."

"I don't need anyone to stay with me. I'm almost seventeen. Besides, Lucy snores and Desiree turns on the blender for her protein shake before the sun's even up."

Bent clears this throat again and ignores me.

Rooster Cogburn rolls over onto his back, and suddenly there's a dead smell in the air. On top of being the laziest dog in the universe, he's also the smelliest.

"Now there's a serial killer downstairs. She's going to chop me up and take a bath in my blood."

"What?" He gives me a look and eyes Rooster. "Get up, bud. Come on." Bent nudges him with his toe and waves at the stench in the air between us.

Rooster sleeps straight through the nudging and the smell.

"It was on TV the other night. Some crazy Hungarian lady killed a hundred girls."

"I told Desiree I don't want you watching horror movies."

"It was the History channel."

I don't mention that it was after midnight when I watched it on my laptop with headphones because Desiree was in the bedroom next door arguing with her ex-boyfriend.

Rooster's sitting up now and rubbing his head against Bent's leg, leaving a strip of gray fur on his uniform. I can tell by the way Bent's jaw is jutting out that he's had enough of this conversation, and when he snaps his fingers at Rooster to get him to stop getting hair all over the same pants he has to put back on in six hours, I know enough to shut up already.

Bent goes into his bedroom, and I hear him change out of his clothes, and then the bed squeaks.

Rooster Cogburn walks over to me and puts his head in my lap.

When we got Rooster from the shelter, he was a day away from dying. He was on the euthanize list until Bent heard about it and decided he could stay with us. It was supposed to be only until we found him a good home. That was more than a year ago.

"You hate it here too, don't you?" I whisper to Rooster, but he only wags his tail so hard it bounces off the back door, thumping against the wood and making so much noise that Bent calls out that me and Rooster need to hush or leave if he's ever going to get any sleep.

I want to call back to Bent that we *should* leave. And go back home.

But I don't.

I just sit in the heat with Rooster's big head in my lap, his stench filling the air around us, and don't say a word because I know what Bent's answer will be.

This is home.

2

Quinn

Quinn doesn't know exactly how she ended up in this house. Lying in the dark in her new apartment, she closes her eyes and tries to piece it together.

The logistics of it, she understands.

But *how* is the question she keeps coming back to—the thing that keeps her awake at night.

Her husband left her. That's the long and short of it. She knows how to make it pretty in her mind. Dress it up with a fancy diagnosis. Words like *post-traumatic stress. Comorbid condition. Major depressive disorder.*

But still there is the sound of the door slamming shut. Of the truck pulling out of the driveway. And the silence that followed. The loudest noise she'd ever heard—that silence.

He's been gone five and a half weeks, but that night is still fresh in her mind.

How she'd sat in the dark at the kitchen table and stared at the door, feeling as though the night had somehow split her and John in two, severed them in a way that left her faceless and disposable. As though she no longer had any idea who she was or what she wanted.

She'd called John's cell phone after he left. Even though she knew he wouldn't answer.

She called him several times a day that first week. Left messages like *Call me* and *It's not your fault*.

After two weeks, she came home to an envelope taped to the door. Inside was a typed letter from the landlord telling her the lease had expired and would not be renewed. She had until the end of July to vacate.

She hadn't been surprised—the landlord lived on the other side of the thin-walled duplex. Of course, he'd heard them arguing, heard John in one of his night terrors, the screams raw and startling, echoing throughout the house.

Quinn had simply sat on the steps, the letter in her lap, too tired to even go inside. That's how Bent had found her.

She hadn't even heard the police car pull up in front of her house or the sound of his boots on the paved path to her front door.

She only looked up when he said her name and—even then—she was outside herself, as though she were looking down from somewhere above, watching some stranger sitting on the steps with a letter smoothed out on her lap, studying it as though it were a map guiding her instead of a piece of paper telling her to pack up and leave. A letter saying: *This is not your home.*

The rest is a blur.

Weeks of packing and moving, and now she is here, in this strange house with boxes filling the front room and the living room rug rolled up and stacked in the foyer and the kitchen table leaning against the wall, its legs scattered on the floor beside it.

Bent had offered to help her get settled, but he'd done so much already, and Quinn didn't feel right accepting any more help.

That was days ago, and she hasn't unpacked.

She hasn't really *done* anything besides walk around this apartment in a daze.

She called in sick to work on Monday, and then again today,

and she could sense Madeline's fury through the phone—her sons would need to have breakfast and be driven to school and picked up in the afternoon and fed dinner—and Quinn's absence was difficult.

That's how Madeline put it—*Of course, I'm sorry you're ill, but rearranging my schedule is difficult.*

She doesn't like to disappoint Madeline. And she misses Nick and Nate—she's been their nanny since they were infants, after all. Some days she thinks her job as a nanny to the twins is the only thing that keeps her sane.

With John deployed twice in their five years of marriage, gone for a year the first deployment and two the second, Madeline and the boys have become her family, her home away from home.

She loves the routine of her job and most of all, the feeling of being needed. Being part of a family.

When John came back from Iraq earlier this year, after his second deployment, she thought that might change. Now, finally, they could start their own family. Except he wouldn't touch her.

It became a thing between them: sex. The lack of it. How he never wanted her anymore. The unspoken argument behind every shouting match.

John said they were fine. That all couples go through ups and downs, and after all, they had been together since they were in high school.

If she had wanted to strike back, to hurt him, she could've said: *Define together.*

Together implies occupying the same space. Perhaps the same *country*.

But she didn't allow herself to say things like that to John. It was selfish, in her mind. This was his *job*. And anyway, it's not like she wasn't at least partly to blame.

Would John have enlisted if she hadn't gotten pregnant back then? Would they have even married?

They were juniors in high school when they started dating—although some days, she wonders if she can really call it dating, remembering the group of friends they were always with, the way they somehow ended up a pair. In her memory, he'd never taken her out on an actual date.

After high school, all their friends left for college. So did John. Quinn was the only one who stayed in Paradise.

Her father had been angry at her for that. But for her, college could wait. Her scholarship could wait. It was her mother who was running out of time.

The lung cancer she'd fought when Quinn was younger had returned, spread to her liver, then her brain, and her mother refused to live out her last days injecting that *poison* into her veins.

Quinn had spent the year when everyone was away at school taking classes in early-childhood education at the community college and caring for her mother and watching her father glare at both of them—mad at Quinn for staying and mad at her mother for not fighting harder and mad at the universe for handing him *more than any one person should have to handle*, a sentence he muttered under his breath no fewer than a dozen times a day.

When John called from his dorm, he'd sound restless to Quinn. Classes were hard—harder than he expected—and he was never much of a student anyway.

He'd been the star wide receiver for Paradise High. At college, he sat on the bench all season—the upperclassmen on the squad bigger, faster, stronger than him.

It's not like I thought it was going to be, he'd say, and Quinn would swallow her resentment. She'd have given anything to switch places with him.

And then everything after that blurred and blended and moved in fast-forward: her mother died, Quinn got pregnant, and John joined the service.

He hadn't discussed it with her. He surprised her the day they were married at the courthouse. After the ceremony, they were in the car when he dug in his pocket and pulled out a box. She was confused because the wedding ring was already on her finger. He flipped it open and inside there were dog tags. Fake ones, she saw when she picked them up. She looked at him, expecting him to laugh, to tell her it was one of his pranks.

But John wasn't laughing. His face was sharp, a flicker of something in his eyes that she recognized immediately.

The same look she'd see on his face in a football game when he'd walk to the sidelines and pull off his helmet after scoring a touchdown, his teammates slapping him on the back and John, emotionless, sitting down on the bench and staring back at the field, tracking the ball, waiting for the play, calculating his next move.

The look of someone who was needed. Someone who belonged.

John had reached over, put his hand on her stomach, flat still, even though two hearts fluttered inside of her. He leaned in and whispered, "When I meet them, I'll be a soldier," with such pride in his voice, such conviction. She only nodded, speechless.

Nothing in her life had prepared her for this.

She didn't know anyone in the military. Her mother's father, but he was dead, and she'd never met him, only saw an old black-and-white picture of him in his WWII uniform.

When she thought of people joining the army, she pictured southern boys in Ford trucks with oversize tires and flags hung in the back window. Midwestern farm boys born from a lengthy line of men who served.

Not John—kind, funny, oddball John with his lopsided grin

and sleepy eyes, so blue between his dark lashes sometimes she teased him for it, called him her *pretty boy*.

He saw the shock on her face, told her it was just the National Guard, insisted he'd never go to war. It was a weekend away, extra pay, help with college.

She envisioned him getting called to help in a natural disaster—maybe a flood down south or a tornado in the Midwest, or even one of the nor'easters in their home state.

But they both had been wrong. The Guard unit he'd joined went to war after all. A year in Iraq, to be exact.

Now Quinn opens her eyes. Gets out of bed.

It's the middle of the night, and she needs to be at work in the morning, but she can't sleep. Locking herself in this house for the last couple of days has her suddenly desperate to be outside, and she dresses quickly in the dark, not sure what she's pulling out of the suitcase on the floor and throwing on her body—leggings and one of John's sweatshirts, too hot for this weather but she doesn't care.

The desire to be anywhere but in this bare, dark bedroom is suddenly overwhelming. She knows her eyes are swollen from crying, and when she catches her reflection in the bathroom mirror, she pulls the sweatshirt hood over her head to hide her blotchy face.

Before she can change her mind, she is outside, keys in her hand, closing the door quietly behind her as though she's a teenager again and sneaking out of her house, slipping soundlessly into the dark street.

Minutes later, she's in the car, heading for the waterfront, the air blowing in through the open window humid and warm at this time of night from the heat wave that's settled in.

She parks in the town lot in front of the water, gets out of the car, and walks to the railing. Lights from the boardwalk reflect off the stretch of Atlantic in front of her.

She breathes in the dank odor of low tide rising from the rocks below.

Laughter trickles past her, and she turns to see a group of kids in the park, far off in the distance. Teenagers from the sound of it, the silhouette of a girl lounging on a swing coming into focus in the dark.

She and John used to come to this park when they were in high school. Late at night, after his football game, they'd park in front of the water. Sometimes they'd get out of the car and find a bench in the park and sit.

Paradise Park was a popular couples spot back then, but Quinn and John rarely kissed on those nights. They'd just sit and talk. Or sometimes just watch the ocean with the radio playing in the background. Both happy to be anywhere but home.

Years later, it was the same park where Quinn had met Bent for the first time. It seems like another lifetime now. She can close her eyes and picture the girl she used to be. But it's a hazy outline of someone she barely recognizes.

John had been deployed, Quinn remembers, and he'd called her late one night. She remembers the phone ringing and then John's voice on the line, seeming so far away even though the connection was fine. He'd called to tell her a guy in his unit was coming home, one of his bunkmates, and he wanted Quinn to meet him.

"I'm sending your present home," John had told her over the phone. "His name is Bentley. He'll be in uniform at the entrance of Paradise Park."

After they hung up, Quinn had rushed out of bed and hurried to the kitchen to write down the day and time of the meeting—Wednesday. One o'clock sharp—but in the back of her mind she was replaying the sound of John's voice. How he'd sounded different, speaking to her in a voice she'd never heard before.

The week had passed and then it was Wednesday. Quinn had strapped Nick and Nate into their car seats and driven across town. The boys were tiny then—she'd only just started the job and she knew Madeline wouldn't approve of her meeting some strange man with her boys in tow.

But Quinn wanted to meet the man who slept in a bunk near John every night. It meant something to her back then, to share this small thing. With miles and oceans separating her and John, and a war she didn't understand, this was something she could keep close to her.

She parked in a space in front of the ocean, put the twins in the double stroller, and hurried to the entrance of the park.

She was late, and in a rush, pushing the heavy stroller in front of her, and there was a noise next to her from the playground, and she looked over to see two boys chasing each other around the swings, one of them holding a stick out like a gun, shouting, *Bam, bam. You're dead.* A woman walked over and grabbed the stick from the boy, scolding him it seemed. He pouted, kicked at the sand.

When Quinn passed the little boy, she heard him tell the woman, *It's just pretend. Not real.*

Then she noticed the soldier.

From where she stood behind him, he looked just like John: tall and broad shouldered, standing with the posture of someone trained to be alert. To be ready.

He was standing on the wide concrete steps at the entrance of the park, dressed as if he just stepped off a tank in the Middle East, the desert camouflage uniform out of place against the backdrop of the New England coastline.

When she reached him, he turned and looked at her, raised a photograph and held it up: a picture of her and John from their senior prom.

"You're here," the soldier said, and she pointed to herself, joking. As if to say, *I'm here?* He'd come from the Middle East. She'd only driven the three short blocks to the park.

She asked about his trip home, and he held up a finger, interrupting her. He reached into his pocket, pulled out a small package, her name in John's handwriting on the front.

"Here," he said, holding the package out to her. "He'll kill me if I forget. And these days, I seem to forget everything." He tapped his temple. "They didn't send me home for nothing."

She took the package, glanced at the scar peeking from under his hat, running the length of his hairline to his jaw, a thick stripe of newborn skin, puckered and pink against the weather-beaten, unshaven slope of his cheek.

His name was Bentley. *Winters* was printed in black letters on his uniform.

"You're John's boss?" she asked.

"Sergeant," he corrected. "Well, former now, I guess, with the medical discharge. Bent." He held his hand out.

She shook it, her eyes on the scar. She wanted to ask if John was there when it happened, but the words wouldn't come out of her mouth.

He hadn't flinched under her gaze, and she sensed he was accustomed to women watching him.

He was handsome in a traditional way, older than her, in his thirties, if she had to guess. The stubble on his jaw reaching up to touch his cheekbone, a starburst of faint lines creasing the outer edge of each eye.

"Want to grab a coffee?" he asked, gesturing with his chin to the row of restaurants lining the water. "I can tell you about life over there."

"These guys are hungry," she lied, pointing to the infants. "I need to get them home."

She'd fed them lunch already. But she hadn't wanted to hear about life over there. She hadn't been ready to hear why John sounded like a stranger to her.

"Luke said you're a nanny. Toughest job there is, raising kids," he said.

"Luke?" Quinn asked.

"Oh, sorry. John. Luke is how he's known over there."

"Why Luke?" she asked.

He shrugged. "I think it started after some shitty patrol. All of us were spent. Working on no sleep and hungry and filthy. Falling into our bunks. There's John, taking apart his weapon. Cleaning it, wiping it down, putting it back together. Someone called him Cool Hand Luke, and the name stuck. Got shortened at some point, I guess. Now he's just Luke."

Quinn hadn't answered, the image of John, tired and hungry and filthy filling her thoughts.

"Hey, look, if you change your mind, call the station and ask for me. John said you sounded worried. If I can help, let me know." He looked around and sighed. "Never thought this shitty town would look so good. Paradise, huh?" He winked at her, gave a casual salute as a goodbye and walked away.

She watched him leave, the way he'd said *Paradise* lingering in her mind.

She thought of their duplex across town—the stained shag carpet that smelled like cat pee no matter how many times she scrubbed it.

Now Quinn blinks herself out of the memory and shivers, chilled, even though she should be sweating with the way she's dressed in the humid night.

She should leave. Go back to the apartment and try to get some sleep. She has to be at work in the morning, and she still has boxes to unpack—clothes to hang up and furniture to arrange and pictures to hang and, well—her whole life to put in order. The thought of it makes her want to curl up in a ball, pull the sweatshirt hood over her head, and just . . . disappear.

Instead, she climbs up on the hood of her car, leans back against the windshield, and looks up at the sky.

John should be in her thoughts, but all she can think about is Bent. She knows he's working tonight, and the thought of him patrolling the streets makes her feel safe somehow.

Brothers is what Bent and John call each other. That's why she'd called him that day, with John missing and the notice in her lap, and no idea what to do next.

It shouldn't have surprised her that Bent hadn't spoken to John in months. That he didn't know John was missing.

After all, John had been disappearing right in front of her for years. Little by little, growing more distant. More silent. More . . . gone.

And then that night when he'd told her he was leaving again. Signing up for another tour, even though he'd only just come home. And they'd fought, and she'd said that word.

Coward.

Right out loud before she could stop herself. It was the last word she'd said to him before he disappeared into the night.

She didn't tell Bent any of it. She didn't have the words to explain. She merely told him the truth. That John had left. Just vanished.

I'll find him is all Bent said, and Quinn didn't answer, only nodded, unable to speak the question that formed in her mind.

What if he doesn't want to be found?

3

Libby

The paint's not even dry on the wall, and Lucy is complaining about the color. According to her, the chi is all wrong.

Desiree squints at Lucy when she hears this, and I think I see fire shoot out of her nostrils. Probably because this is the third shade of brown that we've tried—none of them are giving off the right energy—and the foyer doesn't have any windows, and the temperature outside is in the nineties.

It's like standing in the hottest oven ever. Watching paint dry.

"You're getting paid to put up with this shit," Desiree mutters to me. "I'll be outside having a smoke."

I want to go outside with Desiree, stand on the porch with her in the shade, and try to cool off. But she's right. I'm getting paid to stand here and watch paint dry. Twenty bucks an hour, to be exact.

Lucy doesn't take her eyes off the wall, but she *tsk*s loudly, and I don't know if it's because Desiree is smoking or because she swore.

Helping Lucy with the house is my summer job. My other option was bagging groceries at the supermarket like I did last year, so when Bent pitched it to me in the beginning of the summer, it sounded like the easiest job ever, so I told him yes.

And then I found out Lucy thinks if we hang a mirror on the

wall within five feet of the front door, the good chi will bounce off and disappear.

Lucy owns her own real estate agency, but she's also a certified feng shui consultant who wants to be an interior designer. She's been flipping houses for years now—buying them for nothing, fixing them up, and reselling them for a better price. She's been so busy that she hasn't had any time to work on our house. Apparently, this summer, our house is on her to-do list, and I'm part of the equation.

Today, we're supposed to scrape off the old paint in the entryway of the house and apply a fresh coat. Desiree is only here because she's not paying rent, and Lucy suggested this would be a good way to chip in.

But so far, all we've done is listen to Lucy tell us that the staircase is facing the front door—a feng shui disaster that's affecting our well-being.

Awful chi energy, she kept repeating under her breath until Desiree told her that the staircase had been that way forever and that if Lucy said *chi* one more time, Desiree was going to smash the glass in the front door with Lucy's head.

So we moved on to paint, and now we're stuck again.

There are three brushstrokes lined up in a row on the wall, and Lucy's not sure about any of them.

She keeps glancing over at me and back at the wall, as if I might be able to help her decide, but it's so hot that all I can think about is the bead of sweat rolling down my neck.

Desiree stomps in from outside, smelling of cigarettes, and stands next to Lucy. She says smoking calms her down, but I can feel her anger pulsing through the room, and as usual, Lucy ignores her. She either doesn't care or she's so used to Desiree's temper she doesn't notice it anymore.

"What about that one?" Lucy asks, pointing to the color on the left.

"They all look fine to me," Desiree snaps. "It's brown. In a hallway. Who gives a shit?"

"It's not brown. It's ecru. There's a difference." Lucy answers serenely, lost in the colors on the wall, as though Desiree isn't about to annihilate her.

"Which one makes you feel peaceful?" Lucy asks us both.

"Don't ask us," Desiree says. "You're the feng shit expert."

"Feng shui," I correct, and Desiree glares at me.

My stomach growls, and Lucy breaks out of her paint trance.

"I thought you made breakfast," she says to Desiree.

"I did. And she ate. Tell her you ate."

"I ate," I say.

I don't mention that breakfast was egg whites sprinkled with some sort of brown seed mixed in that I tried to slip to Rooster Cogburn under the table and even he wouldn't eat it.

"I'm sixteen," I tell them. "I can make my own breakfast anyway."

"Preaching to the choir," Desiree mutters, and this makes Lucy put her arm around my shoulders.

"Of course, you can," she says in a soothing voice. "We know that you can. It's just nice to eat with someone." She says this the way only Lucy can say such things—so sweet and nice that you have no choice but to feel bad about being the jerk who gets mad about someone making you breakfast.

"Her stomach is growling because it's lunchtime. You managed to waste an entire morning on a staircase that can't be moved and paint that all looks the same."

Lucy ignores Desiree, and suddenly the front door opens, and a woman steps through the doorway. It takes me a minute to register that it's the serial killer who's just moved in.

She freezes, looks from me to Lucy to Desiree, apparently as surprised to see us as we are to see her.

The front door is wide open and the light behind her is blinding. I blink, and my eyes focus on the oversize black sweatshirt she's wearing, so large she's swimming in it, the hem almost touching her knees, only a sliver of shorts peeking out, and then just her thin, white legs.

I take a step away from her, bumping into Desiree and stepping on her foot by accident.

Desiree scowls and elbows me, her bony arm digging into my side, but before anyone says anything, there is chaos in the hallway.

Two small boys are chasing each other. Arms and legs and the smell of vomit surround us. One swings a plastic golf club and it whizzes by Desiree's head, so close a puff of her hair flies up.

The serial killer's eyes go wide, and she rushes to her front door, puts the key in, and pushes it open.

"Boys!" she yells. "Go inside!"

The boys tumble through the doorway and out of sight, disappearing around the corner, taking the noise with them.

Lucy, Desiree, and I haven't moved, and if the serial killer wasn't still standing in front of me, I might think I dreamed the whole thing. I glance at Desiree, who looks back at me, then down at her foot, her big toe bright red in her flip-flop.

"Quinn," Lucy greets. "Are you getting settled?"

"I'm so sorry," the serial killer named Quinn gushes. "He didn't get you with the club, did he?" she asks Desiree.

"She's fine," Lucy insists, and Desiree gives Lucy a look that makes me take a step away from her. "My gosh, you're making me sweat," Lucy adds, eyeing the sweatshirt.

"I got sick, and some of it got on my T-shirt. This is the only thing I had in my car," Quinn says. "I wouldn't normally bring them here, but we were at the park—"

"Oh, well go change," Lucy interrupts, taking her by the arm and guiding her into her own apartment. "Come," she says over her shoulder to me and Desiree. "We can watch the boys while she washes up."

And then they're gone, around a corner into another room.

"Go," Desiree says. "I hate kids."

"You hate everyone," I tell her, and she shrugs, like I have a point. "I don't want to go in there either. Why are we getting in the middle of this?"

Desiree snorts. "Because Lucy can't help herself. Ever since your father showed up with that girl, Lucy's been snooping around. Wouldn't surprise me if she went through the trash barrels outside. Nosy as all fuck."

"Bent brought her here?"

Desiree squints at me. "You didn't notice him moving her in? Carrying boxes? Hello?"

"I thought he was just being nice. Like helping the new tenant type of thing."

Desiree nods, as though she can see why I might think that. We have a ninety-seven-pound dog upstairs that proves Bent can't say no to anyone.

"How does he know her?" I ask Desiree.

But she's already stomping upstairs, leaving me alone in the empty hallway, surrounded by the bad chi from the staircase and the smell of vomit and the paint on the wall that looks to me like dirty brown stains.

The last thing I want to do is go inside, but I hear Lucy's voice, and I know it's only a matter of time before she comes looking for me and finds me standing here in the hallway, doing nothing.

I walk through the doorway, and the first thing I see, the only thing I see, is moving boxes. Stacked against the wall and still taped shut, as though she hasn't been living here almost a week.

The living room has the same built-in hutch as ours, and when I pass it, I see a picture frame on the shelf. There are voices coming from the back of the house, at least a room away, and I grab the frame, bring it close to my face.

It's a picture of two guys dressed in army uniforms, somewhere in the desert.

One guy is leaning against a tank with his helmet in his hand. He's young, maybe in his twenties, tanned and blond, with a face that Desiree would say is *movie star material*.

Only his profile appears because he's looking at the other guy, who's lying on his back, legs crossed, a cigar in his mouth, winking at the camera, as though he's on a beach in the tropics instead of a war zone. I squint and bring the picture closer, and that's when I recognize him.

The other guy—the one the movie star material is staring at—is Bent.

It's a minute before I realize I'm holding my breath. The memories of when Bent was gone turning my stomach inside out.

Five years ago, Bent went overseas with his Guard unit. It was supposed to be for a year, but he got hurt and came home early.

I'd slashed each day he was gone with a blue marker on the calendar in my room. Blue because Bent does a spot-on impression of Elvis Presley singing "Blue Christmas"—like if you close your eyes, Elvis is right in front of you—and it's impossible to see the color blue and not think of that, and when I do, it's also impossible to be sad. And I needed every reason to not be sad when Bent left.

When he came home early, I didn't flinch one bit at the scar on his head—if I could have thanked it, I would have. It brought him back to me. Maybe a little different—thinner and a little bit deaf depending on where you were standing when you talked to him. But otherwise, the same old Bent.

But he hadn't been home long before my mother took off.

I don't think his bags were all the way unpacked when my mother told him she was leaving. *A girls' trip* was how she put it.

She was the one who had been *on duty* while my father was overseas. She needed a break, she kept repeating. And from my bedroom, I remember wanting to ask—a break from *what*?

She flew south, to sunnier skies and warm weather, and told us she'd be gone a couple of days—a week at the most.

A week became two, then three. Then a month passed.

My mother and I talked on the phone once or twice a week, and she'd give me an excuse, explain why she needed to stay longer—her friend needed help moving to a new apartment or there was the threat of a tropical storm and she didn't want to fly in that kind of weather, a breeziness to her voice that should have been reassuring.

Except we lived in a two-bedroom house with thin walls. I couldn't pretend I didn't hear my father shout into the phone one night—*I'm not talking about me . . . don't do this to her.*

I didn't tell my father I was happy she was gone. That the air in the house was easier to breathe after she left. No more of her mood swings. No more coming home to one of her "bad days" when she'd lock herself in her bedroom all night or sit at the table with a blank look on her face, staring at the wall.

Maybe her vacation would help. Maybe a break was all she really needed.

The weeks passed and Bent and I settled into life together. Just us. He wasn't back to work yet, still recovering, getting stronger day by day.

Then I started getting headaches—migraines that had me lying in the dark, afraid to move. Bent would sit next to my bed, ask me what he could do. I'd ask him to talk—his voice helped block out the throbbing. He'd tell me about the guys in his unit. Or what it's like to fly in a helicopter. Sometimes he'd go back in time, tell me what it was like when he first joined the Guard, before I was born. How back then nobody ever dreamed they'd be on the front lines of a war so far away from home.

My mother came home finally, months later, and I know Bent hoped it was because she missed us.

But she'd found a lump in her armpit down in Florida. So, it was really the cancer that brought her back. Except that she never really came back. Not in her heart at least, where it mattered. Her body was with us, but she just walked around like a ghost. Like she was already gone.

After she died, people would say things to me like *I'm sorry you lost your mother* or *Cancer doesn't seem to care who it takes.*

And in my mind, I'd think, dying isn't the only way someone disappears.

4

Quinn

Quinn hadn't expected guests.

When she'd opened the door, the twins ran in and stopped in her bedroom. Quinn found them jumping on her mattress, and by the time she had them off the bed and settled down, Lucy and the girl were in the doorway, staring at the mess—Quinn's suitcase in the corner, spilling over, her underwear inside out in her pajamas from when she'd pulled them off early this morning, late for work and desperate to get dressed as fast as possible.

There is a stained mattress on the floor, a worn sheet in a ball at the foot of the bed. Cardboard moving boxes line the walls, some marked: *shoes*, *books*, *toiletries*. The one at Quinn's foot reveals a bra stuffed into a small wicker wastebasket, a frying pan, spice containers piled haphazardly on top of one another.

The sign of someone who packed hastily. Without care.

Lucy is politely pretending she doesn't notice, rounding up the boys, telling them she has a treat for them upstairs.

But the girl stands awkwardly in the doorway, shyly glancing around. Quinn feels her cheeks color, unprepared to explain why she's been in this house almost a full week and the only things she's unpacked are her toiletry bag in the bathroom, a single towel, and the picture frame in the other room that she dug out only to show Bent.

The bed frame piled in the corner is hidden behind boxes, and Quinn wonders if they think she sleeps like this normally. The stained mattress thrown on the floor as though she's some sort of squatter. A vagrant.

"I wasn't feeling well, so I didn't unpack yet. . . ." Quinn trails off.

The girl looks at her and gives a slow shrug, and Quinn wishes she didn't feel the need to explain—Lucy and the girl are in Quinn's apartment, uninvited after all.

But still, Quinn wants to tell them—this is not who I *am*. This is not *me*.

"It's better to take your time unpacking anyway," Lucy chirps, as though reading Quinn's mind.

Lucy gives her an encouraging smile. Quinn can't tell if she's just being nice or genuine.

"Don't rush getting cleaned up. I'm kidnapping these two ducklings for a treat. We'll be on the third floor. Just come up when you're ready. Let's go, Libs! *Choo, choo!* Follow the train, ducks! We're moving," Lucy sings as she leads the boys to the back stairway in the hall.

The girl follows sullenly behind, and she glances back at Quinn before she shuts the door, and the expression on the girl's face is unmistakable—if looks could kill, Quinn would be dead on the floor.

The door clicks shut when Quinn feels a lump form in her throat, and suddenly the room spins, and she barely makes it to the bathroom before she vomits again, the ginger ale she drank earlier to settle her stomach splashing into the toilet bowl.

She sits on the edge of the tub, reaches over to the sink, and turns on the water. Her single towel hangs on the shower rod above, and she pulls it down, holds a corner of it under the faucet, and presses the wet towel to her face.

She washes off quickly, feeling a panic rise inside of her that she's left the twins with complete strangers.

Madeline will be upset if she finds out—she doesn't like any changes to the twins' routine—and Quinn hopes the boys won't mention it to her. But it's likely they will—their days rarely include something outside of the schedule Madeline has dictated.

Preschool in the morning, followed by fifteen minutes of playground time. Lunch and a nap from one thirty to two thirty. The afternoon is tumble-time at the gym or reading at the library, depending on the day, then bath time, dinner, and Madeline is home at six o'clock (never a minute before) to spend an hour with her sons before their bedtime.

Madeline had the twins exactly one week before she turned forty, pregnant by an anonymous donor, and now the twins are almost five, and Quinn can't remember a single weekday that Madeline has not gone to work. She doesn't take sick days—and Quinn has witnessed days when Madeline should have been in bed—and she doesn't deviate from the schedule. Ever.

Their life seems to exist as a complicated sentence, the twins parentheses in Madeline's meticulously arranged life of speaking engagements, conferences, and whatever else went into being Boston's premier research scientist. The one and only *Dr. Madeline Lawson.*

But today Quinn is lucky. It's Wednesday—Madeline's late night, and the overnight nanny will relieve Quinn after dinner.

And by tomorrow night, when they see Madeline for the first time in two days, this quick stop at Quinn's new apartment, with any luck, will be forgotten, and Quinn won't have to explain why she altered the twins' routine.

Still, Quinn rushes, and she is dressed and on the landing of the third floor less than ten minutes later.

The door is open, but Quinn sticks her head in, calls out a hello.

"Back here!" she hears Lucy say.

Quinn walks in and glances around. The floor plan is the same as Quinn's, yet the two apartments look nothing alike. Here, there is light and openness. Soothing colors on the walls, and furniture placed just so, giving the impression that the room is much larger than it is.

There is a couch across from where she is standing. Sunlight from the window washes over the plaid cushions—the same pattern as the hand-me-down couch in her and John's apartment when they were newly married. They'd had it in their living room only one week before the fabric on the cushions split wide open, bits of stuffing falling on the floor every time they sat on it. John had finally hauled it downstairs to the sidewalk and put a *Free* sign on it.

For a moment, she is back on that couch with John. Stretched out with her feet in his lap on the first night in their duplex.

They'd ordered pizza, and John had pushed boxes together as a makeshift coffee table. She was lighting a candle when John came up behind her, put his arms around her waist, whispered *first things first*, and kissed the side of her neck.

They'd made love on the couch, the pizza box unopened in front of them. By the time they were ready to eat, the pizza was cold, and John had given Quinn a sheepish look, told her that now that she was eating for two, maybe dinner should have come first. She'd laughed and corrected him.

Three, she'd said. *I'm eating for three.*

She still remembers the look on his face. How his eyes had filled, and he'd brought her close, kissed her temple and let his lips linger, breathing her in. As if she were the most intoxicating thing on this earth.

Quinn would do anything to stay inside of that memory, peel it open as though it were a Polaroid picture that she might step into. To go back in time, before she lost the babies. Before John deployed. Before he came home a different man. She has an unbearable desire to lie down, curl up on the couch, close her eyes, and stay in that memory.

But she hears the boys in the other room, and she is reminded that she is in charge today. The paid caretaker.

And she's no longer the most intoxicating thing on this earth to anyone—she's not even sure she's a wife anymore.

Can you be a wife when your husband has vanished?

Now she walks through the house and stands in the doorway of the kitchen, and Lucy looks over at her.

"Here she is," Lucy says brightly to the boys, as though they've been waiting for Quinn. But the boys don't even look up at her. "They're having a picnic," Lucy tells her. "Come sit."

The boys sit cross-legged on a blanket on the kitchen floor, paper plates in front of them. Watermelon and sandwiches, peanut butter and jelly. Lemonade juice boxes in their hands.

The kitchen is light—the walls painted golden yellow. A stark change to Quinn's kitchen downstairs, where shadows linger in corners and the dull, flat gray walls have an air of gloom.

In the middle of the room rests a large round table, where Lucy and the girl sit across from each other, a plate of sandwiches and a bowl of fruit between them.

Quinn crosses the room and pulls out the chair at the far end of the table.

"Oh, not there," Lucy says, motioning Quinn to move over a seat. "It's under the beam. That one's better."

Quinn looks up at an exposed wooden beam that runs the length of the kitchen. Two bamboo flutes with silky red tassels hang from it, and when Quinn looks back at Lucy, she sees the girl smirk out of the corner of her eye.

"It's not healthy to sit under a beam," Lucy explains. "Cuts you up. The bamboo helps. I'd take away the chair, so people wouldn't sit there, but then it's an odd number of chairs."

"And then someone is left out," Quinn replies, and Lucy's eyes go wide.

"Do you practice feng shui?" Lucy asks with such enthusiasm that, for a moment, Quinn considers lying to her, but she shakes her head.

"I interned in a special education classroom when I was getting my degree. One of the mothers was very into it . . . I guess I picked up a few things."

Quinn doesn't mention how the teacher made exasperated faces while recounting how the mother believed her son's autism might be helped by positioning his bed in the right place in his room. She felt protective of the mother, even though she didn't know her very well.

Would it hurt to try? she remembers thinking.

Quinn is still standing and Lucy gestures to the chair next to the girl. Quinn slides in, and the girl shifts in her seat, away from Quinn.

Quinn doesn't move, feeling as though she's done something wrong—although she doesn't know what that may be. The feeling is familiar, and a moment passes before she's able to place it.

And then it occurs to her. She knows this feeling from John.

After he came home from his second deployment last year, she would slip under the covers in bed at night and turn to him, and he would move ever so slightly away from her.

Quinn remembers it as an almost imperceptible movement—a shift in John's weight on the mattress, the roll of his hip, the turn of his shoulder—yet this almost imperceptible movement would cause an earthquake inside of Quinn, her entire world crashing down. John's muscled back suddenly a wall between them.

Her heart would race, and her limbs would tremble, and she would lie silently next to him, both angry and ashamed in equal measures. Angry at him for refusing to talk to her. Ashamed that he no longer wanted her.

Now Quinn keeps her body still. She doesn't know why the girl doesn't want to be near her—they've never really met before, she and Bent's daughter. Libby is her name, she recalls. She can see the resemblance to Bent—through the eyes mostly, deep set with the same dark color.

But Quinn dismisses it. She doesn't have time to dwell on it—she needs to get the boys home for their nap.

"Thank you so much," Quinn says to Lucy. "For taking them. And feeding them. All of it."

"Oh, please. We should be thanking you. You saved me and Desiree from killing each other in the hallway," Lucy says. "Do you feel any better?"

Quinn nods, even though the plate of sandwiches in front of her is making her stomach turn. "Much better. I think it's just the heat."

"So I've met the boys." Lucy gestures to the twins. "Nick has the freckle on his cheek and Nate doesn't. Right?" she asks, and the boys nod, their mouths full. "Thank gosh for the freckle or you could never tell them apart!"

Quinn smiles. She hears this often. The truth is, the boys' personalities are nothing alike. And Quinn knows their faces so well she can't imagine not being able to tell them apart.

"So tell me about you," Lucy says, turning to Quinn. "I usually rent the apartment, but I've been swamped at work. And then my brother found you and told me to butt out. So all I know is what I could get out of these two—that you're a nanny, and you're pretty, and they call you Kinny."

"They have a hard time with the Q. It drives their mom crazy. She's constantly correcting them. She's worried they'll never get it right. I think it's cute. I hope they don't outgrow it." Quinn is rambling on purpose, hoping to steer the conversation back to the boys. She isn't prepared to answer questions about her own life.

"Where are you from?" Lucy asks pointedly.

"Paradise," Quinn replies.

"How do you know my father?" the girl interrupts loudly, her voice making Quinn jump. Quinn has never heard her speak.

"Libby," Lucy warns, frowning.

Quinn turns and studies the girl.

She is thin and freckled, with hair so blond it's almost white. Sweet is the first thing that comes to mind when you look at her. The voice that comes out of her is anything but. Low and gritty—it's a voice that reminds Quinn of whiskey and dimly lit bars, the kind that line the waterfront in downtown Paradise.

Before Quinn can answer, the woman Nick almost whacked with a plastic golf club walks into the kitchen wearing skintight bike shorts and a tank top. She's tiny, barely five feet tall, and cut from stone, not an ounce of fat on her chiseled figure.

Quinn suddenly feels enormous in her own shorts and tank top, even though she knows she's not—flat chested and boy hipped if anything.

"Are you coming or not?" the woman says to Libby. "I'm gonna be pissed if you make me late. I have spinning at one o'clock."

"Language, please," Lucy says, tilting her head at the boys. "I apologize for my niece and sister," she says to Quinn. "They're not normally so *rude*."

"I'm Desiree," the woman says to Quinn, ignoring Lucy. "The normal sister."

Quinn smiles, holds up her hand.

"Go get dressed," Desiree tells Libby, who says a quick goodbye and disappears out the back door.

"And no flip-flops this time," Desiree calls after her.

She looks at Quinn and Lucy and scowls. "Only a teenager would wear flip-flops to the gym. No common sense."

"Libby doesn't need to go to the gym. Don't make her neurotic about her body like you." Lucy frowns.

"It's better than her hanging around here listening to you complain about the staircase. I'll teach my class, and then we'll hang at the pool for a bit. She can come to work with me and get dinner. You take her home when you're done bowling."

"No pizza or chicken fingers," Lucy instructs.

"Nice to meet you. Goodbye, small people," Desiree says to the boys as she walks by them.

The door shuts and they are alone, and Quinn knows she has to leave *right now* or there are going to be questions from Lucy—questions Quinn doesn't know how to answer. Like who Quinn is exactly, and how she's come to live in this house.

Which is a problem. Because Quinn has no idea who she is anymore. And she certainly doesn't have the words to explain how she ended up here.

"I have to go," Quinn blurts, gathering the boys. "Their mom insists these guys need a nap, even though I can hear them chatting away through the entire hour they're in their room." She forces a laugh, desperate to steer Lucy's focus away from her.

"I'm sorry about Libby," Lucy says, not taking the bait. "Since Sarah . . . passed . . . Libby's sort of . . . protective of her father."

"Oh—no apologies. Please." Quinn reaches for a plate on the blanket. "Come on boys, let's clean up."

"You leave everything right there—it'll take me two seconds."

Quinn thanks Lucy and tells the boys to do the same, and after they do, she takes them by the hand and hustles them toward the front door, while Lucy follows closely behind.

"Did you know Bent's wife?" Quinn hears Lucy call.

Quinn doesn't answer. She concentrates on wrangling Nate when he tries to sprint back to the kitchen. She finally gives up and hoists him up on her hip. She holds Nick's wrist in her other hand.

"Thank you so much. I really appreciate it," Quinn gushes, finally in the hallway, her foot on the first step. "You were so nice to let me get cleaned up and feed them."

Lucy follows her out to the hallway and stands on the landing. "Sarah was from Paradise too. Is that how you and Bent met?"

"Yes," Quinn lies. It slips out before she can think it through. But she hasn't prepared for this. It's the easy answer. Easier than admitting she knows Bent only because of her husband—the husband she can no longer locate.

As though he's a library book she's misplaced. A pocketbook suddenly gone missing. A set of keys she's lost.

Inside her head, Quinn thinks, *Oh, that husband of mine? He'll turn up. We just need to keep looking.*

The absurdity of it almost makes her laugh, right there in the hallway.

Instead, she waves goodbye to Lucy and hurries the boys down the stairs, her face suddenly wet with what she thinks is sweat until she reaches the car, straps the boys in their car seats, and Nate reaches out with a finger, presses it to her cheek.

"Kinny hurt?" he asks, a puzzled expression on his round-cheeked face, and when he takes his hand away, there's a single tear on his fingertip.

She didn't think she had any tears left in her—she's cried enough already to fill an ocean. And this makes her tired somehow, as though she thought she might be done with all the sadness. All the worry.

She feels a sob growing in her chest and holds her breath until it passes, refusing to succumb to it.

She doesn't want to upset him, this sweet boy, or his brother. It's silly, she knows. She's just the nanny. But she loves them. She has since the first day she met them.

She doesn't trust her voice, so she doesn't speak. Instead, she brings his hand to her lips, kisses the salty wetness from his hand, and the tear disappears between her lips.

She watches the evidence of her grief vanish in front of her, not a trace of it left on the small pad of his finger.

Gone just as quickly and silently and easily as her husband has vanished from her life.

5

Libby

Sully's isn't exactly a five-star restaurant. It's more of a bowling alley wannabe brewpub that some say is just a dive bar.

But it has two things going for it: it's a cop hang out, so it's safe, and Desiree is the bartender. Which means I get free food and unlimited lemonade, and she lets me sit at the bar.

So I tag along whenever she lets me.

It's busy here tonight, even though it's Monday, because of the police charity bowling event, and Bent has already texted me a million times for the update on his team's score, even though I keep texting back that they're getting killed.

Like in-last-place type of killed.

Desiree comes over with a plate of food and puts it in front of me. I ordered the chicken fingers and fries, but that's not what she hands me.

"What is it?" I ask.

It's a game we play. I order what I really want, and she brings me what she wants me to eat. The game is so old, I don't complain anymore.

"Grilled chicken. Baked potato. Green beans."

She points to each as she says it. When she sees my face, she raises an eyebrow. "If you ate what you wanted, your diet would consist of fried food and sugar."

"And?" Sully says from the other end of the bar. "She's the size of a twig. Let her eat what she wants."

Sully is Desiree's ex-boyfriend, who she just broke up with, which you think would be a problem because he owns the place and is therefore Desiree's boss.

But they've broken up and gotten back together so many times over the years, I can't tell the difference between them together and them not together.

I'm not sure they can either.

Sully walks over to me and hands me a bowl of butter and a salt shaker.

"Here. I'm used to her cooking. Take my advice . . . apply liberally."

Desiree scowls at him and holds up two fingers.

"*A*, I didn't cook it, your chef did, and *B*, the two of you are freaks of nature. You eat what you want, don't exercise, and you still look like that." Desiree waves her hand in our direction. "So, excuse those of us who have to work at it."

Sully screws up his face at her. "Work at it? Please. You live for it."

"What's that mean?"

"It means this . . . is normal." He points to himself and then to me. Then he waves his hand over Desiree's body. "This is an obsession. Don't pretend it's something it's not."

They're squared off in front of me and Sully isn't smiling, and Sully is *always* smiling.

Desiree pushes past him and shoves open the door to the kitchen, her dark hair swinging with the way she's just stomped away from us.

Sully leans against the bar in front of me, defeated.

"The kid thing again?" I ask.

He studies me out of the corner of one eye, squints at the question. "You know too much for someone so small."

"That doesn't make any sense," I tell him. "Plus, if you're over at my house at one in the morning arguing with her in the next room, you can't complain about not having any secrets."

"I came over to make up with her. She was the one that made it a fight."

Sully lives up the street from us in the same house he grew up in. It's where Desiree was living until she moved upstairs.

Bent takes every chance he gets to tell Desiree she better smarten up or Sully's going to leave her. Desiree always rolls her eyes and tells Bent he's just saying that because Sully's his friend.

But I think Bent just says out loud what everyone else is thinking. Sully's nice—like he'll-give-you-the-last-dime-he-has kind of nice—and Desiree?

Well, she's just Desiree.

"She thinks getting pregnant will ruin her body," Sully says to me.

"Well, she's kind of right. I mean . . . morning sickness. Weight gain. Probably some stretch marks. Not speaking from experience, of course."

I play with the straw in my lemonade, and Sully's eyes glaze over.

I don't know what's thrown him, but it could be any number of things. Lucy likes to say Sully is blessed with good humor and good looks, but good sense got away. This is as close as Lucy gets to an insult.

If we were talking in Desiree speak, she'd just call him stupid.

"Whatever," Sully replies. "She's the one that keeps bringing it up anyway. For someone who isn't sure she wants kids, it's all she talks about. I told her I'll do whatever she wants but that only starts another fight about how she has to make all the decisions."

He shrugs, sighs. "But you know what? One thing I know about your aunt. Talks a big game, but she can only stay away from the Sully machine for so long." He flexes his arm and kisses his bicep.

"Gross," I say, and he laughs and fills up my lemonade before he walks away to take an order.

The bar overlooks the bowling alley, and from where I'm sitting, I can see Lucy in the far lane.

She's wearing the team bowling shirt like everyone else, but on her bottom half she has on a skirt. A flowery long thing that she probably bought in the consignment store in town that sells old hippie clothes.

Bent's still mad that Lucy's even on the team.

Over Christmas, Lucy went out to lunch with the police chief, even though Bent told her he was a womanizer.

At first, it looked like Bent was wrong—the chief let Lucy feng shui his office and came over to Lucy's for dinner twice one week, and when they needed to fill a spot on the bowling team after the chief broke his ankle, Lucy filled in for him.

She turned out to be a pretty good bowler—better than the chief, all the guys said—but a month later, the chief got caught sexting a couple of women on his staff, one who was married with kids, whose husband found out about it and went to the local paper.

After the story broke, the chief never came over for dinner again. Lucy kept the spot on the team but Bent was still sideways about the whole thing.

"I told you you were going to get hurt," Bent kept saying until Lucy had enough of him.

"Who said I'm hurt?" she asked. "We had a wonderful time together. He's a lovely man when you get to know him."

"No, he's not," Bent said. "He's actually a total asshole. Why do you always do that?"

"Do what?" Lucy asked innocently.

"Think everyone is so wonderful. Most women would be completely pissed off. I mean, he sent a picture of his—" Bent saw me out of the corner of his eye and cleared his throat.

Lucy raised an eyebrow. "Well, first off—that's not my behavior to defend. The chief can take that burden. Furthermore, I was introduced to the bowling team, and turns out, the chief never liked to bowl. It's all entwined in the cosmic trinity, Bentley—there is a choice at every crossroad. A part of everyone's destiny is man luck. A negative can always transform into something beneficial. You should really learn more about it. Both you and Desiree actually. The two of you might attract more positive energy into your lives."

"So, you're staying on the team?" Bent asked, raising his voice.

"Of course," Lucy told him, as though this was never in question.

Now Desiree comes over to me and takes my plate and puts it in the sink. She drops the fork and leans over to get it. Her jeans are so tight I don't know how she can bend in them, and she's paired them with knee-high black stiletto boots and a shirt that barely passes for a tank top. More of a tube top, in my opinion.

I have no idea how she and Lucy are sisters.

When she's standing again, she walks over to me and leans in close, glancing behind her and turning her back to Sully.

"What did he say about me?" she whispers.

"Who?"

"Sully. Who do you think? The least you can do is pay attention. Is he mad? I mean, on a scale of one to ten—ten's the worst—how mad is he at me?"

I have no idea how to answer this question, because Sully never seems mad. Just confused. As though life isn't working out the way he planned, and he has absolutely no idea why.

But I try to put it in context.

"Two," I tell her. "And mad isn't the right word. Exasperated. Apprehensive. Sort of anxious. But hopeful, I think."

Desiree looks at me blankly. The same look Sully gave me.

"Two's not bad," she says, and I nod.

I can tell she's not done grilling me about Sully, though, so when Bent comes through the front door of the bowling alley, I jump off the stool and join him.

He leans down and kisses me on the cheek, but from the look on his face, he's annoyed.

"Why aren't you answering your phone?" he asks.

"The battery died. I didn't realize until a minute ago."

He doesn't like this answer, but it's better than telling him I was ignoring him.

I wait for the lecture on how having a phone is a privilege—one that I have because he wants to be able to get in touch with me, and it's my responsibility to keep my phone charged and the ringer on.

But he just looks over at his team.

"Are we still losing?" he asks. "We better not be. For Christ's sake, we're playing Revere, and they've got a guy who's half-blind."

"Partially sighted," I correct.

"What?" he barks at me.

"That's what it's called. We learned it in health class."

He rolls his eyes and walks to where his team is sitting, and I follow. There's a round of applause when they see him, and somebody yells, *Papa's in the house*, and there's a beer in his hand before he even sits down to take off his shoes.

"I thought your detail ended at six?" I ask.

"I stopped at home to feed Rooster," Bent says.

I look at the clock on the wall. "It's seven thirty. What took so long?"

"I got hung up. Hand me those shoes."

"Hung up doing what?"

"Don't worry about it. I'm next," he says, taking his bowling shoes from me. I can tell by the way he blinks fast that he's not telling me something.

Rooster eats his dinner in a minute flat, and he does his business just as quick.

When Bent texted me earlier, I asked him three times: *Where are you?* Each time, he answered: *Update on score?*

He's never late to anything, especially not bowling.

But I can tell by the look on his face that he's only going to get mad if I keep asking questions while he's rushing to get ready.

"Do you care if I go?" I ask him now, before he gets up for his turn. "Flynn said he could come get me."

Bent frowns. "Why Flynn? What about your pack of girlfriends?"

We've had this same conversation all summer. By *pack* he means Erin and Katie, my two best friends since grade school. They both live across town in the wealthier section of Paradise, and they both leave for their family beach houses after school gets out. I've been friends with Flynn for almost as long, but every time I mention him lately, it's as though Bent's surprised we're friends.

"Katie's at her Cape house and Erin's on the Vineyard. You know they go all summer."

"Why is Flynn around, then?" he asks, as though one has anything to do with the other.

"What do you mean? Where should he be?"

"He's always around. You spend too much time with him."

"He's my friend. Why wouldn't I spend time with him?"

"Doesn't he have a summer house he can go to?"

"He lives a street away from us," I explain.

Bent looks like he might argue, but he doesn't bother. If you come from our section of town, chances are you don't have a summer house.

Someone calls out Bent's name, and he looks over my shoulder.

"It's my turn," he says. "Tell Flynn to keep his hands to himself."

"We're just friends—for, like, the millionth time."

"Tell him anyway. From me," he says, and walks up to take his turn.

The bowling alley is loud now, the music cranked up. "Sweet Caroline" blares through the speakers. Some of the guys from a team named Schweaty Bowls are standing on a bench, shouting along with the chorus, using their beer bottles as microphones.

I walk over to the bar and wave goodbye to Desiree, who's in the middle of handing a plate of food to a customer, but she holds up a finger for me to wait and then gestures for me to meet her at the service station. When I do, she leans in close.

"Where you going?" she yells over the noise.

I tell her I'm leaving with Flynn; she puts her hand on her heart.

"Aw, my handsome guy. Tell him I miss him," she shouts just as the music stops, and Sully frowns and walks over to us.

"What handsome guy?" he asks me. "You got a boyfriend?"

"He's not my boyfriend. We're just friends."

Sully laughs. "Sure you are."

"What's with you and my father?" I ask. "You're, like, from the dark ages."

"We may be old dudes now, but we were your age once." Sully says this as though he's an expert on people my age, and Desiree scowls at him.

She picks my bag off the bar and shoves it at me. "Go. Don't stand here listening to this garbage."

She turns to Sully, who looks sorry he ever opened his big mouth.

"What are you trying to teach her? That a guy only wants to hang out with her if he's interested in her? That her value is purely sexual and has nothing to do with the fact that he might like her *company*. Her *personality*!"

Sully puts his hands up. "Here we go. Another f-bomb assault."

Desiree gives me a disgusted look. "That's what he calls feminism. The f-bomb."

"No," Sully corrects. "It's only the f-bomb with you because you blow men up with it. All I'm saying is teenage boys are horny, and you turn it around. Make me look like some sort of knuckle-walking ape."

"I wouldn't insult an ape like that," Desiree snaps.

Before they go at it another round, I pat Sully on the arm and give Desiree another wave and slip away. Her voice follows me, ranting at Sully again, until the music turns on, and I'm out the door, the noise fading behind me.

Outside, the boardwalk is slick, the weathered wooden slats glossy under the dome lights above. It must have rained while I was in the bowling alley, and now the air is suffocating, the heat wave going on its second week now.

Flynn is waiting in his car at the curb. I get in the passenger seat and turn to him and squint at his head.

"What's on your head?"

"What do you mean?" He looks in the rearview mirror, as though he doesn't know what I'm talking about.

Flynn's in his usual clothes. Basketball shorts and a T-shirt, but his hair is pulled back and tied in a knot on the back of his head.

"I mean the man bun."

"Stop looking at me like that. It's a thing."

"That's debatable."

"Well, Anna likes it," he says, and I roll my eyes at him.

"Here we go again," I say.

He puts the car in drive and pulls away from the curb before he looks at me. "What?"

"Last month, you almost shaved your head because Karen wanted you to—"

"Ka-RINN," he interrupts. "You say it wrong every time."

"I'm saying it just like you."

"No." He shakes his head. "You say Karen. KA-ren. And it's Ka-RINN. Hear the difference?"

I stare at him until he shrugs and motions for me to continue.

"The month before that, it was Shelly, and you were obsessed with yoga because she was into it."

"So, I like to please my women." He winks. "What's the crime in that?"

"Your *what*? Gross."

"Don't be so dramatic. I'm just kidding. Since when are you such a prude?" He smirks at me and when I don't smile, he sighs.

Flynn turned eighteen in the beginning of the summer, and his cousin got him a job covering shifts behind the bar when they're shorthanded at Roscoe's. It's a popular hangout for college kids, and now it seems like he has a new girlfriend every month.

"It's not like I'm sleeping around. It's harmless," he says.

This is new territory for us. We've been friends since middle school, and I've known just about every girl he's had a crush on. But they were always out of his league. Before this year, he was just a skinny kid with arms too long for his body, a good jump shot, and a decent enough smile under a mouthful of metal. Then he grew to over six feet and became the star forward on our varsity basketball team. His face cleared up and his braces came off and everything just seemed to fit into place, like the pieces of a puzzle. And I wasn't the only one who noticed.

Now that he's dating, it's all he talks about.

Until he gets tired of whatever girl he's into and hangs around me for a week until he gets a new crush.

So far this summer, it's happened three times.

"Do your *women* even know your age? Or are you lying to them?"

"You say it like I'm underage and hitting on old ladies. Anna is twenty-one."

"I mean more that you're still in high school. They don't think that's creepy?"

"Technically, I shouldn't be. If my mother hadn't kept me back in first grade, I'd be starting college in the fall."

I tilt my head at him. I've heard this argument before. "So you are lying to them."

He turns onto my street and pulls over to the curb. "How many times have I had to listen to Katie or Erin or you go on and on about some guy? And now that it's me, it's not cool?"

I don't answer because his voice has an edge to it and it settles somewhere in my stomach. Flynn and I never fight. And it's all we've done the last few months.

Maybe he's right. I'm used to Katie or Erin disappearing when they get a boyfriend. But Flynn is always there. Or he used to be, at least.

"Point taken," I tell him now, and his face softens, back to normal.

The car is still running, and I open the door, expecting him to follow, but he doesn't move.

"I thought we were going to watch a movie?" I say, looking back at him.

"I can't. Something came up."

His phone dings and he doesn't answer it, and I know it's this new girl, Anna. Who likes guys with man buns.

"Something better, you mean."

"Don't be like that. Come on."

"Fine. Be careful."

"Oh, Plural," he says. "Get lost. I'll call you later."

I get out of the car, and he drives away, toots the horn as a goodbye.

Bent didn't leave the porch light on and the house is dark and uninviting. I should go upstairs and take Rooster Cogburn out one last time, but I know he's sleeping on his back, upside down on the couch. He'll be impossible to get up without luring him with a treat, and in this heat, I'm not up for the challenge.

I climb the steps to the porch landing and sit on the top step. Up the street, Flynn is stopped, waiting for the light to turn green, and I watch his taillights until he pulls away and disappears, the way he said *Plural* stuck in my head.

It's a nickname he gave me the day we became friends.

It was the first day of sixth grade. We were sitting in homeroom, alphabetically, with name tags on our desks. Mine said *Winter*, the *S* missing.

Flynn was sitting in the desk in front of me, and I was in the last seat in the row—typical unless Sean Yablonski or Emma Zabel were in class with me.

Flynn and I were friendly, but not friends. Since we shared the same last name except for one letter, we'd been sitting next to each other in classes since the first grade.

On this day, Mrs. Belcher was up front, calling out names from an attendance sheet. I was drawing circles on the side of my notebook when I heard her call out "Flynn Winter."

"Here," Flynn said.

"Elizabeth Winter," she said, not looking up from the paper.

"It's Libby," I called out. "Winters."

Mrs. Belcher looked up and squinted through her thick glasses. She was a crabby old lady who never smiled and shuffled more than walked. The boys hated her because she gave detentions if you spoke above a whisper. The girls avoided her because she'd send you to the assistant principal for *inappropriate clothing* if she so much as glimpsed a bra strap. Behind her back, everyone called her *Belchmeister*.

This was her last year before she retired, and Katie and I had groaned when we saw on our schedules that she was our homeroom teacher.

"What's that?" Mrs. Belchers squawked. "Speak up!"

Katie was in the next row over, and she whipped her head around and looked over at me, her eyes wide.

"Over here," I said loudly, lifting my arm.

Mrs. Belcher was so short I had to lean to the side to see past Flynn. She shuffled forward, her eyes finding me finally in the last seat in the back.

"Stop mumbling," she said. "Why is your hand up?"

I lowered my hand. "You said Elizabeth Winter. I was just saying that I go by Libby. And my last name is Winters."

"Is your name Elizabeth?" she screeched, and I thought I saw Flynn flinch.

"It's Elizabeth. Libby . . . but . . ."

"Stop speaking." She looked down at her sheet, marked her paper with a shaky hand. "I don't concern myself with nicknames, Ms. Winter. I'll address you as Elizabeth, and you'll answer as such."

She turned and walked back to her desk. "Silent reading until the bell rings," she said to the class. "Not a word from anyone."

Katie looked over at me with a *see, I told you so* face, and I stuck my tongue out at her and slid a knee under myself so I was sitting up higher.

"It's Winters," I said loudly, and Katie slid down in her seat, covered her face with her hands, and shook her head.

In front of me, Flynn turned and stared at me.

"Is someone speaking when I said quiet?" Mrs. Belcher scanned the classroom. No one looked up.

"It's still me," I said. "Libby . . . Elizabeth."

"I know your name, Ms. Winter, and you need to stop interrupting." She looked down at her desk again.

I looked over at Katie, and she mouthed, *Just forget it*.

There were signs all over our school about bullying. This old witch apparently hadn't read them.

"Mrs. Belcher. You keep saying Winter, and that's not my last name."

"If you have a last name that is different than what I called, you don't belong in this class." She waved her hand at me, dismissing me. "Go to the office and let them figure it out."

"I'm on your sheet," I pressed, and Flynn collapsed in his seat so hard the desk shook. Katie moaned. "You're just not saying it right," I told her.

"I'm not saying it *right*?" Mrs. Belcher asked, as though I'd said pigs could fly.

"I'm Winters. Plural," I said. "He's Winter. Singular."

I pointed to myself. "Plural," I said, and touched Flynn on the shoulder. "Singular."

Flynn's forehead was pressed firmly to his desk. I didn't think he was breathing anymore.

Mrs. Belcher cleared her throat and straightened in her seat.

"Elizabeth. Your grammar is atrocious. I'm not saying it . . . *not right*—I'm pronouncing it *incorrectly*." She looked at me over her glasses. "Do you understand, Elizabeth?"

I nodded, and she leaned forward.

"Repeat after me, Elizabeth: I'm pronouncing it *incorrectly*."

"I'm pronouncing it incorrectly," I repeated, and Flynn sat up and squeezed his nostrils together, suffocating a laugh.

"Thank you, Ms. Winter*ssss*," she replied, lingering on the *S* for so long that Flynn let out a laugh that he disguised as a hacking cough.

Flynn found me in the cafeteria later that day. He put a cookie down on my tray, gave me a salute.

You earned this, Plural, he said, taking the seat next to me and across from Katie and Erin.

Flynn talked about it that whole year. How brave he thought I was. How anyone in their right mind would have gone down to the office instead of taking on the *Belchmeister*.

Now, sitting on the steps, the red of his taillights disappearing and darkness filling the street, I hear him say it again.

Plural. Get lost.

I wasn't sure when things had changed. How these days, when he used my nickname, it meant: stop talking. It meant: go away.

~ 6 ~

Quinn

There is a baby inside of her.

She suspected as much after she pushed Nate on the swing and watched him sail into the sky in front of her, and the ground beneath her feet shifted. Black dots hemmed her vision, and the orange juice she gulped back earlier in the kitchen was suddenly in her throat, and she barely made it to the trash barrel before she threw it up.

She hung on to the edge of the barrel to keep her knees from giving out.

It wasn't until after she dropped the boys off for the night that she took the pregnancy test. When the plus sign showed in the tiny window on the stick, she submerged herself into the tepid water in her small tub in her strange new bathroom and closed her eyes.

Five years had passed since she miscarried, but she remembered this feeling so vividly, so precisely, it was as though she'd been pregnant her whole life and not just once, years ago, for eleven short weeks. The motion sickness. The fullness of her breasts. The insatiable desire to *lie down*. It all came back to her.

She sank in the water until her ears were submerged and all she could hear was the hum of the AC.

She can count on one hand the number of times she and John had sex this past year.

And here she is, pregnant from the ten minutes they'd been together hours before he had disappeared from her life.

She remembers every detail of that night.

How she coaxed him out of the lawn chair in the backyard, where he'd sat all night in the dark, a bottle of whiskey in one hand, a cigarette in the other.

He stumbled in, drunk, the bottle still in his hand, and when she returned from brushing her teeth and climbed into bed, he was naked. He put his hand on her hip, then her breast and she let him, because it had been *that* long.

Afterward, they fell asleep, the rise and fall of John's chest steady. His skin hot under her hand.

It was John's voice that woke her from a deep sleep, her body lurching out of slumber. He was next to her on his back, his eyes closed but his legs jolting under the sheet, his groans guttural and feral in the dark room.

She bolted upright, clutched the sheet to her chest, and yelled his name.

He thrashed next to her, his arm in the air. His elbow missed her forehead by inches and slammed into the headboard. A thud echoed through the room.

She yelled his name again, leaned over to shake him awake, and she hadn't seen his other arm underneath his body, his arm jerking up as if to ward off an attack.

There was a whoosh of air past her ear before the back of his hand struck her face. His knuckles slammed into the edge of her cheekbone, and she screamed. John's eyes flew open and he blinked out of the night terror, stunned and wide-eyed while Quinn cowered in the corner of the bed, a trickle of blood edging out of one nostril.

He'd apologized, sober it seemed, his face drawn and worried as he rushed to get her ice and clean up her nose, all the while telling her how sorry he was.

How *fucking* sorry.

They'd sat at the kitchen table after, Quinn holding a bag of ice to her cheek and John staring at the floor, his arms crossed over his chest.

The night terrors had happened before, but not like this. He'd talk in his sleep, maybe yell or jolt awake. But never like this. With Quinn cowering in their bed. Her eye swelling and nose bleeding and her arms up to fend off the man next to her. Her husband.

She'd said he needed to get help in a soft, quiet voice, but her words were an ultimatum, and he heard it. She saw it in his face. The way his jaw set.

She waited, feeling as if that moment in the bedroom was the end of a long road they had traveled. As though they were stumbling for years on the thin lip of a steep drop and they'd finally slipped off, and here they were, falling away from each other, tumbling in separate directions.

She said it again, louder this time, and he stood up, moved away from her, already putting physical distance between them. When he said the words out loud, she wasn't surprised.

Help for what? A bad dream?

They'd had this fight before. The back-and-forth about his symptoms. She brought home library books on post-traumatic stress syndrome, read them cover to cover, and left them on his bedside table, where they sat untouched. She called Veterans Affairs and PTSD hotlines, joined online support groups, and scoured the internet for information. Looking for ways to talk to him about the drinking, the night terrors, the way he seemed checked out from their life.

She refused to argue this time, though, the pulsing beat of her swollen cheek all that needed to be said. Instead, she'd asked him if he was going back, something he had mentioned in one of their fights. His Guard component had approved his release—John wanted to join active duty—and he answered so quickly, a curt nod of his head, as if it were that easy, as though she meant nothing, that it slipped out of her mouth before she could stop it.

Coward.

And then he'd left. Packed a bag and walked out. Just like that, it seemed, in her mind, on that night and in the days after.

But now, lying in the tub, thinking back to that night, enough time has passed that she's able to see it more clearly. He left at the end of May, and now it's early August. The weeks he's been gone have let her distance herself from that night without living inside of it, as though she's watching a movie of her own life.

He hadn't left her on that night, she realizes, because he hadn't really come home. Not the John she knew.

Quinn gets out of the tub and wraps a towel around her body, suddenly exhausted, the small motion of leaning down to pull the plug from the drain making her legs burn.

Earlier, Bent put an air conditioner in her window and cranked it to full, but the house is still stifling, so she dresses quickly and walks out to the front porch, lies on the cushioned bench in the dark corner, her feet dangling off the edge.

The air isn't much better outside, but a puff of something that resembles a breeze floats by, and Quinn closes her eyes, the sounds of the neighborhood surrounding her.

The duplex across town where she'd lived with John had been quiet, and after he disappeared, she'd lie awake at night, listening for any noise. Occasionally, she'd hear one of the kids from two houses down or the poodle from across the street.

Here, though, the houses are so close she can hear everything—

the coffee grinder first thing in the morning from Lucy's third-floor kitchen or the murmur of voices late into the night from the patio next door. She thought it might bother her, this constant hum around her, but she finds it comforting in a way that surprises her, as though she is suddenly, just by living on this street, part of something bigger than herself.

She felt that way when she first took the job as a nanny to the twins.

Quinn had applied on a whim after John first deployed, never expecting to get the job—she had no experience with infants. Just a degree in early-childhood education, a handful of summers as a camp counselor, and her job in the toddler room at the preschool where she'd worked for almost a year.

But she'd made herself apply for the job anyway. It wasn't lost on her that she was trying to fill a void. Trying to do something, *anything*, to take her mind off the miscarriage.

The pregnancy had been a shock—not the plan, of course. Pregnant at twenty was not something she'd aspired to. But it was a good shock nonetheless.

John had talked about getting on track to manage the hardware store where he'd worked since he was a teenager. And she'd figure something out once the twins were born, maybe continue working at the preschool. The twins could stay in the infant room, and she could work in the toddler room, pop in to see them now and then. At least they'd be in the same place, and she'd be making an income as well.

And then *poof*, just like that, plans changed. She lost the twins and John deployed all in the same year.

And suddenly, there she was—on the cusp of twenty-one with absolutely no idea who she was.

She wasn't a mother. She was a wife—John's wife. But they'd

had so little time together in those new roles before he left that she didn't even have time to figure out what this new part of her might look like.

When she saw the ad for the nanny position, she thought, *Why not?*

Madeline didn't seem to care about anything other than how Quinn's eyes had filled in the twins' nursery. The look on her face when she'd looked down at the boys in their crib.

Quinn didn't mention the miscarriage. Didn't tell Madeline that she'd carried her own twins for eleven weeks. Madeline had hired her within the hour, and over the next months, Quinn let herself be devoured by her job.

That was years ago, and Quinn still loves her job, and the twins, but something has been missing from her life.

Lying in the dark now, the word *lonely* fills her mind, rests on her chest, heavy as a brick.

She knows this feeling didn't just start when John disappeared two months ago. She remembers being in the same room all year—sitting right next to him—and feeling completely alone.

It's only now, in this neighborhood full of sounds and smells and life, and her arms wrapped around her middle, around her *baby*, that the loneliness suddenly feels like a memory instead of something inside of her.

She feels her face color, the shame of it—quick and startling. Her husband is missing, but all Quinn can think about is how, for the first time in as long as she can remember, she feels oddly present. As though these past years she's been slogging along, waiting for her life to begin, watching her days unfold and the years pass by until suddenly, her world broke apart, and now everything is foreign and uncomfortable, yet strangely invigorating.

A car pulls in front of the house and jolts her out of the thought.

A door shuts, and she hears footsteps on the cement walkway to the house. She picks her head up, but earlier she'd shut off the porch light to avoid attracting bugs, and now she can't see in the darkness.

She sits up slowly and leans to the right, straining to see over the large rhododendron blocking the stairs. The bench is tucked in the far corner of the long porch, and she squints, the outline of Libby coming into focus. She's sitting on the porch steps with her back to Quinn, looking at something up the street.

Quinn freezes—she doesn't want to startle her—and she knows Libby isn't aware that Quinn is behind her. She wouldn't even know about the bench—Quinn only wrestled it out of her apartment and onto the porch earlier.

Libby is going to think she's creepy for sitting here in the dark not saying anything, but her voice is caught in her throat.

Quinn stands quickly, making as much noise as she can, pushing the wooden bench against the siding on the house, the thud of it vibrating against the bare soles of her feet.

As expected, Libby twists, a hand to her throat.

"I'm sorry!" Quinn blurts, her own hands up, as though she's in the middle of a stickup. "I was lying out here because it's so hot inside, and I didn't even know you were there until a second ago."

The streetlight casts a glow on Libby's cheek, and Quinn sees that it's wet.

A siren wails somewhere in the distance, and they both turn to the sound. Bent's face in Quinn's mind. The look he gave her earlier when she pressed her back against the air conditioner and lifted her hair off her neck.

It had settled somewhere inside of her, that look.

The noise fades, and the girl studies her, presses a fingertip against her cheek, catching a single tear. Casually, though, as if she is familiar with the movement.

"Lying where?" she asks, looking behind Quinn.

"On the bench. It's here for anyone to use . . . I mean, feel free, whenever to, you know, to . . . use it."

Libby doesn't respond, just looks at Quinn. After a moment, Quinn walks to the door. "I'll leave you alone," she says over her shoulder. "Sorry I scared you."

"You don't have to leave," Libby says. "It's your house too."

Quinn pauses—the words are delivered gently, without the edge that she'd heard in Lucy's kitchen—and she walks back to the stairs, leans against the post.

"I'm Quinn, by the way. It's Libby, right? In my head, I call you the girl from upstairs. But if we're living in the same house, we should probably know each other's names."

"In my head, I call you the serial killer." Libby shrugs, as though this is a perfectly normal thing to admit. "But most serial killers probably don't have a porch bench with gingham cushions." Libby waves her hand at the look on Quinn's face. "Don't ask. Active imagination."

Quinn smiles and feels the knot between her shoulder blades loosen for the first time in days.

Headlights turn onto the street, and they both watch a truck pull into the driveway. Bent gets out of the driver's seat, and Libby stands up quickly.

"I'll be right back," she says, and disappears into the house.

Quinn is suddenly aware that she's wearing a ratty pair of John's old boxers and a baggy T-shirt she'd thrown on without a bra. She sits down on the step, pulls the T-shirt over her knees, and then Bent is in front of her, and she calls out a hello before he trips over her on the dark stairs.

"Whoa," he says, squinting to see her and pausing on the concrete walk. "It's you."

Quinn doesn't know what to say to this, so she doesn't respond, which is a first when it comes to Bent. He has the sort of laid-back demeanor that unnerves her—that inexplicably causes her to ramble in a way that makes her cheeks hot. He doesn't seem to mind, just usually watches her like he is now. A look on his face she can't quite read.

Quinn feels the house shake, and suddenly a massive dog pushes open the screen door, his leash trailing behind him. The dog nudges Quinn's hand with his head, and when she lifts it to pet him, he collapses, half on her lap, half on the porch. The weight of him nearly pushes Quinn off the step.

"Be careful," Bent says. "He's an attack dog."

"Rooster. Get up." Libby sighs as she walks down the steps and snaps her fingers at the dog, who snuggles deeper into Quinn's middle. "Sorry. I hope you aren't afraid of dogs," Libby says to Quinn.

Quinn scratches behind Rooster's ear. "Who could be afraid of this guy?" She smiles. "He actually reminds me of a bigger version of a dog we had. He was sweet like this. Just a puppy, though."

"Had?" Libby asks.

Quinn nods. "It was a long time ago. I surprised my husband with it when he was just back from overseas. Turns out, it wasn't the best surprise. Just too much for him, I think. Anyway . . . the puppy went to a home with kids. Some land, I guess . . . I was told, at least. So it all worked out, I think—well, I hope." Quinn stops talking because she can hear her own voice. Hear the disappointment. The hurt.

Nobody speaks, and Quinn wonders if she'll ever be normal. Ever not blurt things out without thinking.

But when she looks up, Bent isn't fazed. Neither is Libby.

"He likes you," Bent says.

"He likes *everyone*," Libby corrects.

"Tell that to the guy who almost got his arm ripped off."

"That doesn't count," Libby tells him. "He was a psycho."

"Who was?" Quinn asks.

Bent reaches out and rubs the fur between the dog's eyes. "Some asshole we sent away after a domestic dispute with his girlfriend. He was drunk, beat her up. Rooster was the girlfriend's dog and got a chunk out of the guy's arm trying to protect her. He came to live with us after that."

"She didn't want him back?" Quinn asks. "The girlfriend?"

Bent glances at Libby, picks up the leash.

"Let's go, bud. I know you've got to water some grass." He gives Rooster a tug, and Quinn watches as they cross the street, disappearing into a shadow behind a large tree.

"She died," Libby says, sitting on the step next to Quinn. "You know, from the boyfriend. That's why Rooster ended up at the shelter."

Quinn feels the words sink into her. She looks up the street to where Bent is standing.

"Me and my big mouth. I don't blame him for not wanting to talk about it."

Libby shrugs. "He's got a million stories like that one. War stories. Cop stories. He only gets quiet because my mother hated hearing about any of it. And Lucy shushes him because she thinks I'm too young. He probably thinks everyone is like that. Every woman, I mean."

It's on the tip of Quinn's tongue to say something about Libby's mother. To offer her condolences. Before she can get the words out, Rooster walks in between them, bumping against Quinn as he slowly climbs the stairs. The dog sits in front of the door and looks back at Libby.

"You're the laziest dog," Libby tells him, but Rooster wags his tail and stands up, pushing his nose against the screen until Libby opens it, and they both disappear inside the house.

Quinn feels herself smiling in the dark, Libby and Rooster reminding her of the week she had alone with the puppy before John came home.

She hadn't even given him a name, wanting John to be a part of choosing one. Instead, he'd barely looked at the dog. Then he'd sent it away.

When she turns, Bent is watching her, and she blushes, aware that he's caught her lost in a memory.

"It's nice to live with a dog again," she admits. "I mean, in the same house. I can hear him at night. When he jumps off the couch. Or bed, or wherever he sleeps. It's this *thump*." Quinn pats the wood porch with the palm of her hand.

"He sleeps with me. Right over your head. Hope it doesn't wake you."

"I like it. Makes me feel less . . ." She pauses, shakes her head to dismiss it, as though it's not worth talking about. "How was bowling?" she asks.

"Borrow him anytime you want," Bent says. "He likes sleepovers."

She nods, knowing she won't do that. Won't ask Rooster to sleep in a strange place away from his home on the second floor. She pictures him standing over the woman he was trying to protect, and suddenly, inexplicably, her eyes fill and she swallows and clears her throat, embarrassed, even though she thinks Bent probably can't see her face in the dim glow of the streetlight.

"He went to a good home," Bent says, and she looks up at him, confused.

"Of course he did. It's obvious how much you and Libby love him."

"Not Rooster," he says, and it takes a minute for her to understand that he's talking about the puppy. Her puppy.

She stands, wanting to see Bent's face. She's on the third step, and their eyes are level. She is close enough to see the scar on his face, to breathe in the faint scent of his aftershave.

Her face is only inches away from him—but he doesn't move, doesn't look away from her.

"John only told me a buddy of his found the puppy a home. He wouldn't say who. So it was you?"

There's an edge to her voice that slips in, even though she's angry with John, not Bent.

But Bent's here, in front of her. And her husband isn't. She wants to tell him she's sorry for this—he's done so much for her already, and here she is, practically shouting at him—but he speaks before she can get the words out.

"I wasn't going to say anything; I shouldn't say anything. But that look on your face . . . that's just, you know, not something I can live with. Luke, maybe—I mean John. Sorry. I can tell you're confused when I call him that." He clears his throat again. "Anyway. I don't know how much you know. What John told you."

She considers this before she speaks. "I know I brought home a beautiful eight-week-old puppy to give to my husband when he came home from Iraq. I put a bow around the puppy's neck, and he was the happiest, furriest dog I'd ever seen. And when my husband walked through the front door—John, who loved animals—all animals—looked at that puppy and his face went . . . blank. Like he wasn't even in the room anymore."

She let out a breath, stood up straighter.

"And John—the John I knew, my *husband*—was no longer there. He didn't hold that dog or look at him once in the week that followed. Not once. And one morning, I woke up and John was gone. So was the puppy. Along with the crate. The dog bed. The blanket and toys and bowls and treats—every single trace of him. There was a note on the table that said: *Please don't hate me, but I can't.* John came home later that day. He could barely look at me. I asked him over and over to tell me where the puppy was, but he wouldn't give me specifics. He just said a friend of his told him about a family with kids, lots of land. And that's where he brought him. He said it was a good home. A good family. And we never talked about it again." She crosses her arms over her chest, hugs herself. "That's what I know."

She doesn't hear Bent breathe in, just sees his chest rise. There are tears on her cheeks. She doesn't blink or move to wipe them away. The memory of that morning, all those years ago, still raw inside of her.

Bent gestures for them to sit, but Quinn shakes her head. She needs to hear this now. Standing.

She knows this is the reason John is gone. These things he could never tell her. Never say out loud.

"I'm not sure where to start," Bent says, and chews on the corner of his thumb. He pauses for a moment and shrugs. "I'll tell you like I found out, I guess." He tilts his head, holds her eyes.

"John called me out of the blue one day. Asked me to grab a beer. I met him at Sully's, and he was wound up. I thought he was on something, but he swore he wasn't. He said he needed a favor and handed me a picture of this puppy. Cute, just like you said. He tells me he's got his shots, comes from good stock, and he needs to find him a home. One with kids. He was adamant about that. So, I made a call. I knew some staties up north with families, big pieces of land. One of them said yes, so I gave John the guy's number and that was that."

"They took him? Were they nice?"

Bent gives her a sad smile. "They *are* nice. Great people. Good parents. Four or five kids. I get a Christmas card every year. Pup's in it. He's big. Always wearing a festive collar. Part of the family, from what I know."

He's quiet now. But there is more. She feels it in the small distance between them. The air thick from what's left unsaid.

"We were in Fallujah when I got this." He points to the scar on his face. "Patrolling some shitty road. John was in the truck in front of me. It was morning—just another day. Nothing special about it. All I remember is looking through the windshield at the bluest sky. And then everything went black."

He pauses, backs away from her, disappearing in a shadow near the stairs, where he leans against the railing, as though what needs to be said is easier to get out in the dark.

"They rolled over an IED and it took out the back of the truck. We got hit too, just not as bad. Some shrapnel came through the windshield and got me. I don't know how long I was out, but when I came to, I was on the ground and John was next to me, crouching over his buddy, a medic next to him trying to stop the bleeding. His friend was missing parts he shouldn't have been missing. And he was dead—anybody could see he was gone. But John was telling him to hold on. To stay with us." He clears his throat, shifts his weight.

"The medic finally called it, moved to the next guy who needed help. There's blood everywhere. Smoke and the smell of gasoline, but it's still just another day in Fallujah, you know? The sun's blazing in the sky, and somewhere there's a radio playing, as though it's just a typical day in the life. And on the side of the road there's this dog, skinny thing—dirty and matted, and well . . . hungry. He walks over to the dead guy, couple feet from him, and he's standing there, over a puddle of blood, drinking from it. John picked up his rifle and fired. Dog never felt a thing."

She doesn't speak. She's never heard this story. She remembers the smell of her puppy, the noises it made asleep in her arms. And the anger. The white-hot fury she felt when John sent it away.

Bent is talking again, and she blinks, his words sharpening in her mind.

". . . about a month after John asked me to find a home for your puppy, he calls me again. Drunk. Or high. Maybe both. Not making any sense. Telling me he's sorry. That he let me down and if he wasn't such a pussy, it wouldn't have happened. I'm telling him that's nonsense, trying to get him to tell me where he is, and he's just talking in circles. But he keeps coming back to the dog. We're on the phone for an hour. Maybe more. And finally, he's spent—I can hear on the phone that he's just done—slurring and mumbling. He promises me he's going to sleep, and before he hangs up, he brings up the dog again. Muttering about how it comes to him in his dreams. Haunts him. He tells me he wishes he'd saved it, put his gun down, brought it some water. Some food. Then the line goes dead. I call him back three, four times, but no answer.

"And I just sit there. I must have sat there for a half hour. Speechless. Realizing I've been on the phone with him talking about a damn dog, and we're not even talking about the same damn dog. He's back in Fallujah. Trying to stop himself from shooting a dog who's drinking out of a puddle of his buddy's blood."

Quinn is watching Bent's mouth, hearing the words. But it's as though time has slowed, and the world is somehow no longer real. How do you live with someone—sleep, eat, make love—and not know such details?

She turns and walks up the steps. She can feel Bent follow her.

Can hear him calling her name, but her mind is numb, and she just wants to lie down.

She's in the hallway when she feels his hand on her arm, stopping her, turning her.

"Quinn," he says, "I'm sorry."

She blinks. Once. Twice. Until his face comes into focus.

"Take me sometime," she blurts, and his eyes flicker over hers. "To the house—with the dog. I won't bother them. I just want to see him. Just look from a distance."

She can see from his face that he doesn't want to do this. Doesn't want to have anything to do with this. But he nods.

"Thank you for telling me," she says. "I know it must be hard to talk about."

"It's actually not. Once you start talking, it just comes," he says. "My wife was . . . fragile. That's probably not the right word. Easily upset by things, I guess. When I first came home, she'd ask me about what happened over there, and I'd start to tell her, and she'd tell me to stop—that it was too much. That I shouldn't think about it anymore. Move on, you know. So I stopped talking. And now, with Libby—she wants to know everything. I know she's a kid, and I'm her father, and I try to walk that line between shielding her and babying her." He smiles, but his eyes are sad, tired. "Just trying to raise her as the type of person that doesn't crumble under the weight of things."

She swallows, doesn't trust her voice, and takes a minute to compose herself.

"I'd like to hear it. All of it. Sometime."

She leaves him standing in the hallway. Inside, she slides to the floor, her arms wrapped around her body.

She thinks of John's slow turn away from her. His gradual descent into silence. Into alcohol and pain pills and his lawn chair in the backyard, positioned in the far corner so that it looked out at the abandoned baseball field that was more of a sand pit, dust blowing in his face on windy nights, and the glow from his cigarette bright when he brought it to his mouth.

She can picture that glow. From where she stood at the kitchen window, that blazing orange tip of the cigarette allowed her to see her husband staring out at absolutely nothing. Her husband captivated by emptiness.

Now she knows what some of that emptiness looks like.

It looks like a dog. And a dead friend. And smoke and shrapnel and a puddle of blood.

7

Libby

On Saturday, my phone dings at nine in the morning.

I think it's Flynn texting me, apologizing for blowing me off last week. Maybe inviting me to have lunch after his basketball game, like we used to do before he replaced me with his girlfriend of the month. But it's Desiree.

Wanna work a kids bday prty today?

I send her a thumbs-up sign. Helping Desiree with a bowling party at Sully's isn't exactly what I had in mind for the day, but she'll give me cash under the table, and it's better than helping Lucy paint the hallway.

How old are kids? I ask.

There's barely a pause before her text drops in.

Enuf with the ?? be ready in 15

I get out of bed and get dressed. Shorts and a T-shirt and sneakers because Desiree had a fit last time I wore flip-flops to help with a kid's bowling party. She made me put on a pair of bowling shoes and snapped when I told her I looked ridiculous.

"How do you think you'll look when your foot's a damn pancake?" she said.

Which I didn't have an answer for. Desiree might be a lot of things, but wrong wasn't usually one of them.

Flynn always says Desiree doesn't get any credit for being the brains behind Sully's—but Flynn says a lot of things about Desiree now that he's decided he's in love with her.

He knows better than to talk about her to me, but whenever they run into each other, he always makes some sort of pass at her. *You're too young for me*, she'll tell him, and Flynn will answer with some flirty comeback. *Not too young to be your man.*

He knocks it off if I stare at him hard enough, but later he hisses that I'm ruining his chances of having sex with an older woman.

To which my answer is *Cry about it*. I mean, she's my *aunt*.

In the kitchen, there's a note on the table that Bent's working a detail, but he fed Rooster and took him outside already. He's drawn a smiley face next to his name. A very un-Bent-like thing to do. But he's been acting strange all week.

Yesterday I saw him standing at the front window looking down at the street, his body hidden behind the curtain, only his face peeking out, like he was spying on someone outside.

"What are you doing?" I asked, and he jumped back so fast it made me jump too.

"Jesus, Libby," he said, as though I snuck up on him in the dark while he was sleeping instead of walking into my own living room in broad daylight.

I leaned past him and looked outside, the street empty besides a few parked cars. Then I heard the door close downstairs, and I narrowed my eyes at him.

"Were you just stalking her?"

"What?" He glanced at me, then pointed out the window. "There was a squirrel on the wire near the attic. I'm trying to see where he's getting in the house."

It could have been true—Bent was known to hang out the window with his BB gun, his eyes trained on where the telephone line met the attic—but there wasn't a squirrel in sight.

"How do you know her?" I asked, and he heard the question but didn't acknowledge it.

If I could have looked inside his head, there would have been wheels spinning, gears shifting: Bent trying to figure out how much he could get away with not telling me.

"Who?" he asked, and I didn't bother to answer, just crossed my arms and waited.

"I don't really," he said finally, and paused until he got tired of me staring at him. "Look, Libs. Her husband and I served together overseas. He's a buddy of mine."

"Then where is he? In Iraq?"

"Well, no. He's been back for a while. He's just, you know, sort of . . . gone right now."

"Gone where? Like AWOL? Can't you go to prison for that?"

"Not AWOL! Don't talk so loud," he whispered, and looked at the floor, as though Quinn could hear us.

"So he's, like, missing?"

"I wouldn't say missing. I mean, technically, yes, because he's not here. But he's not exactly lost. It's more of a voluntarily missing."

"Voluntarily missing? I hate it when you talk in circles. Like he left her? Is that what you mean?"

He pressed his hand to his forehead like I was giving him a headache. "I mean he's just, I don't know. I think it's just a husband-and-wife thing."

I scowled at him. "How did you get involved? Why does she have to come live in our house?"

He put his finger to his lips. "Libby, shush. She's had a hard time already without thinking she's not welcome here. Look. It's no different than being on the police force. They're my brothers.

When you go to war with someone, they're your brothers too. That doesn't stop when you come home. So, I'm just doing what I can to help. And you, you can help out too, you know."

"*Me?* What am I supposed to do?"

"You can be friendly. Stop calling her a serial killer, for Christ's sake."

"First of all, I told her about the serial killer thing—and for the record, she was calling me *the girl upstairs*. It's not like she's writing me love notes, trying to be my best friend."

Bent waved me off, done with the conversation. "I'm inviting her for dinner on Sunday. I want you home. And I want you to be *friendly*. Got it?"

I nodded, and he left me standing at the window, staring at the tree with the make-believe squirrel.

Now, outside, a car horn beeps and I know it's Desiree, waiting with the engine running. I rush down the stairs, and when I get in and close the door, she hands me a wad of cash.

"Here. It's more than usual because you're dealing with the kids today. I'm in no mood to play nice with a bunch of five-year-olds."

Desiree's rarely in the mood to play nice with anyone, but I just tuck the bills in my pocket and buckle my seat belt.

"Plus, you deal with the mother," Desiree tells me. "She's some big-shot doctor—that's how she introduced herself on the phone—*Doctor so-and-so*. I wanted to say, well, I'm *Bartender Desiree*. I mean, you're calling a goddamn bowling alley—who gives two fucks what you do for work?"

She's dressed in workout gear, probably so she can get her cardio in on the treadmill she has stashed in Sully's office. There's a stack of Tupperware on the seat between us that holds all of her food for the day—so she can meet her *macros*, whatever that means. She says it makes her happy, her obsession with food and exercise.

I don't know what to say to that because I'd never put *happy* and *Desiree* in the same sentence. Except for maybe when she was younger.

When I look through the photo albums of Lucy and Bent and Desiree when they were growing up, Desiree's laughing in every picture. Just a dimple faced, happy kid.

Then she's gorgeous in a prom dress—all curves and hips and boobs—with a smile that lights up her eyes, a guy on her arm who's looking at Desiree, gazing at her really, instead of the camera, as though he can't take his eyes off of her.

The only pictures I ever see of Desiree now are the ones in her room, showing her onstage in a bikini and heels. Her hair dyed and skin oiled and leathery. No curves or hips or boobs, just bone and muscle and veins and the whitest teeth I've ever seen, glowing under a smile that looks painted on, it's so perfect.

But that girl in the photo album isn't on that stage. You could hold up those pictures of Desiree—the prom one and the bodybuilding ones—and you'd swear they're different people. Complete strangers, if you ask me.

"You're not just the bartender," I tell her. "You practically run the place."

She snorts. "Tell Sully that. I helped him build this from the ground up. But until we're married, I'm just the hired help. He could fire me tomorrow if he wanted."

"He wouldn't do that. You know he loves you—he's asked you to marry him a million times."

"And what then? In Sully's head, we get married and I get pregnant and out comes little Joey or Ginger, and I'm home all day and he pops in now and then to babysit. Do you know he said that out loud, right to my face? *Come on, Desi—I'll babysit all the time.*" She drops her voice low, mimicking Sully, and looks at me.

"That's just Sully. You know he loves kids. He's just not up on the lingo. Like that it's not cool to say you're babysitting your own kids."

She shrugs, as if I might have a point. "Maybe. But he also said he doesn't want his kids to go to day care. So, I say, 'Fine—you're going to watch them when I work?' I mean, my parents are dead. So are his. And he goes, and I'm not joking—'Work where? Like keep doing all the part-time stuff you do?'" She laughs, but it's a loud, hysterical noise, and her eyes are a little wild.

"As if everything I've worked for over the last decade—all the training and clients and hours I put in at Sully's—those are just fun little *hobbies* I've dabbled with until I can be a wife and mother and my life is complete." She's out of breath, her face pink. I'm waiting for her rant to continue, but she sighs, rolls her eyes.

"Don't get me started—I haven't even had a fucking cup of coffee." She turns the car into the lot, parks, and hands me the keys.

"Take the box out of the trunk and get started on gift bags. I'll get us breakfast."

"Can you get me a toasted bagel with butter, a side of bacon, and an orange juice?" I ask, and she frowns at me but gets out of the car, sparing me the nutrition lecture.

Inside Sully's, the door echoes behind me when it closes. I flip the switch for the lights and watch the fluorescent bulbs on the ceiling flicker and turn white.

It's eerily quiet—the lanes in front of me empty and the bar still dark—nothing like the noisy place it'll be in a few hours.

There's nothing nice about Sully's—*old-school candlepin* is what Bent calls it. There's no fancy disco ball hanging from the ceiling or plush leather booths. Just a jukebox in the corner and twelve lanes, each with a fiberglass bench and a table bolted to the floor.

But I love it here. Especially when it's quiet like this. Bent says it's because I grew up in Sully's. From the time I was little, he'd take me here in the morning when my mother needed a break. Sully would cook breakfast, and they'd sit on one of the benches and eat while I crawled on the wooden lanes.

Sully became the owner after his parents died, but Desiree's right when she says she changed the place. She created a website, put the menu online, added an events page and links for birthday parties and bowling leagues. Then she hired a new cook and had him add healthier options to the menu. And she told Sully to start carrying some decent wine and beer.

Bent's not crazy about any of the changes. Earlier this year, Desiree told Sully they should start offering free Wi-Fi to customers, and Bent chimed in that she needed to just *slow down*. Not everyone cared about that kind of *stuff*.

"People come here to unplug. You know, talk to actual people."

Desiree just raised an eyebrow at him.

"This from the last guy on earth still using a flip phone," she quipped.

Sully stayed out of it, but not long after, there was free Wi-Fi at Sully's, and everyone knew Desiree set it up, because she named the network Gohome_Bent.

That's Desiree for you. As my friend Katie says, she gives zero fucks.

There's a long table in the side room where we hold birthday parties, and I put the box on top of it and start on the gift bags. I hear the back door slam and voices in the hallway. Desiree turns the corner with Flynn behind her.

"They were selling studs at the coffee shop, so I picked one up," she announces, winking at Flynn. She hands me a bag, while Flynn slumps in the seat across from me.

"You know I'm free of charge for you," he tells her, a dopey grin on his face.

Desiree laughs and pats him on the head as though he were a puppy.

"I'll be in the office if you need me," she says. Flynn watches until she disappears around the corner.

When he finally looks at me, I'm two bites into my bagel. He puts his hands up, tilts his head at me.

"Sorry—don't yell at me. I know you hate it when I flirt with her, but please . . . I'm barely upright."

I'm about to say something snarky when his face stops me. His eyes are bloodshot, puffy, and red rimmed. His clothes wrinkled.

"Why do you look like you haven't slept in days?"

"Because I haven't. I worked last night and went out with some of the guys after. Guess I had a few too many. Woke up in my truck this morning—literally ten minutes ago. Don't tell Desiree," he says, as though this is the only thing that might ruin his chances with her.

I'm so stunned I almost choke on the bagel. Flynn puts his head in his hands.

"Wait—back up. You slept in your *truck*? Like in the parking lot?"

"Apparently. I woke up there."

"How did your truck get here? I'm lost."

"I drove it here last night. I was fine when I was in here. Then we went to that dive a couple doors down and someone ordered shots. I don't remember anything after that."

It takes a minute for what he's said to sink in. When it does, my jaw drops.

"You were here? Like at Sully's? Drinking?"

"Shh! Jesus, Libby." He leans back and looks over at the hallway to Desiree's office. "Talk a little louder, why don't you."

"What the hell were you thinking? They can lose their liquor license for something like that! Not to mention that Desiree knows you. Sully knows you. My father knows you—"

"Relax! The place was packed, and we were at a back table. One of the guys slipped me a rum and Coke. Besides, no one I knew was here. The bartender was that old guy who can't see past his glasses anyway."

"It's still not cool, Flynn—Desiree's my aunt. They could get in a lot of trouble—"

"I know, Libby! Look, it'll never happen again. I promise. That's why we left and went to another bar. It was stupid. I know that. Don't be mad. Okay?"

I nod, and he breathes in deep, rubs his temples.

"What are you doing here anyway?" he asks through his fingers.

I don't answer him because there are piles of small toys on the table and a stack of *Happy Birthday* gift bags in front of me. Flynn spent the last year talking with scouts from division one colleges for basketball. But he's also in every one of my honors courses. Even hungover, he's smart enough to figure out what I'm doing.

I glance at the clock on the wall behind him.

"I should be asking you that. Aren't you going to be late for basketball?"

"I already missed tip-off. Besides, I'd be trash out there today. The guys will be better off without me."

Flynn's played in a Saturday-morning basketball league for as long as I can remember. He never misses it. Neither do any of the guys he normally hangs out with—basically all the seniors on our high school team.

"So what *guys* were you with if you weren't with all of your friends? Nice ones, obviously, since they left you drunk . . . in a parking lot . . . by yourself. Why didn't they just drop you at home?"

"Maybe I told them I'd just sleep it off—I can't remember anything. It's not like I expected them to babysit me."

I can feel the words forming in my mouth, a lecture about how stupid it was for him to get so drunk that he blacked out, but when I look at him, he's staring at the table, a defeated look on his face.

"Here. Eat this. It'll help." I spread out my napkin in front of him and put the rest of my bagel and the side of bacon on it. I twist the cap off the orange juice and hand it to him.

"I love you," he says, and puts the bottle to his lips, draining it in three gulps.

I work on the bags while he inhales the food. When he's done, he reaches over and grabs a bag, starts filling it with the toys on the table.

We settle into our own two-person assembly line. Flynn launches into how Anna invited him to some family shindig down the Cape, and he didn't know how to get out of it until he found out it was the same weekend his brother was coming home. I interrupt him midsentence.

"Wait. Jimmy's coming home?"

Flynn nods. "Prodigal son returns. Let's see what he can fuck up next."

I've secretly had a crush on Jimmy for my whole life. Or since I met him in sixth grade. But he's also older—like, I-don't-even-know-when-he-graduated older—and probably the reason Bent isn't crazy about Flynn.

Jimmy's always in trouble with the police about something. Or he had been until he joined the army.

"I thought he was deploying somewhere. Like overseas."

"He is, but he's coming home first. Not sure for how long. Maybe a month or two."

I catch his eye. "You don't sound thrilled."

He shrugs. "I don't want to see my mom get hurt again. Supposedly he's a changed man—sober and whatever. But he put her through hell. Made the house like a war zone with all the fighting. Like she didn't have enough to deal with raising us alone and he has to be a bigger dirtbag than my father with the drinking and drugs."

When Flynn was little, his father took off and died not long after somewhere down in Florida from a drug overdose. He doesn't talk about him often, but when he does, it's never with any nostalgia. He still refers to the day his father left as National Goodbye Motherfucker Day.

Katie and Erin always get upset when he says it. They fawn all over him and try to make him feel better. Tell him things like his father had a disease and he lost his way and they know that his father really loved him. All of which are probably true.

I don't ever say anything because I know the other truth. That Flynn's glad his father's gone. That life got easier after he left. It's why I only ever talk to Flynn about my mother.

He knows what it's like to love someone and want them to leave at the same time.

Above us, the speakers crackle and music fills the room. Desiree has one of her yoga playlists on, and some sort of flute plays with birds chirping in the background.

Flynn looks skyward, blinks his eyes. "What is this shit?" he asks.

I open the tissue paper, start stuffing the bags. Flynn isn't helping anymore, and when I look up, he's studying me.

"Why are you looking at me like that?"

"You know what I love about you, Plural?"

"Knock it off and stuff the bags. There's going to be thirty kids here by lunch, and I haven't even started on the streamers."

"I love that we're sitting in a bowling alley bar, stuffing party bags for kids, and Zen music comes on and you don't even miss a beat. Like it's the most normal thing in the world."

"Remind me not to feed you again. You get all weird."

One of the rubber balls on the table rolls off and bounces behind me. Flynn stands up and follows it. When he reaches it, he whips it at the far wall, where it zings back at him. He catches it in one hand, turns in midair, and throws it again. Nimble and graceful and powerful at the same time. The reason he's Paradise High's star basketball player.

"And the real Flynn Winter is back," I say, watching him.

"You always bring me back to life, Plural. You know that," he tells me.

And just like that, we're back to being us.

— 8 —

Quinn

She never works on Saturdays. But it's the twins' birthday party, and they asked last week if she'd go, and how could she say no to two pairs of hopeful eyes staring at her?

Well, obviously Quinn didn't know, because now she's strapped into the passenger seat of Madeline's minivan, the twins in the back screaming *HAPPY BIRTHDAY TO ME* over and over at the top of their lungs and Madeline explaining that meeting Quinn at the bowling alley would have been *fine* but driving together seemed logical, since Madeline drives *right by* Quinn's new place.

Quinn nods and doesn't let her expression show how ridiculous this sounds because Quinn's new place is nowhere near the bowling alley, and the reason Quinn is in the car at all is because less than an hour ago, Quinn's cell phone rang, and it was Madeline, nearly hysterical.

She'd put Quinn on speakerphone, a child wailing in the background, and Madeline had shouted frantically over the crying, "Quinn! Nate can't find his backpack, and he refuses to get in the car, and he says you had it last!"

Quinn had closed her eyes and counted to three before she answered. "The backpack is in Nate's closet. Remember, Nate and I decided that was the best place for it?"

"Well, *he* doesn't remember that. Nate, come here and talk on the phone. Hold on, Quinn. He's hiding from me. I'm getting him."

Quinn had breathed out slowly while she waited. Madeline had finally returned to the phone, asking Quinn if they could just PICK HER UP ON THE WAY because Nate only wanted to see HIS KINNY.

Quinn had agreed and hung up. This wasn't the first time Madeline had called on a weekend when she was alone with the twins. And Quinn wasn't surprised the call was about the backpack.

Weeks ago, Nate had started talking about *not* going to kindergarten in September. Quinn had steadily ignored him, answering with, *mm-hmm* or *I know* whenever Nate listed the reasons he didn't want to go—he'd miss Quinn, or school was stupid (he'd heard that from Jake, his teenage neighbor).

Quinn wasn't concerned—this was just Nate.

Preschool and karate class and tumble time at the gym—Nate had the same reaction to the beginning of every new event. He was anxious, nervous about trying new things. But on the first day, he'd go willingly with his teacher, and by the time Quinn picked him up from school hours later, he would have forgotten every fear. In all the years of being a nanny to Nate, she'd never had a single issue when leaving him, and kindergarten was going to be just like that.

Until last Friday night, when Madeline brought home backpacks and told the boys they were *magic bags* that would keep them safe all day. And only big boys—*good big boys*—could have a backpack like this.

Nick hadn't even looked up from his dinner, but Nate had scooted down from his chair and grabbed the bag, eyes wide. He unzipped every pocket while Madeline looked on, beaming.

Quinn had left for the weekend and arrived Monday morning to find Nate sitting at the table wearing his backpack and Madeline sitting next to him, pale and tired and drawn.

She'd motioned for Quinn to follow her to the mudroom and explained that Nate had refused to take off the backpack since she'd brought it home.

He ate with it on. Went to the bathroom with it on. Slept with it on. He hadn't even bathed since Friday because Madeline put her foot down, finally, and said she would not allow the bag in the bathtub.

"Why is he doing *this*?" Madeline had cried, as though Nate were subjecting her to the cruelest form of torture.

"Because you told him it was magic and that it kept him safe," Quinn had said matter-of-factly.

"I meant in *school*," Madeline had hissed, tucking an unwashed strand of matted hair behind one ear.

Quinn had worked with Nate all week, finally getting him to leave the bag in the closet. But since she'd left them last night, the backpack had emerged again.

So now Quinn is turned in her seat, looking at Nate. He's stopped crying, but his face is tearstained and flushed.

"Hi, birthday boy," Quinn says, and he peeks at her over the top of the backpack in his lap, his arms wrapped around it. The backpack is stuffed full. The zipper is only halfway closed. A giant light saber is sticking out.

Nick is in the seat next to him, unfazed. Quinn reaches her hand back, and Nick grins and gives her a high five. He needs a haircut, his blond hair nearly touching his shirt collar. His skin is honey brown from the sun, his blue eyes bright when she tells him he already looks bigger now that he's five.

Quinn often wonders about their father, the sperm donor. The twins look nothing like Madeline, both blond and blue-eyed with round, dimpled faces and bodies that are off the charts for their age in both height and weight. Madeline is angles and sharp edges, rail thin with a nervous energy Nate inherited.

"I just wanted this day to be fun," Madeline whispers from the driver's seat. "But he's been like this since he woke up. I don't really care about the bag—it's the tantrum he throws when I touch it. It's full of his favorite toys. I'm afraid he's going to throw a fit if the other kids try to play with them—and you know they're going to want to play with them!" Madeline is gripping the steering wheel, the veins on her thin arms bulging.

"Did you tell him he's getting new toys today? Maybe he'll empty it?"

"Of course I told him. I've talked and explained and begged and threatened, and it's just made it worse. I even bribed him with candy, great mother that I am. But you try—he listens to you more than me anyway."

"That's not true—" Quinn says, but Madeline interrupts her, looks in the rearview mirror at Nate, and calls back to him. "Natey Bear? Kinny wants to talk to you about your backpack. Will you talk to Kinny, honey boo? It would make Mommy soooo happy!"

Quinn feels her jaw set at the baby talk—she'd hoped Madeline would grow out of it once the twins were no longer infants.

"Whose birthday is it again today?" Quinn calls. She squints at them as though she's forgotten.

Ours, they scream, and Quinn covers her heart, feigning surprise, and they both giggle.

"And who do we invite to birthday parties?"

"Friends," Nick yells, and Nate looks over at him, smiles.

"And when we invite friends, they are our guests, right?" Quinn asks, nodding her head, and they follow her lead.

"And we're nice to our guests because we're happy they're at our party. So—what are some of the ways we show our guests that we're happy. We say . . ." Quinn pauses, waits.

"We say HI," Nate shouts.

"Yup. And we say please and . . ."

"THANK YOU!" they scream.

"And what else? What do friends do with friends? It starts with *shhh* . . ."

"SHARE!"

They shout it so loud, Madeline puts her hand on her heart.

"That's right," Quinn says as Madeline pulls into a parking spot, turns off the engine.

The boys are already unbuckled, out of their car seats. Nick slides open the van door and jumps down to the pavement. Nate steps over his backpack.

"Leave that here," he tells Quinn from the back seat. "I don't want to share it."

"Good choice," Quinn tells him.

She holds up her hand, and he slaps it, then jumps out of the van.

Madeline is still in the driver's seat, smiling at Quinn, but it's a sad, wistful one.

"You're a born mother," Madeline tells her, and Quinn shrugs off the compliment, but the words settle inside of her, making it difficult to breathe.

Madeline doesn't know Quinn's pregnant—more, though—Madeline *can't* know, not until Quinn has processed it, thought about what it means, especially with John missing.

Although she's stopped thinking of John as missing. *Left* is the word she uses in her mind now when she thinks about it. John *left* her.

She has no idea where he is. Not the specifics, not the actual location. But he's somewhere. Maybe with some unit. Perhaps back with the people he considers family. She can't say how she knows this other than a feeling.

Or maybe it was Bent's reaction last week when she passed him in the hallway and asked if he'd heard anything. The way he'd held her eyes, his lips parted, as though he wanted to tell her something.

"What?" she asked. "Did you hear from him?"

He paused. "Can I ask you a favor?"

She nodded, waited.

"Let John take care of John right now, and you take care of you."

He turned and walked away, but she heard him stop on the landing, as though he wanted to return and tell her more.

She's lost in this thought when Nate pulls her by the hand through the door and into the bowling alley.

The lobby is full of kids—Quinn thinks there must be thirty or more. Madeline spares no expense when it comes to the twins—although Quinn knows this isn't the birthday party Madeline envisioned.

Madeline had wanted to rent out the aquarium in the city. She'd said this to the boys one night before Quinn left to go home, in a breathless voice, and they'd just stared at her.

"We want it at the bowling alley," Nick said. "Like Suzy's."

Nate nodded.

"Suzy?" Madeline asked, with a blank look.

"A friend from preschool," Quinn said. "She had her birthday party at Sully's, down on the boardwalk."

Madeline wrinkled her nose. "Isn't that a bar? Boys, wouldn't you rather have the *entire aquarium*? Mommy will plan the whole party."

"The bowling alley is our favorite place," Nate replied.

"But there are sharks at the aquarium. You love sharks."

"They have popcorn at the bowling alley," Nick said.

"And games," Nate added.

Madeline had tried to change their minds and had finally given up. She'd called Sully's and told them to take care of all of it—from gift bags to balloons to pizza and cake.

She told Quinn later that she'd felt like a failure on the phone—she hadn't even known the twins had ever been to Sully's, never mind that it was their *favorite place*—and to make matters worse, Madeline had been multitasking at work when she called, and when the woman at Sully's had asked for a name for the reservation, she'd blurted *Dr. Madeline Lawson*, like some uppity out-of-touch professional who barely had time for her kids, which is exactly how she felt, she told Quinn.

"I could *feel* her judgment just radiating through the phone," Madeline had said, visibly upset by the memory. "I apologized, but I could tell from her voice she wanted none of it. I mean, why is it that we can't just cut each other some slack? I mean, people these days are just so easily *offended*."

Quinn had put on a sympathetic expression, but this was a common complaint from Madeline. She often wondered if Madeline excelled in her profession because most of her interactions were with petri dishes and test tubes—inanimate objects not so easily offended.

The party took a turn for Madeline after that. It seemed to Quinn that Madeline wanted the entire event behind them.

And now, ever since they arrived, Madeline hasn't put away her travel-size bottle of hand sanitizer, squirting liquid onto the twins' palms whenever they're in arm's reach.

Quinn makes small talk with some of the moms, while the kids are led to a long table set with paper plates and cups, a bouquet of brightly colored balloons in the center.

Madeline gestures wildly at Quinn from the other end of the table and Quinn politely excuses herself and makes her way over.

"What am I supposed to do?" Madeline whispers.

"Do?"

"Yes, do!" Madeline cuts her eyes at Quinn. "I don't know how to run this party!"

"I think you should let her do it," Quinn says, pointing to a girl wearing a T-shirt with *PARTY LEADER* printed on the back. The girl pours lemonade into cups on the table while the kids take their seats, and when she turns, Quinn realizes that it's Libby. Quinn waves, smiles at her from the other end of the table.

Can I help? Quinn mouths, not wanting to yell over the noise, and Libby points to the full pitcher of lemonade near Quinn and nods.

She grabs a stack of cups, lines them up and fills them halfway. Madeline is hovering over her, wrinkling her nose.

"That's all sugar," she tells Quinn.

"No, it's not," Quinn lies. "That's Libby, my upstairs neighbor. She's a health freak. I bet it's freshly squeezed."

"Really?"

"Mm-hmm. Oh, look—the twins are sitting. You should take some pictures. Hurry before they get up." Quinn gestures to a spot at the other end of the table. She turns her back to Madeline, shielding the pitcher, the sugar swirling and pooling at the bottom like a layer of white sand.

She doesn't want Libby to have to deal with Madeline—she's probably making minimum wage—not nearly enough money to listen to one of Madeline's lectures about the evils of refined sugar.

Quinn leans against the wall while the kids eat pizza, then cake.

She mingles with some of the mothers who've stayed for the party, dodging Madeline as best as she can.

There's a tightness in her back, and a sharp twinge in her pelvis that makes her catch her breath at one point, and she's relieved when the kids pile out of the room and run to the bowling area.

She follows them a minute later, walks over to where Desiree is standing behind a counter, handing out bowling shoes.

"These are sanitized. Correct?" Madeline asks, and Desiree glares at her, lifts an eyebrow.

Quinn takes the shoes from Desiree, hands them to Madeline, and quickly grabs the shoes Nick is holding.

"Madeline—why don't you help Nate before he has a meltdown. I'll take care of Nick," she blurts.

Madeline wanders off in the direction Quinn points, into a sea of kids milling about. Quinn has no idea where Nate is, but Desiree is busy handing out shoes again, and Madeline is on the other side of the building, where Quinn hopes she stays.

Nick tugs on the shoes she's holding, and she hands them to him. "Sorry, bud," she says, and he shrugs and plops on the floor, slips on the shoes, and carries his sneakers to a cubby on the far wall.

Little big man is what she calls him when they are alone. She can't help feeling protective of him—the quiet, confident, calm one in a house with Madeline and Nate, his opposites. Nate requires all of Madeline's attention, and the two are so similar—so tightly wound—they create a certain friction in the house.

Quinn notices it on Nick's face every Monday morning. A weariness at having been left alone with his mother and brother for two days. Some mornings, it takes her all breakfast to get Nick smiling again. And the same amount of time to calm Nate.

She should go over to where Madeline is sitting, offer to help, but she's not technically on the clock today, and her back is suddenly throbbing. She makes her way to the restroom. The bathroom is empty, and she locks herself in one of the stalls and sits on the toilet.

She's reading the graffiti on the back of the door when she sees something out of the corner of her eye. She looks down, and it takes her a minute to process what she's looking at.

Her shorts and underwear are around her knees, and there's blood.

Not a small spot of it. Or a trace.

But a bright red circle that's soaked through her shorts.

— 9 —

Libby

I'm cleaning up the birthday table, throwing plates and cups into a large trash barrel, keeping one eye on the bowling lanes to make sure no one needs anything when Desiree calls my name.

She's behind the bar, and she hands the phone to me, puts her hands on her hips.

"For you. An emergency." She eyes me suspiciously.

I've never had anyone call me at Sully's. I'm not even sure I knew there was a phone behind the bar.

I put the receiver to my ear and say hello.

"Can you come in the bathroom?" a woman says. "It's Quinn. I have sort of a . . . problem."

I look over my shoulder to the hallway. "The bathroom here? At Sully's?"

Desiree is still standing next to me, listening over my shoulder, and now she huffs, makes a swipe to take the phone from me while I wave her off.

"Yes, here. I'm on my cell phone. Just come quick. But please be quiet about it."

The phone goes dead, and I hand it back to Desiree, who slams the receiver down.

"Someone's calling you from the bathroom? This bathroom?"

"Shh—she said to be quiet about it."

"Don't shush me," Desiree snaps, and stomps out from behind the bar.

I follow her to the bathroom, which is empty. Desiree glares at me, as though I'm pulling some sort of prank.

"Libby? Is that you?" Quinn calls out from a stall at the end of the row.

I lean over, looking for feet, and find her in the last stall at the far end of the bathroom.

"I'm here. And Desiree is with—"

"Why are you calling from the bathroom?" Desiree interrupts, her voice loud in the empty room. "Are you stuck in there?"

"Oh, hi, Desiree. God, this is embarrassing. I'm not stuck . . . I just . . . do either of you have a tampon and something I can wrap around my waist? A sweatshirt . . . or something."

"Hold on, I'll get one," Desiree says, and rolls her eyes at me before she walks out.

"Sorry, Libby. This is embarrassing," she says again from the other side of the door.

"Don't worry." I shrug. "It happens to my friend every month. I downloaded an app on her phone that tells her exactly when she's getting her period, and still, it catches her by surprise every time."

There's silence in the room, just the drip from the faucet and the distant sound of bowling balls rolling down the lanes.

From the other side of the door I hear what sounds like a laugh, but it's followed by a sniffle, and I realize Quinn's crying.

Before I can ask her if she's okay, Desiree walks in with a Sully's takeout bag and hands it under the stall to Quinn.

"Here's a bunch of stuff. Clothes I had in the office. You can get it back to me whenever."

"Thank you, Desiree," Quinn says, followed by a gulping sob, loud and unmistakable. Desiree freezes, screws up her face at me, and holds her hands up as a question. I shrug and return the look.

Desiree leans in close to me. "What's her name again?" she whispers in my ear.

Quinn, I mouth to her.

What? she mouths back.

"Quinn," I say out loud by accident, and my voice echoes in the room.

"Yes?" Quinn chokes out from behind the door, and Desiree cuts her eyes at me.

The lock on the stall door clicks, and Desiree and I move back.

The door opens slowly, and Quinn fills the space, leans against the partition as if she's not sure she's ready to come out.

Her face is pale and tearstained, a smudge of mascara beneath each eye. She's changed into black leggings and a long T-shirt that I recognize as one of Sully's, and she's clutching the bag to her middle, her arms wrapped around it, curled over it almost, as though it's keeping her upright.

"Are you okay?" Desiree asks, even though she's obviously *not* okay.

The question makes Quinn's face crumple, and she lowers her head, covers her eyes with her hand.

"Well, that's a stupid question—you're crying, so you're obviously not okay," Desiree announces to no one in particular.

Quinn sniffles and wipes her nose with her sleeve, but she doesn't speak. Just breathes out, a ragged wet noise.

Desiree sighs. "Okay, so here's the thing. I really want to just leave you alone here—like, I *really* do—but I feel a sense of responsibility as the manager. We have kids out there, and one of them might be coming in here soon, and the last thing I need is for some mother to complain because there's a woman bawling in the bathroom."

Desiree glances at me, and I can't help the look on my face. She raises her hands in an *I give up* gesture.

I step closer to Quinn. "What she means is—we can't leave you here like this. I was serious before, it happens to my friend all the time. I mean, I know it's embarrassing and all, but it's really not that big of a deal."

"She's right," Desiree adds. "We've all been there. Periods suck. Fact."

Quinn looks up, shakes her head at us.

"It's not that." Her voice is shaky, broken. "I think . . . it's possible . . . that I, um . . . it might be the baby . . ."

"The *baby*?" Desiree repeats.

The bathroom door swings open, and a girl walks in. She's about ten or eleven, most likely the older sister of one of the kids at the party.

Desiree snaps her fingers at her. "You need to wait outside for a second. We're in the middle of something here."

The girl pauses midstep and looks behind her, as though she's not sure if Desiree is speaking to her.

"Go!" Desiree barks, and the girl turns on her heels and rushes out, closing the door behind her.

"You're *pregnant*?" Desiree hisses, glancing behind her, as though she's afraid someone might hear her.

Quinn nods, stifling a sob. "The home test was positive, but I haven't been to the doctor yet. And now . . . well . . . this."

"Are you in pain?" Desiree asks. "I mean, should I call an ambulance?"

"NO!" Quinn stands up straighter, panicked, it seems. "Nobody knows—my boss is out there, and she can't know."

"You need to go to the doctor," Desiree says in a voice that leaves no room for negotiation.

"I know—I'd just leave, but I came with my boss. I don't have a car."

Desiree looks at me, then back at Quinn. "Libby can take my car and bring you to the hospital."

Quinn doesn't respond, just chews on the corner of her thumb. "There's a walk-in clinic—I've been there before, so they have my chart. If you can just drop me, that would be great."

Desiree nods. "Libby only has her learner's permit, and she's the worst driver ever, but it's a straight shot up the street, so you should be okay."

Quinn glances at me and doesn't move from her spot against the partition, as though now she's weighing her options: stay in the bathroom, bleeding, or get in a car with me—the worst driver *ever*.

"You can leave through the back door so you don't have to walk through the party. Is your boss the clueless one? The *doctor*?" Desiree rolls her eyes.

"Yes. Madeline. You must have been the one she spoke with on the phone. In her defense, she did feel bad about that," Quinn tells her. "Sometimes she just says things without thinking."

"I don't know anyone like that." I slide my eyes over to Desiree, who shoves me.

"Move. Do something useful. Go tell Madeline that Quinn is sick, and you're taking her home. Meet us out back."

They shuffle out, leaving me alone, wondering how I got the job of delivering this news instead of Desiree. But I don't want to make Quinn wait, so I hurry out of the bathroom.

The bowling area is crowded, but it's not hard to find Quinn's boss. She's standing behind the shoe rental desk, bent over at the waist, peering at the shelves.

"There you are," she says, straightening when she sees me. "Aren't you the party leader person?"

"Yes. Sorry. I was in the bathroom."

She flinches at this, and looks at my hands, as though searching for some clue that I've washed them properly.

"I can't seem to find any wipes. I assumed there would be containers at every lane, but there aren't."

"Wipes?"

"Cleansing wipes . . . for the bowling balls."

I pause. "I'm not sure what you mean. Like wipes specifically for the balls?"

Her forehead wrinkles. "Cleansing wipes specifically for *germs*. The children are touching the balls. The balls are rolling on the floor and the children are touching them again. They should be wiped down."

"That's going to make them slippery," I tell her.

She tilts her head at me, as though she doesn't understand.

"Like . . . hard to hold."

"I know what slippery means," she says, and we look at each other a moment before I decide Desiree can handle this.

"You're Madeline, right? Quinn told me to tell you that she's not feeling well, so I'm driving her home. I'll tell my manager you want to talk to her about the wipes." I turn quickly, not giving her a chance to respond, and head toward the back door.

I'd give anything to stick around for the conversation she's going to have with Desiree. Doubtful Quinn's boss will come out of it with all of her limbs attached.

Outside, Desiree meets me at the back entrance. Behind her, the car is running, and Quinn sits in the front, staring blankly at the dashboard, a vacant look in her eyes. Desiree grabs my arm and stands in front of me, blocking my view of the car.

"Don't get caught up in this," Desiree warns. "Drop her and get out."

"I'm not going to just leave her there. She's really upset."

"Tell her to call her husband. She's wearing a wedding ring. I mean, it's his kid."

"Haven't you noticed he isn't around? She's been living downstairs for like . . . a couple of weeks."

"I don't hang around the house all day like you. So, no, I haven't noticed. And husband or no husband, there's a daddy somewhere—i.e., not your problem. Let him handle it."

"Bent said he's missing. He's some army guy Bent served with. I guess he's helping out while this guy's gone."

"If it was up to your father, we'd have vagrants living with us. The more someone needs saving, the more your father comes to the rescue. Just look at your mother—" Desiree stops midsentence and looks at the ground, clears her throat.

"Take the car home. I'll have Lucy pick me up." She opens the door and disappears inside.

I hurry to the driver's side and get in. Quinn is quiet while I buckle my seat belt. The air-conditioning blows lukewarm air at us. Quinn's forehead is slick with sweat, but she doesn't complain, just glances over at me, a worried look on her face.

"I'm not really a bad driver," I tell her, pressing the buttons for our windows to go down and breathing in when the fresh air fills the stuffy car. "Desiree's an awful teacher—sort of like a psycho drill sergeant—and she's mad that I won't do any of my supervised drives with her anymore. I won't kill us, I promise."

"You won't hear any complaints from me. I feel awful that I screwed up your day."

"Leaving thirty-three kids at a birthday party isn't screwing up my day. Desiree's, maybe. Your boss is waiting to talk to her about how to clean the bowling balls."

Quinn groans. "She's got a big heart. It's just hard to see sometimes under all the other stuff."

"You could be describing Desiree," I tell her, and she smiles briefly before she breathes in and closes her eyes.

"I'm sorry, Libby. Do you mind if we don't talk? I'm trying to figure out if I'm having cramps or it's just my mind messing with me, and I need to concentrate."

"Yeah, sure. We're almost there."

We drive in silence the rest of the way to the clinic. When I pull up at the front door, I tell her that I'll be right in after I park, but she says not to wait—that she'll call a cab to get home. But I drive around the block anyway and find a spot on the next street over.

Inside the waiting area, the receptionist tells me to have a seat—that she has no idea how long it will be.

The waiting room is empty aside from an older man in the far corner, his chin resting on his chest and his eyes closed. I sit in the row of seats by the window and check my phone, wondering how Desiree is doing with the roomful of kids.

There's a bunch of messages from Katie—a selfie of her and Erin in bathing suits on the deck at Katie's beach house, followed by a series of messages demanding to know why I'm not there. Like, *NOW!*

Next time, I text back.

Even though I know it's a lie.

Her summer cottage down the Cape is great—walking distance to the beach, a pool in the backyard. But I can't be in the house without thinking of the night I found out Bent was hurt, maybe even dead, when he was deployed.

Years have passed, but the smell of that house—the very air inside of it—brings me back to that night.

Katie's room has changed—even the bed where we were sitting is different: a twin replaced with a queen—but when I'm in her bedroom, my body tenses, my heart pounds, as though I'm waiting for the door to creak open, for Katie's mom's face to appear in the small sliver of doorway.

If I close my eyes, I can hear her voice, feel the walls closing in around me.

Libby, she'd said, and paused, her expression making my breath catch in my throat. I knew before the words came out of her mouth that it was Bent.

Even before Katie's mother sat on the bed, folded me in her arms and said things like *bomb* and *explosion* and *surgery*.

Before Katie gripped my wrist so tight, I thought it might snap while her mother spoke in a soft, reassuring voice about how strong my father was and how she knew he'd fight to come home to me.

It was Lucy who'd called Katie's mother and asked her to tell me. Lucy who dropped everything and got in her car to come get me. Lucy who made sure I heard about the explosion first from an actual person, before I might hear about it on the news.

No one could find my mother. She'd dropped me off at Katie's house earlier that week and kept driving. She didn't think to let anyone know where she was—that someone might need to get in touch if something happened to her husband. Or her daughter.

I prayed that night. Made deals with God that I had no right to make. *Take her instead*, I remember thinking, and then felt awful for it.

When I look back on it, I try to forgive myself. I was just a kid—angry and hurt that my mother wasn't there when I needed her. That she was never there when I needed her.

But even now, all these years later, with my mother gone and Bent alive—if I'm honest, I'd make that same deal.

I'd make it every minute of every hour of every day.

10

Quinn

She's parked on a tree-lined street across town in the wealthier section of Paradise. Quinn's familiar with the area—Madeline lives two blocks away—but she hasn't been on this street in years. Not since the summer after high school.

John's childhood home looms in front of her. A white sprawling house with large columns and a manicured lawn so meticulous, it could be a painting.

The FOR SALE sign on the lawn has been updated to SOLD, and Quinn wonders why John's mother has asked her here. Quinn hadn't even known Susan was back from Florida until she'd called that morning and asked her to stop by. Quinn had been exhausted, her body tired from sleeping poorly and her mind numb since yesterday.

The hours she'd spent in the clinic swirled in her head. The only moment she could clearly remember was the picture of a heartbeat on the ultrasound screen. The sound of the doctor telling her not to worry—the bleeding wasn't uncommon; her levels were normal, and the baby looked just fine.

Still—she finds herself moving more carefully today, and she wouldn't have come at all if Susan hadn't practically begged her.

Please, she'd said to Quinn on the phone. *For John.*

Now Quinn gets out of the car, walks to the door, and presses her finger to the doorbell. She listens to the chime, and a minute later, Susan opens the door.

She's a tiny woman—blond and polished and nearly wrinkle-free, even though she's in her early sixties, perhaps older.

One of the perks, John used to say about his mother's marriage to his stepfather, a prominent cosmetic surgeon. He'd say it with a smile, make a joke of his mother's artificially plump lips and taut skin, but there was an edge to his voice that didn't match his expression.

"Quinn," Susan says now. "It's been a while."

"Yes," Quinn agrees, not sure how to respond—she can count on one hand the number of times they've talked in the past few years. She might not even need all five fingers.

Susan looks rested, serene, but she's fidgeting nervously with her bracelets, and Quinn wonders how much of her placid expression came from a vial of Botox.

Susan gestures for her to come in, and Quinn follows her down a long hallway to the kitchen.

The rooms are empty, the walls bare, and their footsteps echo in the immense hallway. A spiral staircase winds through the middle of the house, and she glances up at John's old room.

She always felt out of place in this house, with its lavish drapes and expensive rugs, not a single thing out of place—so different from her house across town with books piled on every surface and the same faded curtains covering the windows year after year.

Finger sandwiches are on a plate on the table, a large pitcher of lemon water next to it. Susan offers her both. Quinn declines, says she's already had lunch and she's in a rush. Truthfully, she doesn't want to be here any longer than necessary.

"Thanks for coming. I wish we lived closer to see each other more," Susan says, as though the physical distance between them is the reason they rarely speak.

"Have you heard from him?" she asks, and Quinn shakes her head.

"I've called. Almost every day since you told me he left," Susan offers. "Not that I thought he'd pick up. He was always hard to reach when he was overseas, but now since he's angry with me, I don't hear anything at all."

Quinn had called Susan several days after John went missing. She hadn't thought Susan would know anything—and she was right—she hadn't even known John was stateside, had been for months.

"When was the last time you talked?"

"He was in Iraq. Somewhere. I called him to talk about an . . . opportunity. And he hung up on me."

Quinn frowns. "That doesn't sound like John. He just . . . hung up?"

"Well, no. He said he couldn't hear me. I was telling him about a job—a position in medical sales that Richard said was a wonderful opportunity. John told me it was a bad connection, and the line went dead. But he could hear me just fine."

"You called him in Iraq to tell him this?"

"I just wanted him to know he had options," she says defensively. "Maybe he felt like he had to do this army thing because of the situation . . ." Her voice trails off, and in the silence, the word *situation* rings in Quinn's ears.

She knows Susan is referring to her pregnancy. The twins. She swallows, reminds herself that it was a long time ago. Even though the memory of it is as fresh as if it were yesterday.

John had been at boot camp when Susan had called her after the miscarriage, the wound still raw, and she'd said to Quinn, in an almost upbeat voice, *Well, you're both so young. Perhaps it's for the best.*

Quinn never told John about it. His relationship with his mother and stepfather had already been so strained, so tenuous—had been for as long as she'd known him—she didn't feel right mentioning it.

But she never forgot the blow of those words. The way they seemed to slam into her body with a force so powerful it took her breath away.

Susan picks a crumb off the table, puts it on the plate next to the sandwich she hasn't touched.

"I just want him to be happy—to have a normal life. Apparently, I'm an awful mother for wanting this. My husband could have opened any door for him that he wanted. Instead, he threw it all away. And somehow we're the bad guys now."

Quinn slides off the chair, stands up.

"I need to get going. Why did you want to see me?" she asks Susan.

Susan studies her for a moment, walks over to the table behind her. When she returns, she's holding a photograph in her hand. A Polaroid picture of something Quinn can't make out.

"The movers took John's bed apart, and this was hidden between the mattress and the box spring. He was very upset we moved when he was at school. I know he blames me for that. Even though he knew he had a plane ticket waiting to Florida whenever he wanted—"

Susan keeps talking and Quinn tunes her out, remembering John's first semester at college.

How she'd called him one night and he'd sounded upset, although she could hear in his voice he was trying to hide it.

"Come home next weekend," she said. "I'll come pick you up."

He paused, the line between them silent.

"John?"

"About that," he said. "Susan and Doc are heading south. Some swanky retirement community in Florida where Doc can make even more money on boob jobs and lip fillers. They're renting the house out to some other family. So, technically, there is no home."

"What?" Quinn replied, shocked. "When?"

"It's happening as we speak. They're renting it furnished, I guess. I asked Susan if I could come home and pack my own stuff, and she told me the movers had already packed everything and she just knew I was going to act like this and put her in the middle of this mess. Which is just Susan's way of throwing Doc under the bus. Not that he doesn't deserve it."

Quinn had been stunned, silent. "Did you know they were planning to move?" she asked finally.

"I knew they were only staying until I finished high school—I was lucky to dodge boarding school after Susan got hitched—but I didn't know they meant, like, *right* after I finished high school."

"What about your job at the hardware store? Your friends? Me?"

"Minor details," John said. "How I feel about it isn't part of the Susan and Doc *How to make a successful person* guidebook. Missing chapters include love and affection."

John spent the summer in Paradise, crashing on couches of various friends. As far as Quinn knew, he never once set foot in Florida.

She hears her name and blinks. Susan's holding the picture out to Quinn, and it's a minute before Quinn takes it.

She looks down at the Polaroid. A group of soldiers are sitting on the ground, several stretched out, arms behind their heads, looking up at a man who's standing above them. He's telling them a joke, or a funny story, from the way the other soldiers are laughing, some doubled over, hands over their mouths.

She studies the man, recognizes the face, but not the body, as though John's head has been placed on a stockier, thicker version of himself.

"Who is that?" she asks Susan.

"John's father. It was taken when he was in Vietnam."

Quinn brings the picture closer. Looks at the same lips she's kissed a thousand times.

"John doesn't talk about his father. He said he died before he was born."

"He doesn't talk about him because he doesn't know very much. I didn't know he had that picture. It's the only one I ever had. He must have found it in the attic tucked away in a box of my old things."

Susan takes a sip of water from the glass in front of her, and her hand trembles when she places it back on the table.

"I met him in a bar." She points to the man in the picture. "He was older than me. This handsome, mysterious man who had his own apartment. I remember wondering why on earth he didn't belong to someone else." Susan folds her hands neatly in her lap, twists the stack of diamond rings on her finger.

"We'd meet every couple of nights and have a few drinks and I'd go home with him. It was so exciting. Carefree. Of course, looking back on it now, it was careless. Nothing more than careless." Susan smiles at Quinn, and if not for the small twitch in her right eye, Quinn would think Susan was happy, relaxed.

"I got pregnant and we moved in together. And then everything fell apart. And started to make sense—why this handsome, charming guy was single. Never married. No children."

Susan takes the picture from her, looks down at it.

"He'd have night terrors so bad, scream so loud, he'd be hoarse the next day. I'd wake up to him grabbing my wrist. Or my arm. Sometimes so hard I thought it might snap. And it wasn't just when he was asleep. We'd be out walking on the street, and a helicopter would fly overhead, and he'd duck, cover his head. His hands would shake for the rest of the day. That's when the drinking got worse. Or that might not even be true—I can't say it got worse, because I barely knew him. Maybe it was always that bad, but nobody was around to see it."

She hands the picture to Quinn and crosses her arms, as though the memory of it can somehow hurt her.

"He went out one night a month before John was born and was killed in a car accident."

Quinn nods. "That's the story I heard—that he went out one night to buy you ice cream because you were craving it and was killed by a drunk driver."

"That's the story John knows." Susan pauses, clears her throat. "The real story is . . . he was the drunk driver. He was drinking at home one night. And we argued. He told me he was going out to buy another bottle of vodka, and I told him if he did that, well, not to come home. He left anyway. Went to a bar, drank some more, and then got behind the wheel and drove straight into a stone wall. And when I say straight, I mean, *straight* into it. The police said it was an accident, but I don't think it was. There were no skid marks—and he hit that wall so hard, he toppled it. He didn't even try to stop."

Quinn puts the picture on the table, away from her, as though giving it back will erase what she's just been told.

"Why doesn't John know any of this?" She hears the blame in her voice. But it's too late to take it back.

Susan hears it too, and looks down at the table, avoiding Quinn's eyes.

"I'm not trying to justify it. I should have told him. But he wasn't even born yet. And then the years passed, and it was just me and John, scraping by. Things were hard, hard enough without John knowing the truth. Then I met Richard, and everything changed. We moved out of that awful apartment into this house, and finally . . . we . . . John had a stable life."

Quinn remembers John talking about that apartment. How he loved the nights his mother would come home from her waitressing job and bring them dinner from the restaurant, and they'd sit on the couch in front of the TV and eat from plates on their laps.

"She was fun then," he'd said. "Not all the jewelry and makeup and fake shit. Just, you know, normal."

Susan has her head down, and when she looks up, her face is wet. Quinn realizes she's crying, although her expression hasn't changed.

"I never expected to have my son in a war, in *any* war, much less on the front lines. All those years he's had this picture. And what little I told him about his father was good—that he was funny and charming and considerate—and he was. But that was only one side of him. One part of his life. He was also hurt. In a lot of pain. In need of help that he couldn't or wouldn't ask for. And it eventually killed him."

Susan grabs a tissue from the box behind her, dabs delicately under her eyes. "When I found this picture under his bed, something occurred to me, and it's been on my mind since you called." She sniffs, holds the tissue to her nose, waits a moment until she's composed. "My fear is that this is my fault. That all those years, John thought he was looking at a picture of a happy man. A man he wanted to become."

The picture sits on the table between them, and Susan picks it up, holds it out to Quinn.

"Take it. Please," she begs. "I don't expect you to tell him—that's my job. Something I should have done years ago. But I'm leaving, and I want him to have it. When he comes home, give it to him. Ask him to call me. Tell him he *must* call me."

Quinn takes the picture, slips it into her pocketbook. She doesn't say anything—what is there to say?

Susan walks around the island, leans forward, and gives Quinn an awkward hug, kisses the air next to Quinn's cheek so as not to smudge her lipstick.

"I'm sorry," Susan says, and Quinn's not sure if she's sorry John is missing, or sorry she's given away the only existing picture of her son's father, along with a story she was never able to tell.

"We'll stay in touch," Susan tells her. "And of course, you'll call if you need anything. Anything at all."

She says this with an airy breeziness, as though they speak often. They both know Quinn won't call if she needs anything—Susan doesn't even know she's moved to a new apartment. But Quinn nods, tells Susan that yes, of course, she'll call.

She lets herself out and walks to the car.

Inside, she gazes out the window at John's childhood home, a wave of nostalgia flooding her thoughts.

How many times had she parked in this exact spot when they were in high school? Back when their relationship was so easy—so uncomplicated. She'd drive over in the car she borrowed from her parents, and he'd meet her at the door, and they'd go up to his room.

She'd study while John plucked at the electric guitar he was always threatening to learn how to play. Her biggest concern an upcoming calculus test; John's thoughts on his next football game.

She can picture the two of them, draw them from memory, but in her mind, they're strangers. A couple of kids she doesn't recognize anymore.

Her phone on the seat next to her buzzes, and she reads a message from Bent.

Still on tonight?

She sighs—she'd forgotten Bent had invited her to have dinner with him and Libby—and her thumb hovers over the phone, ready to rain check, but she glances at the time—it's already late afternoon. As tired as she is, she can't bring herself to cancel.

Plus, Libby had waited with her for hours yesterday at the clinic—three hours to be exact—just to drive her home, and Quinn wants to thank her. She can't even remember if she said it yesterday.

She answers him before she can change her mind.

Sounds great. What can I bring?

He replies almost immediately.

You

She smiles at the small three-letter word, stares at it until she realizes how pathetic she's acting, and bites the grin from her lips, sticks the key in the ignition.

Stop it, she thinks to herself, trying not to think about how long it's been since she's had a text that made her feel like that. That made her feel anything at all.

She and John used to keep in touch as much as possible—and then this last tour, he was somewhere so remote he didn't have cell service, and she'd talked to him every couple of months.

And when he finally came home, it was as though he'd forgotten cell phones existed. Or maybe it was just that he'd forgotten she existed.

She'd be at work, on the playground with the twins, and she'd send John a text.

What do you feel like for dinner? Or *How's your day?* Maybe *Hi Babe*, with a heart or a smiley face.

He wouldn't answer—he never answered—and she'd come home and ask him if he got the message, and he'd look at her with that blank stare, as though she were speaking a different language.

Finally, she just stopped. She stopped texting. Stopped calling. Stopped asking. The silence between them growing until it was the only thing that existed.

She looks back at the house now, a wave of sadness running through her. Even though she'd never felt at home here—mostly because John never felt at home here—it was still John's childhood home. The place where he had lived.

Where he'd called her most nights from his room, lying in a bed with a picture of his father tucked under the mattress beneath him.

She wonders now what he dreamed about. She'd always thought maybe it was her. But maybe it wasn't.

Maybe John dreamed about the picture tucked under his head and the war he never asked about.

And the father he never knew.

11

Libby

Flynn is sulking across the table from me. He called me less than an hour ago, in front of my house, needing to talk *right now*.

So now we're sitting at one of the high-top tables in the back of Sully's with a pizza delivered by Desiree while Flynn tries to convince me to meet his new girlfriend—or more specifically, the girl he's hanging out with this week.

"Why won't you meet her?" he asks, for the third time.

"Why *would* I want to meet her?" I answer, for the third time.

"Because I like her, and she's important to me."

I snort, and lemonade almost comes out my nose. Flynn gives me a look.

"Okay, maybe not important. But I do like her. And she wants to meet you. Plus, you'd be doing me a favor. It would get her off my back. She's already pissed at me because her family thing got canceled, and I have plans tonight."

"But why does she want to meet me?"

He's pulled this on me before, in the beginning of the summer, with a different girl, but he clearly doesn't remember, because he's sitting across from me looking wounded, as though I've abandoned him. Like some sort of lost puppy.

"Because you're my friend. One of my best friends."

"Has she met Josh? Or Pete? They're your best friends too."

"No. But that's different." He shrugs. "You know . . . not the same."

"I know the definition of *different*."

He tilts his head at me, blinks like he doesn't understand.

"Don't give me that look—what you mean is they're guys. And your new girlfriend is the jealous type who doesn't like to see my name pop up on your phone. At least be honest about it."

"Fine! Okay? But—she's not my girlfriend. She's just a girl I want to take things a little further with, and she's convinced you're more than just my friend. So, just meet her. Then I can just—"

"Sleep with her," I interrupt.

He sighs, puts his head in his hands.

"Sorry my existence is screwing up your sex life."

He gestures for me to lower my voice, as though we're surrounded by people instead of alone in the back of an empty bar.

"Why do you always fall for the psycho, jealous type? Here's a thought—date someone normal, for once. I mean, you're not allowed to be friends with a girl?"

"Come on, Libs. You were blowing up my phone yesterday from wherever you were, and I was with her. I wasn't going to just ignore you. Which, by the way, I could've, because you were making zero sense."

I think about yesterday at the clinic—how Quinn had looked so happy to see me when she came out to the waiting area. I didn't mention the only reason I'd stayed was that I just have my learner's permit and I'm only supposed to drive with a licensed person in the car.

I'd sent Flynn a couple of texts asking if he could come get me, but he was with this new girl and trying to explain the whole mess was a disaster—Flynn kept texting me *Where r u?* and *what?* and *so cnfsed* and *Who pregnant?!* that I finally told him to forget it.

And then Quinn looked so relieved on the way home, so happy that the baby was fine, that I was sort of glad that I'd waited after all.

We finish the pizza, and I clear the table while Flynn meets Desiree at the bar and pays the bill. In the kitchen, I put the plates in the dishwasher, and Sully appears, out from his office.

"Desi putting you to work again?" he jokes.

"She's grumpier than usual. I'm staying out of her way."

"That's my fault. We were watching the Sox game earlier, and she was mad because the ump made a bogus call, and yours truly made the mistake of telling her that I love that she knows so much about sports. And she gets all like, '*Why wouldn't I know about sports? Because I'm a girl?*'" Sully holds up his hands, a defeated look on his face. "I just meant it as a compliment."

I laugh at the way he mimics Desiree, and he shrugs and walks away.

The bar area is filling up, and Desiree sees me from across the room and jabs her thumb in the direction of the front door.

Outside, Flynn is waiting in his car, talking to someone on his phone, and I can tell from the way he's talking that it's a guy—his voice is normal, not the syrupy, flirty voice he uses lately with his girlfriend who isn't really his girlfriend.

By the time he hangs up, we're almost at my house.

"That was Jimmy," Flynn says. "He wants me to come over tonight. And you're coming. I need a buffer with him lately."

"I thought you said he was doing okay—like staying out of trouble and no drugs."

"That's what I need the buffer from. I'm not used to him like this—he's like a different person."

"Isn't that the point? You used to complain about him all the time before. What a jerk he was and a liar and a drunk."

Flynn shrugs. “I know. You’re right. I’m happy he’s doing well—I am. There’s just a part of me that doesn’t trust it. He’s made promises like this before and he always fucks it up. So, come with me. Please. I’ll pick you up.”

“Only if you swear I’m not going to be the third wheel with your new girlfriend.”

“I already told you she knows I have plans tonight. Plus, Jimmy doesn’t want to meet anyone new right now.”

“He’s not going to want me there, then.”

“You’re not new, Libby. You’ve been around forever. Besides, he just asked for you the other day.”

“Really?” I ask, with so much enthusiasm that Flynn raises an eyebrow and smirks at me.

“No. But stop giving me shit about Desiree. Come on. We haven’t hung out in ages.”

“Fine,” I tell him, not bothering to mention that we haven’t hung out in ages because he’s always with some girl or the guys he met at Roscoe’s. “Bent’s making me do some dinner thing tonight, so pick me up at nine.”

He winks at me, and I get out of the car and walk up the porch stairs to the house.

The door is wide open, and Lucy is in the hallway, her back to me, studying the wall. Rooster sits next to her, his ears up. When he glances back at me, he wags his tail, but he doesn’t move. Just shifts his eyes to Lucy, searching her face, as though he’s part of a fun game he doesn’t quite understand.

At least ten different shades of red are taped to the wall, and Lucy’s focused on them so intently she doesn’t notice me until I’m right beside her. She blinks, comes back from somewhere far away, and slips her arm around my waist, rests her head on my shoulder.

"The perfect person to help me with this," she says. "The *bagua* was the problem. I had it all wrong."

"The what?"

"It's sort of like an energy map. Tan wasn't the right color for this room—tan says stability. Nourishment. We want new beginnings. Vibrancy. Youth!" She raises her fist, yells it like some sort of war cry, and slaps her palm against the red paint samples.

Rooster jumps, barks at the wall. I shush him, and he slinks away from Lucy until he's standing behind my legs, a bewildered look in his eyes.

Lucy coaxes Rooster out from behind me, apologizing to him and telling him she got a little carried away.

She scratches behind his ears, and he collapses on the floor, flops on his back, puts his legs in the air.

"I never want to scare my love, do I," she croons, rubbing his belly. She looks up at me. "You know I'm convinced he's my alter ego. Me in animal form. Aren't you, puppy? Yes, you are. What would you be?" she asks. "Oh, no wait. Don't say it—let me guess. If you were an animal, you'd be . . . oh, I know! A dragonfly."

I frown at her. "I hate dragonflies. They're just big bugs."

"Oh, they're beautiful! And colorful—do you know they change colors as they mature? They're all about joy. And that's what you bring to us. To this house." She smiles at me, rubs my arm.

"Well, what's Bent?" I ask, hoping to make her stop staring at me like she is.

"Bentley? Oh, he's an elephant. He'll tell you he's a bear or a tiger, you know, something manly in his mind. But he's a nurturer."

"And Desiree? I think she's like a . . . dragon."

"Dragons are much too nice for Desiree." Lucy laughs.

"I have to go," I tell her. "Bent's making dinner."

"Making dinner . . . as in . . . *cooking*?"

"That's what I was told. Quinn's coming. Host with the most, I guess."

Her eyebrows go up, and she looks at Quinn's door and back at me.

I say goodbye and walk upstairs with Rooster at my heels. Bent is in the kitchen, chopping an onion, and I sit down at the table across from him.

"You're almost late," he says.

"I'm not even close to late. Besides, I've been home for ten minutes, but Lucy had me trapped in the hallway talking about energy maps and animals. Has she always been so . . ." I can't find the word I'm looking for, and Bent looks up, wipes his eyes with his sleeve.

"Loopy?" he offers.

"I don't get it. I mean, you're so normal. Desiree is . . . Desiree. Lucy's just different."

"She's always been like that. When we were younger, we had a cat—some stray that my mother took in. Lucy was convinced it was our dead grandmother because the damn thing would sit in the chair by the window, and that was Nana's favorite spot." He shakes his head. "But you know Lucy. She's no pushover. Desiree acts like the tough one, but you don't want to be in the doghouse with Lucy. Well, maybe not you. She's always had a soft spot for you. Sort of like the daughter she never had, I think."

"Why didn't she have her own kids?"

Bent shrugs. "She had a boyfriend a long time ago. Nice guy. I think he wanted to get married, but Lucy called it off. Then she was with this woman all the time—they were roommates. Sort of wondered about that one." He looks at me sideways, smiles and shrugs again. "I don't really give it much thought. I just want to see her happy, and she seems happy. Goddamn these onions."

Bent has tears streaming down his face, and he grabs a towel and presses it against his eyes.

There are peppers sizzling in a pan on the stove, a bottle of tequila on the table, jars of spices line the counter, and I think I smell something burning on the grill outside.

"What the heck are you making?" I take the onion out of his hand, bring it to the sink and run it under cold water. A trick I learned from Lucy. After it's sliced, I add it to the bowl while Bent sits in the chair, blinking and sniffling.

"Fajitas. I thought we'd do like a Mexican theme."

"Theme? Are you going to wear a sombrero or something?"

He frowns. "Just give me those, wise guy."

He takes the onions, dumps them in the pan, and the oil crackles and spits at him, making him jump back.

"Libby, knock it off," he says when I laugh, as though I'm somehow to blame for this. "She's going to be here in twenty minutes!"

"What's burning?" I ask, and his eyes go wide before he dashes out the back door.

The counter is a disaster—bowls and measuring cups and cutting boards. I pile everything in the sink and turn on the water. By the time he returns, the mess is put away and I've set the table. He breathes out, wipes his forehead with the back of his hand.

"You're welcome," I say, and he leans down, kisses the top of my head.

Rooster is watching us from the other room, only his head peeking through the doorway, as though he's not sure it's safe to come in.

I put his leash on, and he follows me out the door and down the stairs without his usual hesitation, and I wonder if Bent's stressing him out—I can't remember the last time we had someone over for dinner, and I'm not sure I've ever seen Bent serve a meal that didn't include grilled burgers, reheated leftovers from Lucy, or microwaved food from a box.

We take our time walking around the block, which isn't hard, since Rooster twice throws his body down on the sidewalk and refuses to move until I nudge him with my toe.

When we're almost home, he circles the same spot of grass until I hiss his name and he finally does his thing.

By the time I clean it up, put it in the outside barrel, and go back upstairs, Quinn is sitting at the kitchen table, a panicked look on her face, while Bent fills two margarita glasses from a fancy glass pitcher I've never seen in my entire life.

He's changed into a clean T-shirt and smells of aftershave. I flick my eyebrows at him, and he spills some of the margarita on the table.

"Smooth," I tell him.

"I've got it," Quinn says, and leans over, a napkin in her hand.

"That one's for you," Bent says to me, pointing to a glass identical to theirs. "It's nonalcoholic. You two hold down the fort. I've got to check the chicken."

He walks out the back door, and Quinn turns to me, her eyes wide. She puts a finger to her lips until the screen door slams downstairs.

"He doesn't know," Quinn hisses. "About the baby. You didn't say anything, did you?"

"No. I hadn't even seen him until like an hour ago. He was working last night."

"Oh, thank God. I meant to tell you yesterday, but I was in kind of a fog—I don't even remember if I said thank you. Tell me I said thank you!"

Before I can answer, we hear Bent's footsteps on the stairs, and Quinn grabs my arm.

"I can't drink this!" she blurts. "There's tequila in it."

I take her drink and switch it with mine, and Quinn hisses that I can't drink it either and reaches for it just as Bent walks through the door. She freezes, her arm resting on mine.

Bent looks at us and smiles. "I knew you guys would hit it off," he says.

I raise the glass to my lips and take a sip. Quinn gives me a sweet smile, but when Bent turns, she rolls her eyes at me.

Bent gestures for us to sit while he disappears into the pantry. He emerges with an enormous basket of tortilla chips—the kind with a bowl in the middle for salsa.

"What, did you go on a Mexican shopping spree?" I ask, eyeing the new pitcher and the matching margarita glasses.

"I asked Sully for his guacamole recipe, and after he got done laughing about me cooking, he told me he'd set me up. Got home last night to a box of all this stuff by the front door. You know how he is. Go big or go home. I wasn't going to use any of it. But then I thought, when in Rome . . ." He lifts his glass, takes a sip.

"That doesn't make any sense. You could say that if we were in Mexico. Like in a cantina somewhere," I say.

"We're not?" Quinn asks innocently, glancing around the room. She smiles and tilts her head at Bent while I laugh. "All joking aside—this is really nice. Thank you. I usually have most of my meals with two five-year-olds, and it's a been a while since someone cooked me dinner, so I'll try to remember not to reach over and cut your chicken into bite-size pieces."

Bent smiles and asks her a question about her job while I sip my drink.

My plan was to make up some excuse to lie down—maybe a headache—and let them entertain each other.

But when I tune back in to the conversation, Quinn is telling a story, something about one of the boys she nannies, and the way she's moving her hands is making Bent laugh, like really laugh—not the kind where he's faking it.

The windows are open and there's a breeze coming through the house. The faint jingle of the ice cream truck sounds from somewhere in the neighborhood, and my fingers tap along to it.

It's not the first time I've had tequila, but Bent's made the drink strong, and by the second sip, my toes begin to tingle.

By the third, I feel myself settle into the seat.

And by the time dinner is on the table, I can't even remember why I wanted to leave in the first place.

12

Quinn

She'd been nervous when she knocked on the door, butterflies in her stomach, feeling as though she was intruding somehow, even though Bent had invited her. But when Bent answered the door, there was something sizzling in a pan beyond him, and the scent brought a memory of her childhood home: a vision of her mother in the kitchen, smiling over her shoulder at a younger version of Quinn, her sleeves rolled up and a pot on the stove behind her.

Quinn had stood in the doorway, entranced, suddenly at ease—this house had a way of making her feel this way, as though the way the light filtered through the windows and the smells and sounds surrounding her were all so familiar.

Then Bent had said hello, and she'd blinked, lost in the thought. He tilted his head to the side, the way he did sometimes, looking at her.

He said something about just getting out of the shower, and she followed him into the kitchen. The back of his neck was flushed, his crew cut damp, the scent of soap trailing him, and when he turned to say something to her, she bumped into him.

She was *that* close.

He put his hand out, startled, his fingers wrapping around her upper arm to steady her, and she was aware of the small space between them, the slight distance between his hand and her body.

It occurred to her then how *easy* it would be to shift into his touch—to feel the graze of his fingertips against the curve of her breast. The desire was sudden—so shocking and powerful—that she stepped back quickly, and he snatched his hand away, as though he'd done something wrong.

They stood across from each other until he cleared his throat and turned away, busying himself with quartering a lime on a cutting board at the kitchen table and offering her a drink.

Quinn had been unprepared to explain why she wasn't drinking. She could have simply told Bent *no*, made up some excuse. Told him she didn't like tequila, but she *did* like tequila. So, when he offered, she said *yes*, and then Libby walked in and she'd snapped out of it—it wasn't as though she'd *forgotten* she was pregnant; it seemed to occupy her mind constantly. But she was still thinking about the way his hand felt on her arm, wondering how she was going to make it through dinner without making a fool of herself over and over again.

But Bent asked about Quinn's job, and before she knew it, the night had passed, and Libby was leaving, going out with a friend, and Quinn was sorry it was ending.

She'd watched Libby and Bent through dinner—the way they spoke to each other—so natural and easy, *so* different from her relationship with her father after her own mother died that at one point in the night, her eyes had filled, just as Bent turned to say something to her. He'd paused, studying her with an expression that was so . . . tender . . . that she had to excuse herself to the bathroom to compose herself.

When he'd suggested a fire outside, she knew she should go back to her own place, to her own bed, and *stop* the current running through her body. Instead, she'd nodded, a puppet controlled by unknown strings, and followed him to the backyard.

Now there's a fire in front of her, and the chair Bent has brought out for her in the backyard reclines, so she's staring up at the stars while the fire pit warms her body.

The heat wave has moved out, and even though it's August, the air is dry and unseasonably cool. Bent has given her a flannel shirt and it's draped over her like a blanket, and Rooster is lying next to her and she's stroking his large head, and his fur is soft, cashmere under her fingers, and she doesn't remember the last time she was this content.

And as soon as the thought crosses her mind, she pushes it away. She knows it's wrong to feel this way with her husband gone and her future uncertain and a baby inside of her that she's keeping a secret—but it's there nonetheless.

The buttons on her jeans are tight against her stomach, but she knows it's from stuffing herself full at dinner, not the pregnancy.

Although, this morning she noticed a change in her body. Ever so slight, but proof somehow that this was *happening*. The doctor had confirmed she was nine weeks pregnant, yet feeling it for herself made her heart beat faster, an indescribable feeling spread through her.

She'd stood in front of the mirror after her shower, and nothing appeared different—maybe she was a little softer since she'd run track in high school—but when she pulled on her T-shirt, there was a fullness to her breasts, and she hadn't minded the way the fabric stretched across her chest, making her feel like a stranger in her own body, as though she were a different woman somehow.

She sinks deeper in the chair, lets out a groan.

"I ate too much," she tells Bent, pressing her hands to her stomach. "I know you said you don't cook often, but that chicken was delicious."

"The grill I can handle. It's the other stuff that's tricky. I hope you don't mind being my guinea pig. Lucy likes to cook, but I've been trying my hand at it. I don't want Libby growing up thinking guys can't do that kind of stuff."

"I think it's great. My father never learned either. My mother cooked a lot—we ate together most nights before she got really sick. After she died, we never sat at the table again. My father would bring his plate in the living room, eat in front of the TV or just stand at the counter, shovel the food in and leave. You don't realize how nice it is to eat with people until it's gone."

"How old were you when she died?"

"A little older than Libby. She had cancer. We thought she beat it once, but then it came back."

He nods, his eyes on the fire. "Libby's mom too."

She can see him out of the corner of her eye. His legs are stretched out in front of him, his fingers laced over his chest, and she has an urge to reach over and take one of his hands. She doesn't, of course. But she wonders how her hand might fit inside of his.

She wants to tell him how she feels—how being here, in this house, so disorienting at first, has changed somehow for her. But even in her own mind, she can't put words to the feeling.

"I don't know how to say this, but . . ." Quinn says, and pauses.

Bent looks up from the fire, waits for her to finish.

"I'm impressed with you and Libby," she says, slowly, choosing her words. "My father fell apart after we lost my mother. He died two years later—technically of a heart attack—but I think he gave up, just didn't want to live without her."

"Don't be impressed." He looks at her, pauses. "Sarah and I split up before she got sick. I was just home from overseas when she left. Then she found the lump and came home. She thought she'd stay through the chemo, until she got better. But . . ." He bites his lip, studies her. "She didn't get better."

"I'm sorry—I didn't know that. John never mentioned anything."

"He wouldn't have known." Bent shrugs. "I knew she was unhappy when I deployed. But it's not something I talked about with any of the guys. Most of them are stressed-out, leaving their wives and girlfriends for a year or more. Doesn't exactly boost morale. Then I came home sooner than expected." He pointed to the scar on his forehead.

"Were you relieved to come home? So you could be here for Libby?"

Bent turns and looks at her, the glow from the flame suddenly lighting his face. A flicker of something in his eyes that she recognizes immediately.

"John used to give me that same look," Quinn continues. "I used to ask: *Are you happy to be home?* And he'd give me that exact look."

"I guess it wasn't one of your favorites." He shifts, puts his hands up, as though he's afraid.

He's joking, she knows. But she doesn't smile.

"It's hard when your husband likes being away more than he likes being home."

Bent studies her for a long moment and takes a sip of his beer. "It's not a question of liking it or not liking it," he says finally.

"What is it, then?"

He shrugs. "It's a job. Those are my guys I'm leaving. And when you get hurt—someone else has to pick up the slack. I would've been on patrol the next day if they'd let me. Even with all the shit I had going on at home. Not because I got some sort of wargasm from it—some guys like the adrenaline rush. I just didn't want to let anyone down."

"And John? Is he one of those guys? The ones addicted to *wargasms*?"

Bent rubs his neck. "I'm not sure how to answer that," he says after a minute.

"Well, you served with him. What was he like over there? Cool Hand Luke, right? Whatever that means."

She's not sure how they got here, on this topic, but it suddenly occurs to her that this is a question she should know the answer to—that maybe who John is over there has everything to do with why he wants to go back.

He grins, picks at the label on the bottle. "The nickname was a compliment. And he earned it. Never lost his shit—bullets coming at us from all directions and he was always calm, steady." He takes a sip, swallows, the orange glow of the fire reflected in his eyes. "Fear is the great equalizer. Train all you want, but until you have rounds kicking up dirt inches from your face, you don't know anything. Some guys freeze. Not him. Back then, ask any guy in our unit who he wanted next to him . . . answer was always the same: Luke."

She shifts in her seat, faces the fire. It's enough to hear the words. She doesn't want to see it on his face too.

"You're not happy to hear that," he says.

"It's just, the way you talk about him. He sounds like your hero."

She glances at him. He has the same look she sees sometimes when he talks about Libby.

Protective.

"You asked me a question, and I gave you an honest answer."

She nods. "I know. I guess I just wasn't ready to hear about how good he is. You know, to hear it in your voice . . ." She lets the words trail off. There's a sudden tightness in her chest.

"Quinn." Bent waits until she looks at him. "I said John is a good soldier. Doesn't mean he was a good husband."

He picks up a handful of branches from a pile next to the fire and tosses them into the pit, where they crackle and spark, fire reaching up to the sky between them.

She can only see the outline of him through the red-orange flames, and he seems a stranger to her now, the closeness she felt earlier gone.

Something occurs to her then, his words replaying in her mind, shifting and moving behind her eyes until they make sense, as though what he's said to her is a piece of a puzzle finally sliding into place.

She's outside of herself now, standing with the shirt in her hands, clutching it as though it's the only thing she can hold on to.

His face appears through the fire and he's startled, surprised she's looming above him.

"Quinn—"

"What you just said . . . about being a good soldier . . ."

The words tumble out of her mouth, clumsy and thick, and he stands up slowly, one hand up, as though he's unsure of what she'll do next.

"He is. I mean it. He is good. Maybe one of the best."

"No," she says, pointing at him. "The other thing, the husband part—you said *was*. You said he *was* a good husband."

She can't see him now, his body blocking the flame.

"He's not coming back, is he?" she whispers just as a branch thick with dry leaves catches fire in the pit, the sky blazing behind him.

She sees him fully then, the glow lighting his every limb. His hand reaching out to her, but his body turned, holding back, as though he's being pulled in opposite directions.

It's his eyes that give him away. His eyes revealing he's told her more than he wanted to—or maybe he hasn't told her enough—she can't decide which.

She backs up now, wanting to go inside, away from the way he's looking at her and the suffocating silence that fills the air between them. She takes a step backward, feels the arm of the chair catch the back of her leg, and suddenly she's in the air, arms flailing, a whoosh of air filling her nostrils.

The black sky somersaults above her and she pictures the edge of the grass where her chair had been, the paved path beyond it, feels her body brace for the impact, her jaw clenching at the thought of her head hitting the hard concrete.

Instead, she feels arms around her, a body behind her catching her and lifting her to her feet.

Bent is in front of her, his hand still extended, and she turns, finding her footing on the uneven grass. Libby and Desiree and a guy she's never seen before are in front of her.

"Good thing I'm used to women throwing themselves at me," the guy jokes.

"Good catch, Sully," Bent says, but it's barely out of his mouth when Libby rushes past them, her hand over her mouth, and runs up the back stairs.

Quinn hears the door to her apartment open and slam against the wall, and through the window, they all watch Libby, leaning over, her head in the sink.

In the silence, the only sound is the fire behind them, the dry leaves exploding like gunfire in the dark night.

13

Libby

Flynn was late picking me up.

I'd left Quinn and my father sitting at the table and rushed downstairs, thinking he'd be waiting for me. But it was another ten minutes before he picked me up, moody and distracted. It took me almost the whole ride to Jimmy's to get it out of him that his girlfriend was driving him nuts, and he'd decided it was time to end it.

Now we're sitting in the car outside of Jimmy's house, music pouring onto the street through the second-floor windows.

"Wait—isn't this the same girl you were begging me to meet earlier today?"

"Yes. But that was before she spent the afternoon texting me—had to be thirty of them—about going out with you tonight. To see my brother!"

"Well, why'd you mention me? I mean, you already knew she was jealous."

"No—*you* said she was jealous. I thought she really wanted to meet you. She couldn't understand why you were coming with me to see Jimmy and not her. How many times can you explain the difference between someone you've known for what seems like forever . . . and someone new. She had me so nuts I could have polished off the six-pack just to get back to neutral."

"Don't even tell me I just drove with you if were drinking. Because if you tell me that, I'm getting out."

"Will you relax? I said I *could have.*" He pulls the keys out of the ignition. "But, news flash—we're here. So you can get out anyway."

He smiles, as though he's joking, but his voice is tight. He grabs a six-pack from the back seat and gets out of the car.

The street is packed with houses—flat-fronted two-family homes that all look the same except for the color of the aluminum siding. In front of us, the front lawn is steep, a concrete set of stairs splitting the dead grass into two patches of brown.

Music blares from the house, and I hesitate but Flynn takes my hand, yanks me through the door.

"I'm not going to know anyone," I say, following him up the narrow staircase to the second floor, and he yells something back at me.

"What?" I shout, just as the music turns off.

Flynn turns and stares at me. "You'll know me."

"Well, don't ditch me."

"When do I ever ditch you?" he scowls.

I snort. "Hmm, let's see. Pretty much every time you get a new girlfriend."

We're on the verge of a fight now, and Flynn sighs, pulls a can off the six-pack, and opens it with one hand. He takes a swig, offers it to me.

I shake my head. "Don't drink too much. I can't drive us home with my permit."

"Okay, *Mom*," he says sweetly, and rolls his eyes when he sees my face. "Don't be so fucking sensitive all the time," he mumbles, and walks inside, leaving me alone on the landing, blinking, his words bouncing around in the empty hallway.

Inside, the TV is on, the volume off. Smoke swirls in the air, and a man who looks to be around my father's age is sprawled on a couch on his back, looking at the ceiling, a glass pipe resting on his bare chest. A skinny girl with stringy hair sits by his feet, painting her toenails black. Neither of them looks up at us. In the kitchen to my right, there's a roomful of people.

I pull on Flynn's sleeve, and he stops, glances back at me.

"Let's go," I whisper, and suddenly, there are hands on my shoulders from someone behind me, my body weightless in his grip.

"Go where?" I hear, and Jimmy steps around, suddenly in front of me.

His shoulder-length hair is gone, his body lean and muscular compared to the last time I saw him.

"You remember Libby," Flynn says, and Jimmy claps him on the back playfully.

"Don't be a moron. I might have been drunk a lot, but I wasn't blind. Of course I remember." He leans in and kisses my cheek, his breath warm and fresh. I swallow hard, the memory of my crush flooding back.

He's wearing a crisp T-shirt, not a wrinkle on it, his pants fitted and clean next to Flynn's baggy gym shorts, the tanned skin of his head showing under his blond crew cut.

He eyes Flynn's hair, loose under a hat turned backward, and raises his eyebrows. The couple on the couch catches his attention. He shoves the coffee table with his foot, and they look up at him through heavy-lidded eyes.

"Get out," he says, and they untangle from the couch and slip out the door, like they know what might happen if he has to ask twice, the sour smell of body odor lingering after they pass.

Jimmy slams the door after them. "Damn roommate's druggie

friends. Sorry about that. I'd move out if I wasn't leaving soon anyway. Come out to the back porch—it's quiet out there."

The music turns on again, pulsing and loud.

He leads us to a doorway behind the couch, and we walk into a bedroom, bare except for a mattress on the floor and a small table next to it with an open paperback resting facedown. A camouflage duffel bag stands upright in the corner.

On the far wall, there's an open window overlooking the porch, the screen missing, and Jimmy steps through it. Flynn starts to follow, but Jimmy swats him away.

"Ladies first," he says from outside, and Flynn holds up his palms and gives me a look like I was the one who said it.

Jimmy puts his hand through the open space, his forearm sturdy and firm under my grip. My knee swipes the edge of the frame as I climb through, making a loud thud, even though I barely feel it.

"Klutz," Flynn chides, and Jimmy swipes at him through the window, catching only air.

"Why do you hang out with this punk?" He leans down, his fingers gently touching my kneecap. "Are you all right?"

"I'm fine. Just clumsy."

Flynn's on the porch now, and he opens a second beer. Then tosses one to me.

"I can get you something else," Jimmy says when I catch it but put it down beside me, unopened. "Whatever you want."

"Libby's a teetotaler," Flynn teases. "Beer is beneath her."

"You think anyone who doesn't pass out by the end of the night is a teetotaler."

Jimmy laughs, and Flynn shrugs, brings the beer to his lips.

"Is this porch code or what?" he says, yanking on the iron railing.

We're on the second floor of an obviously ancient house, and the rusty structure sways. I lean against the house, wondering what the hell is wrong with Flynn.

"It's an old fire escape, you dope." Jimmy squints at him. "Look at me. Let me see your eyes."

Flynn turns a cheek to him, his face slick with sweat even though it's cool outside.

"Why? You miss me?" He winks, chugs his beer, crushing the can in his hand, and reaches for another one.

Jimmy grabs his wrist, and they both freeze.

The smile disappears from Jimmy's face, the veins on his forearm bulging under the force of his grip on Flynn.

Even with the years between them, Flynn is bigger. Thick where Jimmy is lean, maybe a head taller. But Flynn doesn't move, and out of the corner of my eye, I see him lower his eyes and look away as Jimmy releases his grip.

Flynn's phone chirps, and he looks down at it. He raises a finger as though he'll be back in a minute and disappears through the window. He's arguing with someone, and I know it's his girlfriend, the one he said he wasn't going to see tonight so he could hang with me.

"What was that all about?" I ask Jimmy after a minute.

"Let's just say I know that look."

"What look?"

"The eyes. He's high on something."

"He did just drink two beers in a matter of minutes."

"I'm not talking about booze."

"What . . . like drugs?"

He shrugs. "My mother said some prescriptions in the cabinet went missing last month. Flynn's the only other one in the house." He looks at me. "You don't know anything?"

I shake my head "I barely see him anymore. He's always with some new girlfriend. But he wouldn't around me anyway."

"A regular Casanova," he mutters.

"Well, he's a Casanova who's also my ride tonight. I don't get my license until next week. So he's cut off when he comes back." I look back through the open screen, but Flynn isn't in the room anymore. "Look, you don't have to stay here with me. I mean, all of your friends are inside. I can just wait here for him."

"The only person I know inside is my roommate, and I don't even really know him. I only heard about this place from an army friend. I guess the landlord is a former vet who rents out rooms for cheap to service guys. My friend didn't mention that there's also parties here almost every night. So, if you don't mind, I'm happy sitting here with you."

"I don't mind. Flynn said you like the army? So far, I mean."

"It kind of saved my life. I don't mean to sound dramatic. I'm not sure if you remember, but I was kind of a fuckup." A dog barks next door, and he leans over the railing, looks out at the noise.

"I remember," I say, and he looks back at me and laughs, and my face burns. "Oh—that was rhetorical, wasn't it? Sorry."

"Don't be. I hope you never saw it firsthand, though."

"I just heard about it from Flynn. You were always nice to me when I was at your house." I leave out that I had a crush on him. He used to seem so much older than me. A senior when I was only in eighth grade. Now, sitting next to him, it's as though we're the same age.

"So how was basic? Is it as bad as all the things you hear about it?" I ask.

He pauses, thinking about it. "Yes." He smiles.

"What's bad about it?"

"Everything. But nothing worth talking about."

"Come on. My father was in the Guard, but he went to basic so long ago, he doesn't even remember it. So tell me. I'm all ears."

I settle back in the chair and fold my arms. He looks at me and shrugs.

"Okay. I'll stop when you start to snore." He smiles, but starts in the beginning, when he first got to the base.

His voice is calm, mesmerizing, and he reminds me of Flynn before he became this *Flynn*, the guy who says stuff like *Plural* and *Teetotaler* and *Mom* in a way that makes me blink back tears.

I'm not sure how much time has passed when Jimmy looks at his watch, says he better get me home. Enough time for me to realize Flynn isn't coming back.

Jimmy climbs through the window and moves the table out of the way, holds his arm out for me to take.

"Let's not whack that knee again," he says.

A copy of *The Things They Carried* falls off the table, and I pick it up, hand it to him. "Good book. We had it a couple years ago for summer reading."

"I'm playing catch-up. Too much screwing around when I was your age."

"I can't imagine why you'd volunteer to go to war after reading that."

He smiles. "I probably wouldn't have if I'd read it. Let's hope there's no tree in my future. No Curt Lemon stories."

I look around the room at the bare walls, the mattress on the floor. "My father would approve. He hates clutter too."

"I'm just crashing here until I ship out next month. Doesn't make sense to unpack when I'm leaving again." He walks through the bedroom and opens the door. The house is crowded, and he looks back at me, holds his hand out behind him.

"Grab hold. I don't want us getting separated."

I reach out, and he takes my hand. We step through the doorway, weaving our way through bodies in the packed living room.

The smoke is dense, and a guy in the corner waves to me, puts a can to his mouth. I squint, thinking it's Flynn, but when he tilts his head back, the light catches his beard.

A body fills the doorway of the next room, broad and tall like Flynn—the same baseball hat on backward. I drop Jimmy's hand and walk toward him, trying to catch him before he disappears into the dim room.

But he moves deeper into the swirl of bodies. I lunge forward, snag the back of his shirt with my fingertips and tug. My shoulders are squeezed between people on either side of me. I yell Flynn's name, but my voice is lost in the music and laughter and shouting. The guy turns, and it's not Flynn—the nose too narrow, the lips too full—and his eyes scan over me blankly. He shifts, his profile illuminated briefly under the dome of kitchen light, and then he's gone, swallowed up by the sea of people.

Suddenly there's an arm around my waist, pulling me back. Jimmy grabs my hand again, and we're through the door and down the stairs, the cool, clean air outside filling my lungs.

He walks over to a truck parked on the street, and we climb in.

"Are you okay? I thought I lost you in there."

"I thought I saw Flynn. But it was someone else."

My head is suddenly pulsing, my vision blurry and my toes tingling.

"Hey, are you okay? You have goose bumps." He points to my arm and reaches behind him to the seat. "Here. Take this."

He hands me a camouflage jacket, his name printed on the front. I slip it on, the pattern on the jacket firing in my memory.

"Libby," Jimmy says, staring at me. "You look like you saw a ghost."

"Sorry. It's probably just the smoke in the room. I'm kind of dizzy," I tell him, the picture from Quinn's apartment filling my head—the guy sitting in a camouflage uniform next to Bent. The one with the movie-star looks. The someone else I thought was Flynn. The one turning away from me in the kitchen, disappearing before my eyes.

Quinn's missing husband.

"Just close your eyes," Jimmy says after I tell him where I live. "I'll have you home in two seconds."

I listen to him, because suddenly I can't breathe, and the tequila and smoke and Bent's Mexican creation are all swirling in my stomach, a small burp filling my mouth with the taste of the margarita. I concentrate on taking slow breaths, in and out, in and out, but it still feels like the longest ride of my life until Jimmy pulls up in front of my house.

The truck's not even at a full stop when I thank him and jump out.

Desiree and Sully are on the path to the backyard and she turns and narrows her eyes at Jimmy's truck as he drives off. I follow Sully to the backyard, certain I'm going to be sick. There's some sort of commotion next to me, and I hear my father's voice, then Quinn's, but I'm already on the back steps. Quinn's back door is unlocked, and I rush into the kitchen, shove my head into the sink, the room spinning.

I'm holding on to the sides of the sink when I feel a hand on my back. Quinn leans in close to me, gets a whiff of my breath and clothes, looks at the back door.

"Go lie down on the couch. Quick!" She motions for me to go.

By the time I get to the couch, the room has stopped spinning. A minute later, I hear Bent's voice in the kitchen and pull the blanket on the couch over me, hoping it will cover the smell of tequila and smoke on my clothes and in my hair and on my breath.

I close my eyes while I listen to Quinn tell Bent that he should just let me stay put, and it's perfectly fine for me to crash on the couch for the night. Desiree chimes in that she's been fighting a virus and I must have caught it, and rest is *exactly* what I need, and he should just let me be. She sounds so sincere and sweet, so un-Desiree-like, that the room goes silent for a moment and I think she's blown my cover.

"Besides, Sully wants to have a beer with you," she continues. "Or at least that's the story he gave me when I found him standing outside the house. Frankly, I think he's stalking me again."

Sully says something about how she *wishes* he was stalking her, and Bent tells them both to shut the hell up. Then I hear Bent and Sully on the back porch, their footsteps heavy on the stairs, their voices growing distant when the door shuts behind them.

I sit up slowly, my tongue suddenly leather in my mouth. A dull headache pulses behind my eyes.

I glance at my phone, expecting to see something from Flynn, but there is only a group text with Katie and Erin that I haven't answered all night, both wondering why I'm not answering.

Where r u

Everything ok?

Libs?

The floor creaks and I look up to see Desiree standing in front of me, hands on her hips.

"What the fuck?" she says.

Quinn rushes in from the kitchen, a worried look on her face.

"I should never have let you drink that." She turns to Desiree. "Don't be mad at her—Bent gave me a margarita earlier—it's a long story. But the whole thing was my fault."

Desiree ignores her. "Who was the dude in the truck? You know . . . the *man*."

"Oh," Quinn breathes, looking at Desiree and then over at me, her face blank.

"It's Flynn's brother. He was dropping me off. Can I get a glass of water?" I ask Quinn.

"I'll get it. Stay right there," Desiree says, pointing at me, as though I'm prone to disappearing, and stomps into the kitchen.

"Are you okay?" Quinn asks, her face full of worry.

"Yeah—I think it was just the Mexican food. I'm fine, really."

She waves me away. "Well, I feel responsible. I handled the whole situation poorly. I should've just said no thank you!"

Desiree returns from the kitchen with a glass of water, stands over me, and holds it out.

"Drink," she says. "You smell."

"It's just secondhand—you know I don't smoke." I take the water and sip it slowly.

Desiree's quiet, and I know it's because she knows she can't lecture me about smoking. She's been saying she's going to quit for as long as I can remember. I've told her it's a gross habit, and she must remember this because she finally stops eyeing me and walks to the middle of the room.

"Are you moving out or something?" she says to Quinn, looking at the boxes surrounding us.

"Oh, no. I'm still . . . unpacking."

Desiree looks at Quinn with a sideways glance. "Unpacking? You've been here like . . . ?"

"A while. I know. The pregnancy sort of surprised me. But that's not really an excuse. I don't know, I guess I didn't know how long I'd be here . . ." She looks at Desiree, who juts her chin forward, waiting for Quinn to continue.

"My husband is . . . away."

Desiree squints. "I don't know what that means."

"I mean, he's not here."

"Well, I get *that.* What I mean is—I don't know what that has to do with unpacking. You're here. He isn't. So what?"

Desiree walks over to a stack of picture frames leaning against the wall, picks one up and looks at the back of it.

"No time like the present," she says matter-of-factly.

"Now?" Quinn asks, looking at her watch.

"I've got a picture-hanging doohickey thing upstairs. Hold on," Desiree tells her, and walks through the house and out the back door.

"That's nice of you to help," Quinn shouts after her. She looks at me, holds up her hands. "Funny. I actually felt like she didn't like me for some reason."

"I think she doesn't like me about once a day too." I stand up, my legs shaky underneath me. "I should go shower while Bent's outside."

"Libby, wait. I . . . um. I've been meaning to ask you. Do you mind keeping the baby just between us? I hate to ask you that—I don't want you to keep secrets from your dad. But it's just, I need to figure some things out."

I nod, and something occurs to me. "Are you not keeping it?" The moment the words leave my mouth, I want them back. "I'm sorry," I tell her, my cheeks hot. "That's so none of my business. Forget I asked you that."

"No, it's okay." Her eyes fill, but she stands up straight, as though she's fighting against it. "That's not what I need to figure out. I want this baby more than anything. It's the only thing that matters."

I walk into the living room, pick up the picture with Bent and her husband.

"Is this him?" I ask, holding it up.

She nods. "A younger version. That was his first deployment."

"Can I borrow this? I don't have any pictures of Bent overseas. I just want to make a copy. I'll bring it back, I promise."

She nods. "Of course."

I study the picture. "It's weird seeing Bent without the scar on his head."

She walks to where I'm standing, looks over my shoulder. "I met your dad for the first time right after he came home. I couldn't stop looking at that scar. And I remember thinking that as awful and painful as it must have been to have an injury like that . . . that he was still home, you know? Standing right in front of me. I could reach out and touch him. When John kept deploying, I almost hoped . . ." She pauses, shakes her head. "Well, you start to wish for something to bring him home. And keep him home."

Quinn takes the picture, looks down at it, and hands it back to me. "Then again, he has to want to be home, right?"

"Maybe when he finds out you're pregnant, he'll stay."

She smiles, a sad lopsided thing that's the opposite of happy. "That's what I'm worried about," she says.

"Isn't that what you want? For him to come back and stay?"

"If you'd asked me a couple of years ago, I would have said yes. Now, though—it's not enough. I don't want this baby to be the only reason we're together. I wonder sometimes if we would have been married . . ." She pauses, waves her hand. "I was pregnant years ago, and I miscarried. And then John deployed. Something changed for him then. But not for me. I still wanted him, and a baby—a family. Then he came home, and I thought, well, now we can try. But he signed up for another tour. He said it was for the bonuses they were giving. I just kept thinking that he didn't want to start a family until he was home. You know, for good." She sits on the edge of the couch, tired, it seems. "I kept waiting, thinking it was a timing issue. But really, I don't think that's what he wanted."

"What didn't he want?" I ask. "The family or to be home?"

"Either," she says quietly.

I look down at the picture. At Quinn's husband. And suddenly, I'm certain. The nose. His lips. He's the guy at the party at Jimmy's. The one in the crowd in the kitchen, moving, shifting, just out of reach. Disappearing right in front of me.

14

Quinn

All week she's avoided Bent. She can't shake the feeling that he's somehow on the other side of this—on *John's* side—is how it forms in her mind. The conversation by the fire replaying in her head over and over all week, the way he said *doesn't mean he was a good husband.*

He's hiding something from her. Protecting John in some way. Maybe she's just imagining it, but he's avoiding her too. They used to pass each other when she left for work or came home, and she hasn't seen him once this week, but she hears his footsteps on the stairs after her door has clicked shut. Quick, as though he's rushing to leave so he won't run into her.

Then she feels paranoid for thinking this.

Midweek, she got tired of herself. Sick of waiting for her life to make sense again. Once, she gave over to the feeling, to the overwhelming *unknown*, and Desiree's face popped in her head, the way she'd asked Quinn why she hadn't unpacked.

There was something in her voice when she'd said it—as though she was sizing up Quinn. Wondering if she was the type who needed a man to guide her. The type who couldn't even *unpack* by herself.

As soon as the thought crossed her mind, she realized how absurd it was—she'd been doing this *life* all by herself anyway. With John overseas, she was basically single—no different than what she was now.

And the way they all just *did* it. Like they were on some sort of mission. Desiree had returned with the picture-hanger thingy, Lucy behind her. While Quinn unwrapped dishes and glasses and silverware, Lucy and Desiree assembled the table and hung the heavy mirror and moved couches and bureaus and Quinn's massive headboard.

She painted the kitchen and the dining room, getting up early before work to paint the trim and rolling the walls after she got home from work, the radio on and the windows open, the apartment finally looking as though someone lived there.

Lucy came back on Friday to help her finish decorating.

And for the first time in her adult life, Quinn *likes* her house. No—*loves.* She loves this house.

The way the light streams through the windows in the morning and the sounds she falls asleep to at night.

In the dining room, there's a built-in hutch filled with her mother's china, unpacked for the first time ever—there wasn't space for it in their duplex—and every time Quinn walks by it, she pauses and studies it, feels her mother right there in the room with her.

She's thanked Desiree and Lucy over and over for their help—even left a thank-you note and a plate of brownies by their front door—but it still doesn't seem enough.

Which is why when Desiree asked Quinn to come to her yoga class, she agreed. Quinn thought the idea sounded odd—power yoga in the backyard—and Libby overheard Desiree talking about it and whispered to Quinn: *She just needs bodies—live subjects.*

Quinn wasn't overly fond of yoga—she'd rather go for a run

or take a spin class. But Quinn said yes anyway. How could she say no when Desiree had been so helpful? She even agreed to bring a friend, but then she realized she'd lost touch with everyone from high school except for a couple of girlfriends who didn't live in Paradise anymore, so she mentioned it to Madeline, not expecting her to come.

But she did, bringing the twins with her, walking into the backyard and over to Quinn, who was standing on her mat wondering what the hell Madeline was thinking bringing the boys to a power yoga class, until Madeline leaned over and whispered, "There isn't babysitting here?" Quinn explained, for what seemed like the millionth time, as if it weren't obvious, that this was not a *gym* and the instructor *lived* here.

Madeline squinted at her, looking confused, and the boys saw Libby on the back porch and raced over to her.

Before Quinn could follow them, Desiree started the class, and when Quinn turned around, Libby and the boys were gone.

Now the class is over, and Quinn's soaked in sweat.

She has been sitting on her mat, pretending to watch Desiree demonstrate a headstand pose that looks suicidal, but really, she's just too tired to get up, and the sun feels warm on her face.

Madeline is next to her, lying on her back with her eyes closed, as though she didn't arrive with two children who have been gone for the last hour. She probably thinks Libby is the babysitter instead of just a girl who also, like the instructor, happens to live here.

Quinn sighs and stands up to go in search of the boys, when Desiree walks over, hands on her hips.

"Okay, Miss *I'm not very good at yoga*," she says to Quinn. "Not bad for someone who doesn't do yoga often, never mind someone who's preg—"

"Madeline—the boys are back!" Quinn interrupts, her voice jarringly loud.

Madeline sits up and blinks, looking behind her while Quinn shifts her eyes to Desiree and shakes her head to signal that Madeline can't know about the baby. Desiree claps a hand over her mouth.

The boys are playing on the grass nearby while Libby talks to Lucy, who had started the class on the mat next to Quinn, not following along and doing her own poses until Desiree marched over and whispered something in Lucy's ear. Lucy frowned at Desiree, then picked up her mat and moved to the back of the yard, behind the last row of students.

"Well, that was a success for a first class!" Lucy says brightly. "There must have been fifteen people here."

"Oh, I didn't realize you were taking *this* class," Desiree snaps. "I'm trying to teach, and you're distracting everyone."

"No one cared besides you. Plus, I'm just trying to prepare you. When you start teaching in a studio, there will be *distractions* exactly like that. You'll be dealing with strangers. Not just friends and family."

"Yes, because so many strangers *pay* for a yoga class so they can show up and *not* follow along," Desiree replies sarcastically. Lucy sighs and purses her lips.

"Well, I would come to all your classes," Madeline says. "So many instructors are into that spiritual crap. You have sort of an angry shut-up-and-do-it vibe." She smiles after she says this, and Quinn holds her breath, but Desiree shrugs and thanks Madeline, as though this is somehow a compliment.

"They're soul mates," Libby whispers to Quinn.

"We made you cards," Nick says, walking over to Madeline and holding two folded pieces of brightly colored construction paper out to her, likely Libby's idea. "For your birthday."

"It's your birthday?" Lucy asks Madeline in an excited voice.

Madeline rolls her eyes and nods. "As much as I don't want it to be. But forty-five is the new twenty-five, right? Or something like that."

"But she's not having a party like we did," Nate says sullenly, and Nick nods. "Not even any presents."

"You gave me a present," Madeline reminds him. "The mugs you made with Quinn—I love them."

Her voice is full of excitement, but the boys scowl and wander away while Madeline watches them with a worried look.

"You don't want to celebrate?" Lucy asks. "Desiree is like that too. She hates birthdays."

"You talk about me like I'm not standing right here," Desiree says. "I don't hate birthdays. They're fine when they're not mine. Not everyone likes to be the center of attention."

Madeline sighs. "I just feel bad for the boys. They're excited to celebrate, and somehow I don't think the lamb lollipops I have planned for later are going to measure up."

"I love lamb lollipops," a voice from behind Quinn says, and she turns to see Bent standing behind them, an arm thrown over Libby's shoulders.

He's in his police uniform, and the twins stop what they're doing and walk over to him. Nick's eyes are on Bent's gun belt, mesmerized.

Madeline giggles, a sound Quinn has never heard before, and after they've been introduced, Bent drops to one knee, talking with the twins, who stand so close to Bent, they're almost in his lap.

Nate reaches out and touches the badge on Bent's shirt, while Nick eyes the flashlight on his hip so intently that Bent finally hands it over, shows him how to turn it on. He tells them to take it into the garage, where it's dark, but to be careful, and they run off, arguing over who gets to hold it.

Next to her, Madeline is staring at Bent, studying him so intensely that Quinn takes a step away from her.

"I've never seen a real gun," Madeline says breathlessly. "It's much bigger than I thought it would be."

"I get that a lot," Bent replies innocently.

"I bet you do," Desiree says in a flat voice.

"It's Madeline's birthday," Lucy announces to Bent. "She's making lamb lollipops to celebrate."

"Just for me and the boys," Madeline explains. "Just a small celebration. Single-mom-type birthday, I guess." She giggles again, and Libby rolls her eyes at Quinn behind Bent's back.

"Well, you're in good company," Bent says. "It's Sully's birthday too. He's doing free apps for an hour and disco bowling tonight. You guys should all come down and have a drink."

"I want to go bowling," Nick shouts, sticking his head out from the garage. Nate yells that he does too, and Madeline looks over at Quinn.

"Oh, will you meet us? We should all go! How about you guys?" she says to Lucy and Desiree.

"I'm the bartender, so I'm getting paid to be there," Desiree says, holding up her hands like she doesn't know how she was included in this impromptu invitation.

"I'll go. I can do my poses under the disco ball," Lucy says, her arms in the air, and Desiree glares at her before she turns and stomps into the house.

Madeline turns to Quinn. "Say yes. I promise it won't feel like you're at work. I'll be on kid duty, I promise." She doesn't have a chance to answer before the boys are all over Quinn, tugging her hands, begging her to go.

"Come with us," Bent says to Quinn, his arm around Libby again.

Libby looks up at him. "Us?" she says.

"Come on, Libs. There'll be free nachos. Hang with your old man for one night."

"I'll stay for the free hour, but that's it. I have plans."

"What kind of plans?" Bent asks, but Libby ignores him, and he looks away like he really didn't expect her to answer anyway. "Come with us," Bent urges Quinn again. "Seven o'clock?"

She feels herself nodding, because he's looking at her and what else is there to say besides yes. Bent smiles at her and waves, takes the steps two at a time, and disappears into the house.

She walks with the boys, one on each side of her, swinging her hands, to the minivan parked out front.

Madeline is trailing behind her slowly, and Quinn thinks she'd probably stay at her house all day if Quinn invited her. Which is why Quinn is buckling the boys in their seats, busying herself until Madeline has no choice but to get in the driver's seat. Quinn says goodbye to the boys, shuts the door and steps back on the curb. Madeline motions for her to come closer, and Quinn walks forward, leans in through the open window.

"Well, he's *attractive*," she says to Quinn. "If I wasn't such an old lady . . ."

"You're not *old*, Madeline."

"Well, invisible, then. But it's not an age thing. I've always been invisible to men. Skinny, high-strung, socially awkward scientist is a hard sell. Probably why I'm still single."

"You're single because you work a million hours a week and hang out with two five-year-old boys on the weekends."

She groans, puts her head on the steering wheel. "You're right. I have no life."

"You have a life. Just not a *social* life." Quinn studies Madeline. "What about online dating? Make a profile somewhere. Go out on some dates."

"I tried that already. It falls apart in person. I'm more attractive in virtual mode."

Quinn laughs. "Who isn't? You know what—don't worry about it today. Come out and have fun tonight."

"I'll need a stiff drink. All those hands on the bowling balls." She grimaces, and Quinn gives her a look, and she holds up her hands. "I know, I know. *Let it go*. I'm trying, Quinn. Give me that, at least. You can't say I'm not trying." She waves through the window, toots the horn, and drives away.

Quinn watches her leave, then turns and looks at the house.

Her windows are open, and a new pair of curtains, white and clean, hang inside like a blank canvas. The hibiscus she planted has bloomed, the petals spread wide, soaking in the bright sun. Her house looks welcoming. More than that—it looks lived-in. It looks like her.

She walks up the steps into her new home, thinking of Madeline. How maybe they're not so different.

15

Libby

I'm in my bedroom, staring at the picture of Bent and Quinn's husband, when there's a knock on my door. I stash the frame under some papers on my desk and yell that it's open.

Desiree appears in the doorway.

She's barefoot, still in her yoga pants, her hair in a messy bun on the top of her head, and no makeup. She looks so different that I can't wipe the look off my face before it's too late.

"What?" she says, looking down at herself.

"Nothing," I say quickly. "What's up?"

"Don't what's up me. Why'd you just give me that look?"

"I don't know. You just look different." I point to my face. "You know, no makeup."

She narrows her eyes. "Bad different?"

I shake my head. "You should go without more often."

She walks in and looks in the mirror on the wall. Turns her head side to side, frowns.

"No makeup reminds me of being a kid. A fat kid." She puffs her cheeks out.

"You weren't fat. I've seen the picture books. You were just normal."

"Not according to my mother. Now, Lucy—she was a different story. Lucy and my mother were born like this." She holds up her pointer fingers. "Straight up and down. And me, well I got the T & A—from my dad's side."

"Your mother called you fat? Bent always tells me how sweet she was. How he wishes I'd met her."

"Oh, she wouldn't say it like that. She'd tell me she had the most wonderful dream and in it, I was thin and beautiful and glowing. Or she'd buy my clothes too small, and when they didn't fit, she'd tell me just to hold on to them, that with a little work, I'd get there. It wasn't just me—Lucy got her fair share. My mother would tell her that no man was going to want a wife with her head stuck in an astrology book all day. A girl with her head in the clouds, she'd say to Lucy." She laughs at the expression on my face. "Don't look so traumatized. She was from a different generation. Married my father young and stayed home and raised us. She was happy, though. She wanted the same for us."

"And Bent? I can picture him as a mama's boy."

"Oh, he was. But he also had to deal with my father. I remember he took a baseball to the mouth when he was seven or eight. A line drive right at him. Two teeth knocked out, and the only thing my dad said was stop crying about it. If you're dumb enough to use your mouth as a glove, that's what happens." She laughs. "I think that's why he became a cop. He's going after the bullies one by one."

She turns, looks at me.

"Anyway, I just wanted to say thanks for today. I didn't expect anyone to bring kids. Guess I should've thought of that."

"No problem. They're easy."

Desiree had asked me yesterday to set my mat down in the back and follow along—she wanted the class to look full for one of her clients, a woman who was looking for an instructor to teach a two-week yoga retreat at her house on some tropical island.

I overslept and rushed down the back stairs in the same shorts and T-shirt I'd slept in, and there were the twins—a lifesaver, in my mind. I'd sat on the floor and watched them make birthday cards instead of twisting myself into Desiree's torture poses.

"How'd it go?" I ask. "Did you get the job?"

She shrugs. "She seemed impressed. I had her sit in front, so she didn't see Lucy acting like a lunatic. With any luck, I'll be spending the holidays in the Caribbean."

"So you and Sully are really over, then?"

She shrugs again. "He's still all, *I don't want my kid in day care*," she mimics, her voice low. "Translation: Desiree is the free day care."

"Why don't you get a nanny, then? Like Quinn."

"What do you think, we're the Rockefellers?" She twists her face at me.

"It'll work out. Look at all the couples who have kids," I offer, aware that I have no idea what I'm talking about. My mother thought of our home as a jail.

Desiree looks at me like she can hear my thoughts. "Well, it didn't *work out* for my friend Liz. She's got three kids, quit her job ages ago to stay home, and now the oldest is off to college and the youngest is in middle school and her asshole husband screws his secretary—you think it's cliché, but it happens *all* the time—and now she has to find a job. You know what she's going to be doing? Folding sweaters at the Gap for minimum fucking wage."

"Maybe just have one kid, then?"

"Only children are self-absorbed. Everyone knows that."

I raise my eyebrows, and she waves me off like she didn't just insult me.

"Plus, can you imagine Sully with one kid? He'd give it too much attention. You know, suffocate it."

"Well, you can balance him out," I tell her, and she ignores me.

"All I'm saying is, when you get married, have your own career. Your own money. Then at least when you have little Gingers or Joeys running around and the shit hits the fan, you have options. Money doesn't make your life better, but it sure as hell makes it easier." She pauses, blinks as though I'm coming into focus again.

"Wait." She walks over to my desk. "What's that?"

I shift, blocking the picture with my hip, not wanting to explain why I took it from Quinn's apartment, but she reaches out and picks up my license.

"Is this what I think it is?" she asks.

"I got it earlier in the week."

She sucks in her breath. "Oh, Jesus. Just what we need. You on the road."

She taps me on the shoulder with it and winks when I take it from her, then walks out the door. I watch her leave, thinking that it might be the closest Desiree and I have ever come to bonding.

The picture frame is under sheets of paper on my desk. The back slides out easily, and I take the picture out of the frame and slip it into my back pocket. The longer I look at it, the more I'm positive it was Quinn's husband at the party that night at Jimmy's house.

I close my eyes and try to retrace the route Flynn drove, but I only get to the center of town before I'm lost, side streets criss-crossing in my mind.

I'd call Flynn, but we haven't spoken since that night. He never called or texted to see if I got home okay. I talked to Katie last night, and she asked what Flynn was up to, and I told her I didn't have a clue.

"What do you mean?" she asked.

"I went to his brother's apartment with him last week, and he ditched me. I haven't talked to him since. Which is fine. All we ever do is argue now anyway."

"Argue? You guys? Since when?"

"When are you coming home?" I asked, not answering her. "Erin said she's away until, like, the day before school. Tell me you're not too."

"I am—which is why you need to come down here! Convince your dad to lend you his truck—tell him I said it's not that far of a drive!" she said, reminding me of the latest lie I told Katie when she'd asked me to come down and see her.

I'd laughed and switched the subject, because Bent was the reason I wasn't visiting Katie, but his truck had nothing to do with it. I felt bad for lying to Katie in the first place.

Now I pick up Jimmy's coat off the bed, pat my back pocket to make sure the picture is still there, and walk into the kitchen.

Bent is sleeping after the night shift, his door shut. I leave a note on the table that I'm running an errand, and grab his set of keys off the dining room table.

Rooster Cogburn is lying in his usual spot in the sun underneath the window in the living room. He picks up his head when he hears the keys jingle and lifts his large body off the floor, his ears high, an eager look on his face.

Car rides with Bent are the only thing that get Rooster even mildly excited, and I sigh, stare at him.

"Fine," I tell him. "But you better behave."

He bounds over about as quick as he ever moves and hurries down the stairs, the sound of his toenails clicking against the wood loud in the empty hallway.

Inside the truck, Rooster hangs his head out the window while I drive, his tongue flapping in the wind. I drive to the water, past Sully's, and then turn right at the traffic light and drive up the hill.

The streets are narrow, crowded with old houses that have been turned into apartments or condos, and they all start to look the same.

I remember looking out my window that night with Flynn at a house with Christmas lights still hanging from the gutter, but I pass two houses in a row with their lights still up, and they're single-family homes that don't look anything like Jimmy's house.

At the end of the street, there's a house that looks familiar. I park, grab the jacket, and walk around to the sidewalk. Rooster is sitting in the passenger seat, straight backed, facing forward, a serious look on his face, and he refuses to look at me when I open the door and call his name, as though by ignoring me, I'll just get back in the truck and *drive*.

There's a leash in the truck bed, and I clip it onto his collar, and it's a minute of me begging him to *come on and get down* before he unfolds himself lazily out of the truck and onto the sidewalk.

I walk to the front door and press my finger to the doorbell, feeling my heartbeat quicken, my palms grow clammy. Rooster looks up at me, his eyebrows together. The fur on the back of his neck stands up. A low growl fills the air.

"It's okay," I say, patting his head.

I picture the guy on the couch with the glass pipe on his chest. There's no way I'm going up there, even with Rooster by my side.

On the side of the house, a concrete path winds to the backyard. We walk around the corner, follow it until the back porch is above us, the rickety metal stairs leading up to a landing. I recognize the chairs we were sitting in, but before I can figure out what to do next, Rooster yanks me to the tree behind us and lifts his leg.

"You know this is private property, right?" a voice calls out from above. The sun is bright, blinding. I hold up my hand to block it. Jimmy is leaning out the window, looking down at us.

"I have your coat." I hold it up as proof. "I'm just returning it."

He climbs through the open window and walks over to the railing above us. He's wearing shorts and a T-shirt, a towel in his hand.

Rooster turns and gives a loud bark, but Jimmy walks down the steps and over to us.

"Who's this big guy?" he asks, and when I tell him Rooster's name, he puts his hand out. Rooster wags his tail and licks the sweat from Jimmy's leg.

"Hey, Killer," Jimmy says, scratching behind Rooster's ears until Rooster loses interest and looks up at me. I drop the leash, and he wanders over to the tree and lies down, as though he's in his own backyard.

"Sorry to barge into your backyard. I rang the doorbell, but I wasn't sure I had the right house. I thought I might recognize the porch."

"I was out for a run. I'm glad I didn't miss you." He pauses, looks at his feet and back up at me as if he wants to say something, but he's quiet.

"Thanks for this." I hand him the coat, and he takes it and nods, his eyes on mine before they flit away again.

I put my hand in my back pocket, finger the edge of the picture, losing my nerve. What if he knows Quinn's husband? What then?

"What are you up to?" he asks, and I freeze, as if he can read my mind, but he smiles and pulls at the front of his shirt. "I mean, if you can wait for me to grab a shower, maybe we can get a cup of coffee or something?"

"Sure." I nod. "He needs to go for a walk anyway. I'll take him out front and meet you there."

"I'll be quick," he says, and runs up the stairs, ducking through the window. Rooster and I walk to the front, turn right down the street and then up again, and by the time we get back to the truck, he sits on the sidewalk, refuses to budge.

I open the passenger door and grab my phone, checking to see if Bent has called.

He said it was fine to take the truck if I needed to run an errand. But I've been gone over an hour now, and I'm hoping he's still asleep. There's nothing from Bent, and I shove the phone in my pocket.

My keys are on the floor on the driver's side. I lean in, feeling Rooster's leash pull me back, as though he's walking the other way.

"Rooster, stop," I call out, my head down. The keys have slipped under the seat, and when I finally get my hands on them, my feet are almost off the ground.

When I stand, Rooster is sitting on the sidewalk, leaning into the hand that's petting his head. I look up at Flynn, who raises his eyebrows, stares at me.

"Jesus," I say, my hand on my heart. "You scared the crap out of me."

"Why?" he asks, his face stone. "Expecting someone else?"

"What are you doing here?"

"What am *I* doing here? Well, let's see. Last time I checked, I had a family member who lived here. You know, a *brother*. So that's probably a better question for you."

His clothes are wrinkled, his eyes bloodshot. I look up the street and see his car parked several houses down, at an angle, the back bumper far away from the curb.

"Did you sleep here last night?"

"I didn't have a choice. I stopped in because there was a party going on, and Corporal up there took my keys. Said I was high on something," he scoffs. "Fucking guy thinks I'm him. Or maybe it's just that he's in the army now," he sings, and marches with his arms out straight.

"Well, if that was your parking job, he should've taken them away."

He glances behind him at the car and looks back at me. "There were a million cars on the street last night. I had to parallel park into some tiny space and I barely fit. Anyway, what the hell are you doing here?"

The door opens, and Jimmy walks over and stands next to Flynn.

"Ready?" Jimmy says.

Flynn looks from Jimmy to me.

"What the hell is this?" he says.

"Do you want to drive?" Jimmy asks me. "I don't have a back seat for Rooster."

I nod and open the rear door for Rooster to get in while Flynn glares at Jimmy.

"I'm serious, dude. What the fuck?"

Jimmy looks at him, his forehead creasing. "What's the problem?"

They stare at each other for a moment until Flynn shakes his head.

"No problem. Do what you want."

Jimmy snorts, gives him an amused look. "Thanks for the permission." He reaches into his back pocket and sighs. "Crap. Forgot my wallet. Be right back," he says to me, and jogs up the walkway to the house.

I pat the seat for Rooster, and he climbs in, collapses on the seat, his head on the padded divider in the middle. When I shut the door, Flynn is in front of me.

"You're not seriously going out with him?"

"We're just getting coffee."

"That's my brother. My fucking *brother*."

"So?"

"So, stay away from him," he says, like that's that. "There are a million other guys you can date. Not him."

"It's not a date. It's coffee, Flynn."

"Yeah, right." He walks away, turns, and stomps back. "What happened the other night? Did you hook up?" he asks incredulously.

"What happened to *you* the other night? You know, my ride home?"

"Oh, so that's it. What, payback? Screw around with my brother so you can piss me off."

"Yeah, Flynn. That's it. I'm using your brother to get back at you for blowing me off. What are we, toddlers?"

"For the record, I came back to get you, and you were gone. My brother too. Where'd you go? *Parking?*"

"He was nice enough to drive me home. Sober. Which is more than you would have been. You disappeared, talking to your girlfriend. I thought she was driving you nuts."

"She was driving me nuts—which is why I took the call and ended it. It just took longer than I expected. But I told you I'd drive you home, and I came back to drive you home. You were the one that left. The two of you were pretty chummy on the porch. You wanted me to leave anyway."

"Look—I don't care where you were or who you were with. I do care that you made a promise to me and you broke it. And now, here, right now, you're rude. No, you know what? You're rude *all the time*. And you know who isn't?" I point at the house. "Your brother. That's who. I'm getting coffee with him because he's a nice guy. Sort of like someone I used to know."

Out of the corner of my eye, I see the door open and Jimmy step out.

Flynn leans in, his eyes flashing. He's so close I can smell the stale beer on his breath.

"Maybe I'll stop by later," he says in a voice only I can hear. "You know, see if Desiree's around."

He walks to his car and gets in, the tires kicking up pebbles when he pulls away. Jimmy walks over, leans against the truck in front of me, and sighs.

"He was drunk last night. He's pissed I took his keys away."

"He's mad because I'm having coffee with you."

He tilts his head at me. "Seems weird to be mad over something like that. You guys never . . ."

"God, no. We're friends . . . that's all . . . he's always just been . . . one of my best friends."

"So what's his deal?"

"I don't know. He thinks, you know, we're more than just hanging out."

He's standing in front of me, close enough that I can feel his breath on my face. I could step back, move from the curb onto the sidewalk, but I don't. The way he's looking at me has my limbs heavy, my body numb.

"Are we?" he asks, putting his hands in his front pockets, leaning back against the truck, his legs crossed in front of him.

I study the shape of his lips, the smooth dent in the center, the tiny scar at the edge of his mouth.

My feet are half on the curb, half off, the sharp edge of concrete hard against my foot. I press into it, a sharp twinge in my sole that's strangely soothing. The world around me disappears, blurs into the background until it's just the two of us.

Me teetering on the edge. And him, waiting.

~ 16 ~

Quinn

There was only one box, tucked in the far corner of the dining room, that she hadn't yet unpacked. The last remaining evidence of her move to this new apartment.

Truthfully, she probably would have just moved the box to the back bedroom, maybe even the basement. But she'd promised Libby that she'd look for pictures of John and Bent.

The box was full of pictures Quinn had accumulated—a mish-mash of Quinn's life over the last decade—from high school until now. She'd dumped the box on the kitchen table, sorted through the pictures, and organized the piles according to years, as best as she could remember. She almost threw the whole mess back in the box when the task seemed overwhelming, the box bottomless.

Instead, she went to the store and bought several photo albums. Her childhood photos were already in albums her mother had put together, thick with milestones, dates and names detailed in her mother's precise handwriting. She's been meaning to do the same with these pictures, and now it seems absurd to not just . . . *finish.*

She stands over the table holding a picture of John from years ago—right after they graduated from high school. He's laughing the way he used to—she can almost hear it—a laugh so infectious it was impossible not to laugh with him.

The memory of it forces her eyes shut—she wants to stay in the sound of his laugh, sit with it for a moment with the sunlight bright behind her closed lids and the soft hum of the radio whispering in the room.

There are stacks of pictures like that of John—John smiling. John laughing. John kissing her cheek, his eyes bright—the boy she fell in love with.

She barely recognizes herself standing next to John or sitting on his lap or walking next to him, their fingers laced or shoulders touching. These pictures are on one side of the table—two-, sometimes three-, deep.

And then there's the other side of the table.

Two separate stacks of pictures—John in one stack. Quinn in the other. A handful of them together—she picks them up and counts. Four. She places them on the table again.

Four pictures of her and her husband together, in the same room, since they were married. Four pictures in more than five years.

She doesn't need to go through her stack again to know what she'll see—pictures Madeline has given to Quinn: the boys' birthday parties, the first day of preschool, zoo excursions, and the trip to Florida where Madeline went to a conference while Quinn spent her days at the hotel pool with the boys. It's Quinn's life, of course. And she loves the boys—even Madeline most of the time.

But it's her *job*. What she gets paid to do.

Instead, she studies the pictures of John. Brings each one close to her face before she puts it down on the table, arranging them until the surface is covered with just John. She catches her breath at what she sees.

Camouflage and helmets and tanks and guns.

John in a group photo with his unit. Another in a makeshift outdoor gym, dirt swirling in the background.

John shirtless, a tattoo on his shoulder—the dog tags of a guy in his unit who was killed by a roadside bomb. Someone Quinn had never met, never even heard of until John came home with the man's name on his arm.

Perhaps it's the guy with his blood on the road—the one John shot the puppy over. She doesn't know. She and Bent haven't talked about it since he told her.

But she thinks about it all the time. Wonders more and more what her own puppy looks like now. The one John sent away.

She looks at the pictures—searches them for a trace of the boy laughing in the high school pictures. The one she knew so well.

It's almost dark when she finally puts the last picture in the photo album. After all that work, she only has two pictures for Libby—another copy of the photo of John and Bent, and one of Bent with the entire unit.

She'd thought there might be more of Bent and John together until she realized that most of the pictures were from John's second deployment. The one that seemed to change everything about him. That made him feel like a stranger in his own home. The one that Bent missed.

She can't stop her mind from lingering on this—she's thought often about Bent. How he seemed to go to war and come back, untouched. Hurt—a scar on his head to prove it. But not with the same demons as John. Bent was able to pick up his life right where he left it. To leave the war where it should stay.

Now she wonders if it was the difference between one deployment and two. The length of time between home and away. Bent was gone for six months before he came home.

John stayed, though. And then he went back.

It occurs to her that maybe John has lived away for so long that *away* finally became *home*.

She looks up at the clock, shadows forming in the corners of the room. She'd give anything to lie down for a couple minutes, her muscles tired and aching after Desiree's yoga class.

But she remembers that Bent and Libby will be expecting her to go to Sully's.

She stumbles into the shower, lets the hot water soothe her body. She takes her time getting ready, and when there's a quick knock on her door at seven sharp, she's finally feeling like herself again.

She opens the door to Bent and Libby arguing in hushed voices, and they straighten when they see her.

Bent clears his throat and gives her a forced smile.

"Sorry, we're late," he says. "My truck went missing until a minute ago."

Libby rolls her eyes behind him, and Quinn looks at her watch.

"You're not late. It's just seven now."

"See," Libby says to Bent. "Told you." She turns on her heels and walks out of the house, the screen door slamming behind her.

Bent sighs and looks at Quinn. "You jinxed us last week saying we get along so well."

"I take it she took your truck and was late?"

"She said she had trouble getting it started and was stuck at her friend's house."

"You can't blame her for that."

He raises an eyebrow. "My truck always starts," he says, and she tilts her head at him.

"Well, give her a break. She just got her license."

"Tell that to poor Rooster. He was two hours over his dinner-time."

She laughs at the concern on his face. "He's definitely in danger of starving," she jokes, and he doesn't smile, but she sees him glance down at her, and she puts her hands on her dress.

"Am I overdressed?" she asks, even though she's in sandals and a long cotton sundress she'd bought on a whim years ago without trying it on. It had always hung too low on her chest until now.

"No," he says, clearing his throat. "Ready?"

They walk out to his truck and climb in, and his mood seems lighter. He looks at Libby in the rearview mirror and winks.

The windows are rolled down in the truck, the radio on, and they're quiet on the ride over, a comfortable silence punctuated by Bent singing along with the radio.

"You're not bad," Quinn tells him when they pull into the parking lot and get out of the truck.

"Don't encourage him," Libby mutters.

"Wait till you see my dance moves," he says, and Libby groans and walks ahead of them into Sully's.

Quinn is almost at the door when she feels his hand on her arm.

"Wait," Bent says. "I need to talk to you."

She stops, looks at him.

"It's John—"

"No—not tonight," she interrupts, waves her hands. "Please, I can't think about it anymore today. And about the other night—you're loyal to him. And that's okay. He's a grown man, making his own decisions. You're not responsible for making him come back to me."

"Quinn, I—"

"Bent, please. I just want to forget and have fun tonight. Okay?"

He starts to argue with her, but there's a shout from behind him, and Madeline and Lucy appear.

"Fancy meeting you here." Madeline giggles, putting her hand on Bent's shoulder and throwing her arm around Quinn.

Bent steps away from her and looks at Lucy. "I thought you were already here. You left the house an hour ago."

"We had a pre-party and I talked her into a babysitter," Lucy says.

"And she talked me *out* of the lamb lollipops. We had martinis instead," Madeline adds, her voice relaxed and playful. She's wearing a slinky cocktail dress and heels, as if she's going to a nightclub instead of disco bowling.

"I don't get out much," she explains to Quinn, looking down at her outfit.

"You look hot," Lucy tells her. And Quinn nods; the dress is flattering on Madeline's straight figure. Her hair is loose instead of pulled back in the tight bun she normally wears.

"It's all her fault." Madeline jabs her thumb at Lucy. "She's determined to get me laid tonight."

"Nice." Bent slides his eyes over to Lucy, who puts her hands up.

"I don't think those were my exact words," Lucy says, and Madeline covers her mouth and giggles.

"I have to pee," she blurts, and hurries inside.

"How did you even end up at her house?" Quinn asks Lucy, confused. She thought they'd only met just this morning.

"She left her yoga mat in the backyard and came back to get it. We took the boys for lunch, and one thing turned into another," Lucy says. "Plus, no one should be alone on their birthday." She holds up a set of car keys. "I'm designated driver tonight, but I'm also on matchmaking duty." She flicks her eyebrows and opens the door, disappears inside.

"You better be careful tonight." Quinn turns to Bent and smiles, and he twists his face at her.

"What's that mean?"

"I think my boss is on the prowl. And you're it." She sticks a finger out, pokes his chest.

He grabs her hand so quick and sudden she doesn't have time to pull her finger back in.

"Well, protect me, then," he says, looking at her in a way that makes her swallow hard.

She doesn't move, and he opens his fingers, letting go of her, and she brings her arm back to her body, slowly, as if in a trance.

He walks around her and opens the door. She walks through, feeling his eyes on her when she passes him.

Inside, strobe lights crisscross the room, and a mirrored ball hanging from the ceiling sends shards of neon light over the lanes. A DJ is set up in the corner above a small wooden floor, and Quinn spots Madeline dancing with Lucy, a martini glass in her hand. Lucy twirls her, and she almost drops it.

Bent tilts his head to the right, and she follows him to the crowded bar. He says hello to a group of guys, who slap his shoulder or shake his hand.

The bar is packed, and someone steps in front of her, and she loses sight of Bent. Then he's there, reaching for her and guiding her in front of him, his arms creating a circle around her. She shuffles forward, and he leans over her shoulder, points to the far end of the bar, where Desiree looks up from wiping the counter and waves.

Libby is sitting in the corner and she stands up when they walk over, takes her purse off the seat next to her.

"I'm leaving," she shouts over the music. "I was just waiting so you guys can have seats."

"You just got here," Bent yells back.

"It's all old people," she says, frowning.

Bent looks around, points to the other side of the bar.

"I work with all those guys. They're my age!"

Libby raises her eyebrows. "Exactly."

Quinn laughs, and Bent gives her a look.

"You're not taking my truck," he warns, and she holds up a set of keys.

"Desiree's. She's getting a ride home from Sully."

Bent leans over the bar and calls Desiree's name, an annoyed look on his face. She glances at Libby holding her keys and mouths back that she can't hear him and disappears to the other side of the bar.

"Where are you going?" Bent yells.

"Out with friends," she shouts back.

"Boys?" he asks, and Libby sighs, holds her hands to her ears like it's too loud. She leans over and kisses him on the cheek and waves to Quinn, and she's gone, weaving her way through the crowd.

They sit down, and the song ends, and he turns to her.

"She's a good kid, but I worry about her. You know. Hormones." He shrugs.

"And she's beautiful," Quinn replies.

"Yeah. And she doesn't know it. Double trouble."

"I don't think so. She's more like brains and beauty."

"Sort of like someone else I know," he says, and looks at her, and Quinn doesn't know what to say.

He snorts, presses his face against his palms and groans. "Jesus, I'm sorry." He gives her an embarrassed look. "I shouldn't have said that. I have no idea why I just said that. It just . . . popped out."

She feels her cheeks burn.

"Can we start again?" he asks, and she nods.

Desiree puts a beer in front of Bent and a tall glass in front of Quinn.

"On the house," she says to Quinn and winks. Quinn takes a sip through the straw, and the taste of Shirley Temple fills her mouth.

"You're probably used to having guys say dumb stuff like that," Bent says. "How many dates have you ended with jerks like me?" He grins and then looks at her, his eyes suddenly wide. "Not that this is a date. I'm not saying that."

She smiles, thinks about his question. "Actually, I've never been on a date."

"What?" He gives her a look. "What do you mean . . . never?"

"I mean never."

"Quinn, you were married. I mean, are. You *are* married." He rolls his eyes. "So obviously, you went on a date. Maybe it was just one, but . . . that's still a date."

She shakes her head. "We never dated. I don't even know how we ended up together. I mean, we hung out with the same people in high school. And I think we kissed at some party. And then again. And then, we were just . . . a couple. It's not like he ever called me up and asked me on a date."

When she finishes talking, she looks up and he's staring at her. He doesn't say anything, just rubs his hand on his jaw, takes a sip of his beer.

The music starts again, a Motown song that Quinn recognizes, and she looks down at the dance floor filling up with people now.

She looks over at Bent, elbows him.

"You want to dance?" she shouts, and he leans over, looks past her at the dance floor.

He tilts his head back, drains his beer, puts it on the bar and stands up. She looks over at him, surprised, and he holds out his hand.

When they reach the dance floor, she hesitates, self-conscious for a moment, but Bent pulls her out into the middle, twirls her in a circle. The DJ puts on an old Marvin Gaye song that reminds her of her mother, and the music fills her thoughts.

Bent drops her hand, and they dance across from each other, and she watches him move, impressed that he's not just shuffling from foot to foot like John used to do the handful of times he actually let her drag him up to the dance floor.

Quinn hears a screech, and Madeline appears next to her, her shoes gone and a half-empty martini in her hand. She prances seductively over to Bent and drapes her arm around him, pressing her hip against his.

Quinn backs up, ready to blend into the crowd, not wanting to see any part of Madeline make a pass at Bent, but he untangles himself expertly from her grasp and manages to move just far enough away that Madeline can't reach him.

Lucy joins them for the next song, weaving between them, twisting in circles as though there's not an actual beat to the music, her arms raised in the air.

The song ends, and Madeline slides her eyes over to Bent and points to her glass, empty now. He pulls a twenty out of his pocket and stuffs it into Lucy's palm, pointing them both to the bar. Madeline sticks her lip out, pouting, and waves for him to come, but he grabs Quinn and they disappear behind a group of people, and another song begins, slow and pulsing.

Bent turns to her, wraps his arm around her waist, pulls her close.

He knows how to do this, she thinks, remembering the awkward, halting way John slow danced with her. She follows his lead, her body relaxing in his grip, and they move together without talking, his chin inches from her lips.

She feels drunk, even though she hasn't had any alcohol. His body close to hers, his T-shirt damp against his muscled back, the fabric hot under her hand. She feels herself dissolving into the moment, everything and everyone around them fading into the background.

She lifts her eyes up to his, and he's watching her with *that* look, and she shifts unconsciously, her body reacting, her hips moving into him. She slips her leg in between his, pressing against him, and his eyes flicker to her face, his jaw suddenly tight, and a heat creeps up her neck.

The song ends, and he drops her hands, steps away from her. They don't speak, and she can't read the expression on his face.

Lucy walks over to them, keys in her hand.

"Well, it's lights-out for the birthday girl," she says. "She's in the parking lot, puking in the trash barrel, so I think it's time to go."

"I think I should go home. Can you drop me?" Quinn blurts. "If you don't mind? I just got really tired."

"Of course," Lucy says, and nods for her to follow.

Bent is staring at her, looking at her in a way that makes her want to get on her knees, press her head to the floor, beg for mercy.

"I'm sorry. I have to go," she says, and he doesn't answer her, doesn't move.

She half walks, half runs to the door, rips it open, and jogs to the car, the night slamming into her lungs.

Madeline is already in the car, and Lucy is buckling her seat belt for her. She puts down Madeline's window.

"If you're going to be sick, raise your hand—I'll pull over," she tells her, but Madeline's eyes are already closed, and Quinn wonders if she's asleep or passed out.

"I'll drop you first," Lucy says, and launches into a story that Quinn can barely follow, her mind racing.

She's thankful Lucy is driving fast, probably not wanting Madeline to wake up and get sick in her car, and it's less than five minutes before they pull up in front of the house, and Quinn says a quick thank-you and jumps out.

She rushes inside. The glow of the streetlight shines into the house, and she doesn't turn on the lamp. Her heart is racing, and she's out of breath, but she can't sit down, so she paces, trying to calm down.

But all she can think about is Bent, and the smell of his skin and the look on his face when she pressed her leg into him.

Outside, headlights flash through the window, and an engine turns off. A door shuts in the quiet night, and heavy footsteps pound up the porch stairs. She stops breathing and walks to the dark hallway, stares at the door.

A shadow fills the foyer and there's a noise, what sounds like the flat part of a hand landing on her door.

She reaches out and turns the knob, pulls the door open. Bent is leaning against the frame, his head down, his hands on either side of the door, as though it's holding him up.

She steps closer, so close she can feel his breath on her face.

"We can't," he whispers.

"I know," she says, but he's already in the house, his arms around her, his mouth on hers, his foot kicking the door shut behind him.

17

Libby

I never even showed Jimmy the picture. Flynn had shown up and then Jimmy had asked me that question . . . *Are we?*

And I'd looked right at him and said, *Let's find out*, in a voice that wasn't even mine. I almost turned around to see who said it, that's how strange it sounded coming out of my mouth.

Well, all right, then, he said, and climbed in the passenger seat of Bent's truck, Rooster looking out the back window at me, his head cocked, as though he didn't recognize me.

And why would he? I didn't recognize me for the next few hours.

They passed in a blur—a trip to the state park, me with one hand on the steering wheel, like I'd been driving my whole life, and Jimmy relaxed, his arm out the window, trusting that I knew where I was going, even though I told him I was bad with directions, that everyone always said I was bad with directions.

"I can't imagine you're bad at anything," he said, the words pressing my foot to the gas pedal, the engine purring inside the car.

We took the trail down to the beach, talking about nothing and everything, Rooster prancing beside us, forgetting to be lazy somehow, the air by the water making him stick his nose into the wind, his ears flapping behind him.

We climbed on the rocks, and I stopped to fill a smooth dent on the surface of a boulder with water from the bottle we'd grabbed from the truck. Rooster sat in front of it, lapping at it, and Jimmy sat down and pulled me down beside him.

The afternoon slowed down. And sped up. Hours diminished into seconds and moved in slow motion at the same time, as though the laws of time and space didn't exist within the small circle where we sat. Or I didn't care if they did, at least.

And then Jimmy put his fingers on my watch, tapped the face.

"What time do you need to be back?" he asked, the hands showing it was past six.

We rushed back to his house, and he took my phone, put his number in it before I dropped him off, the engine still running and Jimmy yelling *Drive safely!* as I squealed away from the curb.

Bent was waiting at the door, glaring at me, asking why I hadn't answered my phone. I made some excuse about how the phone was acting weird lately and waited until I was in my bedroom before I looked at the screen, saw the texts and calls from him.

But there was only one text I was looking for.

Jimmy's. With three words.

Come back soon

Later, after I left the bowling alley as soon as I could—Desiree agreeing to lend me her car by some miracle—I sat in the parking lot, texted him back.

soon . . . as in . . . tonight?

Less than a minute later, his text dropped in.

sure . . . back porch . . .

Now I'm parked outside his house, taking a breath in what seems like the first time since this morning, trying to wipe off whatever expression Desiree said I had when I asked if I could borrow her car.

"What's wrong with your face?" she'd asked, and I'd leaned over, looked in the mirror hanging above the waitress station.

"No . . . the goofy grin," she said, eyeing me. "Where are you going?"

I shrugged. "Just out."

She studied me. "It's him, isn't it? That guy in the truck."

"What?" I asked, but I could tell my face had already given me away. "We're just friends. He's Flynn's *brother*."

"Friends, my ass. Not with that look on your face. How old is he anyway?"

"Twenty," I lied, subtracting a year. "Only three years older."

"Are you math challenged suddenly?"

"I'm seventeen soon."

"In *six months*!"

"Five months. As of yesterday."

"Keep this up, and I'll make Lucy give you the sex talk again."

"Please—the first five times were enough. Come on, Desiree. When have I ever asked you for anything?"

She sighed, held out the keys. "Well, do yourself a favor at least. Wipe that look off your face. Don't look so goddamn eager."

I pull down the visor now and look in the mirror, flip it back up, feeling ridiculous for listening to Desiree in the first place.

There are a handful of cars parked on the street. I get out and walk to the back of the house. There's a light on in Jimmy's bedroom, and I climb the steps quietly. Suddenly he's in front of me, stepping out of the shadows of the landing.

He's in sweatpants and a wrinkled T-shirt. The window to his bedroom is open. Inside, a sheet is tangled on the mattress. There's a book on the pillow, a small lamp on the bedside table lighting the room.

"Did I get you out of bed? I can go . . ." I pause, stand at the top of the stairs.

"I was just reading. There are a bunch of guys hanging out in the house, and there's less temptation in here." He points at the chairs in the corner. "Want to sit?"

I walk past the window, trying not to stare at the mattress where he was just lying down. He sits in the chair across from me, and we're quiet before he clears his throat, glances at me.

"I had fun today . . ." he says, and pauses, a look on his face as though there's something more. "This might not come out right, but . . . do you think it's . . . I don't know . . . weird that I'm hanging out with you? You know, since you're still in high school."

I pause, not sure what to say. "You want me to agree that it's weird you're hanging out with me?" I ask finally.

He smiles, shakes his head.

"Flynn kind of lit into me a little while ago. Told me to stay away from you. He thinks I'm, you know . . ." He pauses again.

"He thinks you're what?"

He blows out a breath. "Going to fuck it up, I guess. Do something to let you down or hurt your feelings—he had a whole list of shitty things I've done. We'll be here all night if I tell you every one of them."

"Well, that's between you and Flynn. I don't have a list."

He nods, agreeing with me, but his face is clouded. "I appreciate that—I do. But I have to come clean about a couple of things. Then you can decide. Okay?"

I look at him and wait.

"What I said before . . . when you first got here . . . about temptation . . ." He lifts his chin to his bedroom, his eyes on the door to the living room. "I had a drug problem—have a drug problem. I'm sober now. Part of me thought I could come back, hang out with my buddies like before. Just clean." He clears this throat. "But I can't. So—I've been here—sort of holed up in this room. Keeping to myself until I ship out. And then you showed up . . . and, I don't know, you don't act your age," he says. "I didn't really think about you being in high school until Flynn lost it on me. He said it was creepy."

"Flynn's last girlfriend was twenty-one. The one before that had a kid, I think." I laugh, but he doesn't smile.

"He's just trying to protect you."

"I didn't ask for his help."

"I know that—believe me—I'm not saying that you're helpless in any way. It's just . . . I was messed up for a lot of years, and he remembers it. I didn't exactly make the house an easy place to live when he was younger. But what he said got me thinking—he kept saying, why her? Meaning, why you." He points to me. "And, well—there's something you don't know. And the more I think about it, the more I'm wondering if it's why I feel this . . . connection or just, you know, something with you."

He breathes in again, lets it out slowly. He looks at his hands, stops talking for so long I wonder if he's changed his mind about telling me whatever he thinks he needs to tell me, but he clears his throat, continues.

"I was in a really bad car accident a few years ago. The truck flipped over, rolled a couple of times. My buddy was driving. He ended up through the windshield. I got thrown out of the passenger seat, and somehow the truck turned upside down and I landed underneath it. The door was holding it up. Just that thin piece of glass and metal holding up the whole fucking truck. I remember opening my eyes, seeing that door wobble, and thinking I'm going to die. No way I'm not dead."

He sits forward in his seat, his hands clasped in front of him.

There's a scar on his right leg, raised and angry, and I reach out and touch it. He glances at me, slips his fingers underneath mine, touching the top of my hand with his thumb.

"I'm calling for my buddy, but he's not answering. I didn't know it then, but he was already . . . He didn't make it. Then I see headlights and a car pulls over. But there's no way for anyone to get to me. I mean, there's like an inch between me and this truck, and you can hear the thing wobbling, this *eek*, *eek*, *eek*, back and forth. But I hear this guy's voice, and I'll never forget it because it was calm. Like we're having a beer at some bar. He's telling me he's going to get me out, and I don't answer because he's not. I mean, he's not going to be able to get me out—I can't move at all, and he'd have to be fucking insane to crawl under this truck to get me." He moves his hand away from mine, presses his hands together, puts them to his lips.

"But he does. He crawls right under the truck, his face next to me, and says in the calmest fucking voice—*How about we get out of here?* And then he drags me out from under the truck, and we're not even two, three feet away from it, and it just crashes down, the door flying off and the loudest noise." He stops, looks at me. "I found out later he was an off-duty cop. Just trying to get home to his family."

The expression on his face makes me sit up straighter.

"He was trying to get home to you," he says.

I see his lips move, hear the words come out of his mouth, but they float through the air, swirling around my head.

"It was Bent?" I ask finally, and he nods.

"He came to the hospital a couple of days later. He told me he was kind of a punk when he was younger. Struggled with authority. Got into some trouble. Things turned around when he joined the service." He shrugs. "I listened. Did the same. But I never got to tell him. He only knows me as some drunk asshole who almost got him killed."

"That makes sense now." I don't mean to say this out loud, but it slips out. Jimmy looks at me.

"He's always had this thing with Flynn," I explain. "Like, he doesn't like him. I never understood why. Turns out it's not him he doesn't like. It's you."

"That's why I wanted you to know. He might not be cool with us hanging out. I can talk to him. Maybe being in the army will help. That and I'm sober. You know, not such a loser anymore."

Something clicks when he says *army*, and I reach into my back pocket.

"I keep meaning to ask you if you know this guy?" I ask, holding out the picture. "I think I saw him here the other night."

He takes it and holds it up, catching the light from his bedroom.

"I'm assuming you don't mean your father," he says, and squints at it. "You saw this guy here?" He points to Quinn's husband.

I nod. "In the kitchen when I was looking for Flynn."

"There are guys crashing here all the time. I'll ask around. Someone might know him. Can I hold on to this?" He holds up the picture.

"Yeah—just don't lose it. It belongs to his wife. She moved in downstairs from me, and she's . . . nice. Her husband took off, and Bent won't answer any of my questions. I guess they served together—he just keeps saying he's looking out for him—whatever that means."

Jimmy's phone lights up on the table in front of us, and Flynn's name flashes on the screen. He answers it and talks in a clipped voice before he hangs up.

"He's coming over," he says. "I stopped by the house earlier when he wasn't home. Found some pills in his room. Codeine or some shit. I dumped them down the drain. I don't want you to leave, but it's probably better if you're not here."

We say goodbye, and I hurry down the stairs, anxious to leave before Flynn shows up. The street is empty, and I get in Desiree's car, start the engine, and drive away from the house.

I take the long way home, thinking about Flynn and the empty bottle of pills. And Jimmy, lying under a truck. And Bent, pulling him out from under it.

When I turn into the driveway, I'm surprised that Bent's truck is parked in front of me—it's not even nine o'clock.

My phone rings, and Jimmy's name appears on the screen.

"That was fast," I say. "What happened with Flynn?"

"He hasn't shown up yet. But I showed the picture to my roommate. Ronnie said the guy's an army friend of a friend. Doesn't know him other than he needed a place to crash. Said he had to patch things up with his wife and took off. He said his name's Luke. I didn't get a last name."

We hang up, and I walk around to the stairs. The house is dark, only the porch light on.

Upstairs, when I flick the light on, Rooster picks his head up off the couch, blinks at me.

Bent's bedroom door is open, his bed made and the light off. I walk through the house to the back, flipping on lights, and look out the window to the backyard, thinking maybe Bent and Quinn are sitting by the fire pit, but the backyard is empty.

In the hallway, the front door is still open, and Rooster unfolds himself lazily from the couch.

"Where is he, Rooster?" I ask, petting his head, and he wags his tail, licks my shin. I walk to Bent's bedroom door, look at my cell phone, and press his name.

It rings, once, then twice, and I hold it away from my ear, hearing it echo back at me from somewhere in the house.

It rings again, this time loud, from Quinn's apartment below.

I don't move. I want to close the door, go to my bedroom, pretend I didn't just hear my father's phone ringing right below my feet, where Quinn's bedroom is, the house dark and silent with just the two of them.

I see the way Bent looks at Quinn.

At first, I thought it was just a crush. But lately, it's something more. I noticed it in the truck tonight when we were driving to Sully's. From the back seat, I saw Quinn close her eyes, tilt her chin up, the wind from her open window blowing her long hair off her neck. Bent glanced over at her, and his eyes stayed on her for such a long time I almost nudged the back of his seat with my toe to get him paying attention to the road again, but we stopped at a light and he snapped out of it.

He caught my eye in the rearview mirror, though, and his cheeks colored, telling me everything I needed to know about his feelings for Quinn.

Rooster stands up suddenly and cocks his head; a minute later, a car door shuts somewhere on the street out front.

Rooster lurches out the door and runs down the stairs. I follow him, watch as he pushes the screen door open with his head and disappears onto the porch.

I'm on the second-to-last step when Quinn's front door opens and my father appears.

"Libby," he says breathlessly.

He runs a hand through his hair, puts a hand in his pocket casually, as though we've just happened to run into each other in the foyer.

"Your shoes are untied," I say, pointing to his boots, the laces loose, as if he's just pulled them on.

Before he can answer, a man steps through the doorway into the foyer. He looks up at me, and over at my father, his eyes moving down to Bent's untied boots and back up again.

"Luke," Bent says.

Quinn steps out from behind my father, her eyes wide. "John," she whispers.

But she's not looking at him. She's looking at me, her eyes not leaving my face, as though we're the only two people in the room.

18

Quinn

Quinn didn't know if she'd ever see John's face again. She hadn't imagined their reunion. Hadn't even really processed that he'd left her for *this* long, without even a phone call. A text, perhaps, to say, I'm *okay*. Don't *worry*.

Yet here he is. Upright with all limbs and toes and fingers accounted for. Standing in her foyer. *Her foyer*. Steps away from her with his keys in his hand as though he's just returned home from a short errand to get cigarettes or ice cream or milk instead of disappearing from her life for months.

But Quinn only looks at Libby, wanting . . . no *needing* . . . to explain. As soon as the thought enters her mind, she grasps the difficulty in that—how to explain something she doesn't understand.

Instead, she crosses her arms in front of her body, stays in the doorway, half shielded behind Bent.

They're all silent for a moment. Bent's shirt is untucked in the back, his shoelaces undone, but he's dressed. She fingers the seam on the side of her dress, relieved it's not inside out.

"Good to see you, man," Bent says finally. Politely. Absurdly, Quinn thinks, and she moves out of the doorway now, a surge of adrenaline rushing through her body.

John has on the same clothes he was wearing the night he left;

he doesn't look any different to her. It's as if he stormed out of their duplex that night, crossed the street, and strolled into this house, the past two months nonexistent.

John's quiet, looking at them with a blank expression, and Quinn finds it enraging.

"What are you doing here?" she asks, and he looks at her.

"What am I doing here?" he repeats.

The simple delivery of that sentence, the way he releases it into the air so nonchalantly, so easily, makes the tiny hairs on her arms prickle.

The space between them is suddenly too small—she doesn't want him this close to her—it seems wrong that he's this close to her after vanishing like that.

"Yes, John," she says, in a tone she uses with the twins—with children. "You haven't called. Haven't answered your phone. You've been gone . . . for months. And now, you're here? Just like that? How did you even know where to find me?"

"I called. Earlier." He looks at Bent.

The floor under Quinn's feet shifts, the air suddenly thinner, difficult to pull into her lungs.

She blinks, dumbfounded.

"You called him," she says, and turns to Bent. "He called you?"

Bent glances at her, then at John. "I called you back, but you didn't answer. Guess you got the message, though."

"You called him *back*!" Quinn shouts.

Bent flinches at her voice and draws back from her, moves deeper into the foyer, out of her doorway and away from her.

"I tried to tell you in the parking lot—"

"Quinn—don't be mad at Bent," John interrupts. "I asked him to not say anything. I wanted to see you . . . you know . . . face-to-face."

"I should go. Leave you two alone," Bent says softly, and walks to the stairs. "Libby, let's go."

John takes a step, as if he's coming into Quinn's apartment, but she blocks the doorway with her body, her fury rising to the surface now. Her body shaking with it.

"So . . . John—what did you say to Bent? I'd like to know what you needed to say—what was so important to say to your *brother* before your *wife*!"

"Quinn—"

"Tell me what he said." She grabs Bent's sleeve. "What were you not supposed to tell me? Don't look at him—look at me. *I'm* asking you. *Me*."

Bent swallows, blinks. "He just said that he was coming home. That was it. That was all."

"Home? So, this is home now?" She laughs, but it's a strangled, deranged sound, and Bent puts an arm out between her and John, as though she might be suddenly dangerous.

"And don't tell Quinn? Is that what you said, John? Luke?" Quinn whips around, and John flinches, trips back against the door frame. "But wait, I can't call you that, can I? Only people in your other life can call you Luke. I'm not one of your war buddies—not one of your *brothers*."

"Quinn . . . just . . . let me explain—" John stammers, but Quinn holds up her hand.

"No. Go with Bent—it's his house, after all. But don't come here again. Not to my door. *You* don't live here." She points a finger at John, and Bent steps between them.

"All right. Let's calm down. John, go upstairs. Libby, take John upstairs please. I just want a minute with Quinn."

Libby hesitates, looking at Quinn, as though she's not sure what to do.

"I'd like to talk to you. Can you come in. Please?" Quinn asks Libby.

She feels Bent's eyes on her, drilling a hole into her, but she won't look at him, *can't* look at him.

"Come upstairs when you're done," Bent tells Libby as she walks past him into Quinn's apartment.

"Okay, Dad," Libby sneers, and Bent rubs his forehead, closes his eyes.

Quinn shuts the door slowly. Bent and John disappear from her view, just their shadows visible on the wall before the lock clicks shut.

In the living room, Libby stands with her arms crossed, staring at the floor.

Quinn pauses before she speaks. She considers an excuse, but it seems an insult to Libby—she saw the look on Libby's face in the stairwell.

They hadn't even heard Libby come home. That was the truth of it.

Bent had been moving on top of her, her legs wrapped around him, and maybe five minutes had passed or maybe an hour.

All she knew was she didn't want it to end—the way he felt inside of her; the taste of his lips on her mouth; the weight of him on top of her—and then his phone rang, and the floor creaked above them.

They froze, panting . . . then not breathing . . . and then it came—the ringtone piercing and shrill; the back pocket of Bent's pants, crumpled on the floor, flashing bright white in the dark, the sound loud in the quiet room.

Then the echo upstairs, softer, right on top of where they lay.

"Fuck," Bent whispered, scrambling out of bed, pulling on his

pants while Quinn frantically searched for her dress under the sheets.

She followed Bent to the hallway, looked over his shoulder at Libby's face, saw the look in her eyes. Now a lie wasn't an option.

"I'm sorry. I don't know what to say. I didn't expect John to just show up—"

"Do you love him?" Libby interrupts.

"Of course. He's my husband. It's just . . . complicated."

"I meant my father."

Quinn studies her. "Libby, that's hard to . . . I can't answer—"

"Because he loves you." Her voice doesn't leave any room for doubt. As if Bent's love for Quinn is a fact.

"Libby, what just happened . . . that doesn't always mean two people are in love."

Libby snorts and Quinn sighs, looks at the ceiling.

"That didn't come out right. I just meant that ideally—"

"I have to go." Libby walks to the door, opens it, looks back at Quinn.

"What you said before about the baby. You know, about not wanting your husband to stay just because you're pregnant. Because he feels he has to." Her eyes flicker to Quinn's middle. "It's not just you that has to live with that."

"What do you mean?" Quinn asks, but she's already out the door, closing it gently behind her, leaving Quinn alone in the house.

She's suddenly cold, a chill overtaking her body, as though she were naked in the thin cotton dress. Libby's words swirling in her head.

She walks into the bedroom, sits on the edge of the bed, but the scent of them together lingers in the room, the mattress warm under her hands.

One of Bent's socks is on the floor, and she stands up and walks into the kitchen, her body close to the walls, as if she's safer, not so exposed. Her heart pounding.

She hears their muffled voices upstairs. Bent and John above her, the leg of a chair scraping against the floor. Heavy footsteps cross the ceiling, and she tenses, waits for the sound of a doorknob turning or someone on the back stairs, coming down to her door.

She doesn't ponder it—just moves—noiselessly grabbing her keys and phone in one hand, her sandals in the other. She turns all the lights off for reasons she can't put into words, only pausing in the front hallway to make sure she's alone before she slips outside.

John's truck is parked in front of her car on the street, a dark hulking shadow. She slides behind the wheel of her own car, tosses her phone on the passenger seat. The air reaches her lungs only when she pulls away from the curb, presses the gas pedal until the car lurches away from the house.

She doesn't know where she's going. With the radio off, the car is silent, only the quiet hum of the engine edging her thoughts. Scenes from the night flashing in her mind.

John's figure in the doorway and Libby standing on the steps looking at Quinn and Bent, with those eyes. Full of something just out of reach—something Quinn can't quite grasp.

But her mind keeps stuttering over one moment. When Bent had stood in the hallway on the other side of her closed door. Before she'd opened it. Before they'd ended up in her bed.

She rewinds and plays it over and over, slowing it down until every movement, every word, is in front of her.

The sound of Bent's hand on the door, the soft thud that might have been a knock—but was it?

Or had he just leaned against the frame, heavily, as if he knew he couldn't come in? Not knowing she was right there, a foot away, waiting on the other side.

She was the one who opened the thick door separating them, moved closer to him, his head still down, not looking at her until she'd said that word: *Stay.*

Stay, she'd said.

The fuel light on her dashboard lights up, and Quinn slows down, looks around her. She's on the other side of town, near Madeline's house. She follows the winding street until it turns left onto the cul-de-sac.

When she pulls into the driveway, the house is dark but the motion light on the garage flashes when she passes under it, and by the time she's at the side door, Lucy is peering out at her. She puts a hand over her heart, opens the door, and pulls Quinn inside.

"You scared the life out of me. It's so dark here compared to where we live—Quinn, what's wrong? It's a million degrees outside, and you're freezing!" She takes her hand off Quinn's arm and leads her into the living room.

"Sit," she says, and pulls a blanket off the chair and wraps it around Quinn's shoulders. She disappears and returns seconds later with a box of tissues and puts them on the table, pulls one out, and offers it to Quinn.

Quinn reaches out, confused, until her fingertips touch her cheek, the wet path of a tear running the length of her face. She doesn't remember when she started crying.

They sit in silence while Quinn wipes her face, gets her breath under control.

Madeline is sleeping on the couch across from them, a bucket on the floor next to her, a glass of water and a bottle of Tylenol on the table.

"I knew she was drunk, but *yowza*," Lucy says, following Quinn's eyes. "I almost called my brother to help me get her inside. Luckily the threat of that alone was enough to get her out of the car."

She pictures Bent. Libby walking past him. *Okay, Dad.*

"I wish you had called him," Quinn laments. "I bet he does too. We made a mess of things."

Lucy's brow wrinkles. "Back up—you two were dancing together. Having fun, I think? Then we left; I dropped you off. What am I missing?"

"He came home. And into my apartment . . . and we . . . well—" She twirls her hand.

Lucy's eyes go wide.

"And then my husband showed up. You know—the one who's been missing? His name is John, by the way. Bent calls him Luke. Confusing, right? That's what happens when your husband has a *completely* different life. And you know what the funny thing is?" She sniffs, grabs another tissue from the box. "The funny thing is—and it's not really funny at all—it's not that I just don't know who he is anymore. I have no idea who *I* am anymore. I'm a complete stranger even to *myself*!"

She wads up the tissue, throws it on the table. Looks at Lucy, who's waiting, as if there might be more.

"Oh, and I'm pregnant," she adds, out of breath.

Lucy snaps her fingers. "Now *that* I knew!"

Quinn blinks. "How did you know?"

"Desi's my sister," Lucy says matter-of-factly, and stands up. "Too bad you can't drink. I'll have one for both of us."

She disappears into the kitchen, and Quinn sinks further into the chair, exhausted. She hopes she hasn't made Lucy uncomfortable—she's Bent's sister, after all—but holding it all in is impossible now.

Stay, she'd whispered to Bent. And he had.

And now everything is different. Nothing can return to the way it was before she said it. Before he stepped through the door, lay down in her bed.

Lucy returns with a mug in one hand, a tumbler filled with amber-colored liquid in the other.

"I put honey in your tea. It's not bourbon, but it'll have to do."

Quinn thanks her, puts the mug to her lips, lets the steam warm her face.

"There's something I didn't tell you," Quinn says.

Lucy's head tilts back. "There's more?"

"Not with me. It's Libby. She called when Bent was . . . in my apartment. And then John showed up. She was in the hallway when he just appeared out of nowhere. Anyway, I know you're protective of her—and I feel awful. I mean, she's a kid."

She waits for Lucy to react, steadying herself for her to be upset, but Lucy sighs, shakes her head.

"I know I'm overprotective. I can't help it! Bent's always telling me not to baby her. But you know, he's a guy. He's all—shake it off. Toughen up! Just like my father raised him. I overcompensate sometimes. Always have, I think. Her mother was not exactly nurturing."

"Was Libby close to her? She doesn't talk about her very much."

"Libby wanted to be. She'd try so hard. When Bent was on one of his training weekends, I'd stop by, and Sarah would be in one of her moods. Locked in her bedroom or taking a bath. Libby would always say things like *We should be quiet so we don't bother Mommy*. Now, this is a kid who was born *easy*—I've always said that about

Libby—never difficult. Played by herself. Well mannered. Of course, we saw it right from the beginning. Sarah had no interest in holding her even as a baby—but then Libby was four, five, then eight, nine—I mean, it wasn't postpartum depression."

Lucy brought the glass to her lips, swallowed. "I remember one afternoon, I dropped off dinner, and Libby was drawing her mother a picture. *To the best Mommy in the World*, it said on the top. A rainbow underneath it and a big yellow sun—these golden rays shooting out. A house with flowers out front. And a puppy off to the side. Sarah took one look at it, and the first thing that comes out of her mouth is that Libby can forget about a puppy—how they're just like kids—*too much work*." Lucy's eyes fill. She shakes her head.

"Sarah wanted to be taken care of. And my brother did that when they were first married. And then Libby came along; there just wasn't enough of him."

"It reminds me of my father," Quinn says. "I was close to my mom growing up, and I always felt my father was jealous somehow. Like I was taking her away from him."

"I think I could have forgiven Sarah for that," Lucy says. "If I'd thought she loved Bent so much that she was jealous of Libby. But it wasn't that. She wasn't happy with her life. Had all these dreams but never any desire to work for anything. Wanted to be a model. Then an interior designer. Suddenly she was an artist—spent a fortune on private classes—then, *poof*, that's over. She left them—emptied the bank account, blew it all on some harebrained get-rich-quick scheme. Not a dime in her pocket when she came back."

Quinn looks at Lucy. "Bent said that she left. But I thought she came back because she was sick."

Lucy snorts. "Well, that's true. But she also came back because she would have been homeless. Libby thinks they moved in with me because of the medical bills, but that's not true. Bent worked double shifts for years trying to dig them out of that hole. Anyway, don't worry about Libby. She's got a good head on her shoulders." Lucy stops, studies Quinn. "And you have a tired head on your shoulders. You should close your eyes. Worry about all this stuff tomorrow."

"I think I'm going to crash here for the night. I can watch her if you want to go home." She points to Madeline.

"Are you kidding? Look at this place. I mean, the chi is all off, but Maddie agreed we'd fix that."

"Maddie? I've known her for five years, and I've never heard her call herself anything but Madeline."

"Maybe have more martinis with her. She was Maddie after one. By the second, I don't think she remembered she had a name."

Quinn laughs, unfolds from the chair, and picks up her mug.

"Leave it," Lucy says. "I'll clean up. Go to bed." She tucks her legs under her body, smiles at Quinn.

Before she knows what she's doing, she bends down, presses her lips against Lucy's cheek.

"Thank you," she whispers, and Lucy pats her shoulder, gives her a quizzical look, as though she's not sure what she's being thanked for.

Upstairs, Quinn tiptoes into the twins' room.

Nate has a Band-Aid on his forehead, a reminder of the spill he took on his bike earlier in the week.

She's not surprised to find them in the same bed—Nick's, of course, the older sibling. Even in sleep, he's the great protector. His arm thrown around Nate's shoulders, a leg drawn up as a shield. His small limbs create a cocoon: a safe place for his brother to lay his head and rest and heal.

She lies down in Nate's empty bed, pulls the cover over her, sleep tugging at her until she closes her eyes, the picture Libby drew for her mother lulling her to sleep.

Rainbows and hearts and sunshine, a puppy in the background. A house with flowers out front.

19

Libby

When I shut Quinn's door behind me, there's about a five-minute time gap when I stand in the hallway, completely paralyzed.

I want to call Jimmy, but I don't want to interrupt if Flynn is there. I can go upstairs, like Bent asked me to, and sit in my room while Quinn's husband, this *John Luke* person, talks to my father.

Or I can take Desiree's car and go back to Sully's. Maybe get Desiree to make me some food that doesn't involve skinless grilled chicken.

I'm debating this when my phone dings and a text from Jimmy appears.

U around? He's gone

I think for a minute. Text back.

Want company?

Seconds later, a thumbs-up drops in. I text back that I'm on my way and walk out of the house.

I don't think while I drive. Just put the windows down and turn on the radio, let the music dull my brain. The streets pass in a blur, headlights stinging my eyes, and by the time I'm at Jimmy's house, there's a dull ache behind my eyes.

Jimmy's sitting on the top step on the porch. He stands up when I get out of the car and walks down to meet me.

"We're in luck," he says. "House is empty for once."

We walk upstairs, and he shuts the door behind us.

"Want to sit?" he asks, pointing to the couch.

"This is going to sound weird. But do you mind if I lie down in there?" I point to his room. "I get migraines and I can feel one coming on. Sometimes I can catch them if I just lie in the dark."

"Oh, yeah. God, sure. Come on." He leads me by the arm into his room, and I kick off my shoes, the pain in my right temple stopping me from caring that I flop on his bed, my head on his pillow. He pulls the blanket over me, reaches over, and turns the lamp off.

"Can I get you anything? Water? Tylenol or something?"

"Just sit." I tap the end of the bed with my foot, even the small movement making me dizzy. "Talk to me. Tell me about Flynn."

"You sure? I can just leave you alone. You can sleep."

"No. Stay," I say. "Please."

The mattress dips, and I feel his leg against my foot.

"Nothing really to report with Flynn. He showed up sober, far as I could tell. Came from work. Hadn't even gone home yet. He gave me some story about how he pulled his hamstring working out and one of the guys on the basketball team gave him the pills. When I told him I dumped them, he said he was glad. That they made him feel like shit anyway."

"Do you believe him?"

When he doesn't answer, I lift my head, squint at him. It's so dark, I can't even make out his outline. "You there?"

"Sorry," he says. "I shrugged. Do I believe him? The brother in me says yes. The addict says no. I can't tell you how many times my mother cried in front of me. Begged me to get help. Said part of her would die if something happened to me. I'd make promises I knew I wouldn't keep. She'd leave the room, and I'd be digging through her purse looking for cash to score something." He pauses. "You sure I'm not bothering you?"

"I like the sound of your voice. Reminds me of my dad when I was younger."

I hear him snort. "Just what every guy wants to hear from a girl lying in his bed."

"Don't be a pervert. My dad used to sit with me when I got migraines. He'd talk to me. Tell me stories."

"Addict stories?"

"War stories. Not like blood and guts. He was just back from Iraq and he'd tell me what things looked like. Smelled like. Stuff like that. My mother took off around then, and everyone was convinced my headaches were from that. I think I started getting them because Bent was gone and I was alone with her. When he came back, the migraines eventually stopped. But I used to pretend my head hurt just so he'd sit with me. Stupid, I know, but I used to love to just lie there and listen to his voice. You know, hear about what he did over there."

"I don't have any stories like that." He's quiet, and I feel the bed dip again, his hand by my head, searching for something. "But—I do have this."

The flashlight from his phone turns on. He holds his book up. "I folded the pages with my favorite parts."

He opens the book, starts to read, and stops. "Wait. Close your eyes. Pretend I'm your dad," he says, and when I look at him, he falls over, laughing.

"Now I see how you and Flynn are brothers. You're both sick. Just read, will you?"

He clears this throat, and I think he's going to fool around again, speak in some fake voice. But when he reads the first sentence, it's just him, and I close my eyes and listen.

"'. . . a true war story is never about war. It's about sunlight. It's about the special way that dawn spreads out on a river when you know you must cross the river and march into the mountains and do things you are afraid to do. It's about love and memory. It's about sorrow. It's about sisters who never write back and people who never listen.' "

He pauses. "Are you awake?" he asks.

"Mm-hmm. Keep going," I mumble, his voice getting farther away, my body slipping into sleep.

"Okay, this one's kind of long. Here goes. 'To generalize about war is like generalizing about peace. Almost everything is true. Almost nothing is true. At its core, perhaps, war is just another name for death, and yet any soldier will tell you, if he tells the truth, that proximity to death brings with it a corresponding proximity to life. After a firefight, there is always the immense pleasure of aliveness. The trees are alive. The grass, the soil—everything.' "

He stops, "That's amazing, isn't it? I wish I could write like this. Okay—sorry. I'll stop talking and just read."

He clears this throat. "'The trees are alive'—wait, I read that already. Hold on. Okay, here we go. '. . . You feel an intense, out-of-the-skin awareness of your living self—your truest self, the human being you want to be and then become by the force of wanting it. In the midst of evil you want to be a good man. You want decency. You want justice and courtesy and human concord, things you never knew you wanted. There is a kind of largeness to it, a kind of godliness. Though it's odd, you're never more alive than when you're almost dead.' That's good, right? I'll find another one. Wait a sec."

I hear pages turning, miles away, his voice rhythmic, my limbs weightless, my mind blank, until the only noise I hear is the sound of my own heartbeat.

What feels like minutes later, my eyes open. A light turns on above me, over my face. My mouth is dry, my neck stiff. I sit up, look around, confused until I make out Jimmy next to me. He's sound asleep, his back turned to me, the book wedged between his body and the wall.

My phone is ringing on the night table, two feet from my head, the screen glowing with my father's name.

I freeze, too scared to reach for it. Afraid to see how long I've been sleeping. More afraid to see how many times my father has called.

I grab my phone, see that it's past one in the morning. My screen is filled with missed calls from Bent and a text from Flynn.

UR father was here! where the hell r u

I get up slowly, trying not to wake Jimmy. He turns on his back, but his breathing is deep, and I slip out of the room, close the door quietly behind me. The house is dark, silent.

I pause in the living room, look at my phone, wonder if it's worth it to call Desiree and find out if she told Bent about Jimmy, when the lamp next to the couch turns on and something moves out of the corner of my eye.

I jump, press my body against the wall.

There's a guy leaning up on one arm on the couch. He squints at me and sits up.

"Sorry," I whisper, raising my hand and hurrying to the front door. "I didn't know anyone was there. I'm just leaving."

My hand is on the knob when I hear him say, "Hey—Winters."

I turn around, and Quinn's husband is looking at me. He's naked except for boxers, his hair in all directions.

"You're her, right? Bent's kid?"

I nod, and he picks up a pack of cigarettes from the table, fishes one out, and lights it.

He sucks on the cigarette, blows it out. "That your boyfriend?" He tilts his head at Jimmy's door.

I shake my head, and he lifts an eyebrow. He leans over, picks up his watch, and squints at it.

"Your dad know you're here?" he asks.

I swallow, glance at Jimmy's door. Picture him reading to me, just because I asked. There's no way if Bent finds out that I was here tonight, I'm ever coming back.

"Does Quinn know you're here?" I ask.

He gives me a surprised look, studies me for a moment. "All right. I get it. My lips are sealed." He's grinning, as if this is all a joke, and I feel my hands clench.

"You can't show up at my house . . . her house . . . and just expect her to take you back."

He blinks, sits up straighter. "Look, kid. This has nothing to do with you. Besides—no more surprise visits. Your father told me to lay low until I hear from him."

I pull the lock on the door and step through.

"Hey, Winters," I hear him say.

I turn, and he glances at Jimmy's door, back at me. "Be careful," he warns.

"Of what?" I ask, but he doesn't answer, just reaches up and clicks off the lamp, the room going black. I shut the door, and then I'm taking the stairs two at a time.

Wishing I was already home.

20

Quinn

She hasn't been sleeping for what feels like more than an hour when something slams into her body. She opens her eyes to see Nate straddling her as if she were a pony, peering down at her, his face one big smile.

"Kinny's in my bed!" he yells, looking wildly at Nick, who's standing over her with a gap-toothed grin.

Nick is shirtless, his hands casually stuffed in the pockets of his striped cotton pajama bottoms, as though he's used to waking up to random women appearing in his bedroom.

"Hi, little man," she says, and he giggles, hurls his body on top of her legs, pulling his brother over. They're a mix of legs and elbows. Quinn covers her head with her hands, scoots out from underneath them while they wrestle at the end of the bed.

"I'm hungry," Nate says, his appetite more important than the whys and hows behind Quinn's presence in his bed.

Her phone is dark, the battery dead, but she knows it's probably not even six in the morning yet; the sky is an inky dark blue through the porthole window in the nautical-themed bedroom.

She gets out of bed, leads them downstairs to the kitchen.

The couch is empty—Madeline must have made it upstairs to her bedroom as some point. Lucy's car is still in the driveway, and

Quinn hopes she's in the guest room upstairs instead of the den, where she knows the boys will want to watch TV after they eat.

They take their time making breakfast. Quinn sips a hot mug of decaf while the boys mix the batter. She lets them take turns standing on a chair in front of the pan, flipping the half-dollar-size pancakes.

After they eat, she cracks open the door to the den, peering in to see if Lucy is on the pullout, but the room is empty. She cleans up the kitchen while the boys watch cartoons. She's putting plates in the dishwasher, when Madeline walks through the door with Lucy behind her.

"Oh my God, Quinn," Madeline gasps. "You're a saint."

She's wearing a plush white bathrobe over silk pajamas. She walks over to the table, the belt on her bathrobe hanging at her sides, the ends sweeping the floor.

"Hello, boys," she calls out, and winces.

They appear in the doorway, and she waves to them. "No, no—stay in there. Mommy's still waking up," she says, looking relieved when they disappear into the room.

Lucy walks over to Quinn, squeezes her arm.

"Go sit. You're not on duty today. I wanted to get up with the boys—I guess I forgot how early kids wake up. Another?" she asks, pointing to Quinn's mug.

She nods and sits at the table across from Madeline, who moans, puts her head in her hands.

"I must have dreamed we dropped you off, Quinn. See, this is exactly why I don't drink."

"You weren't that *bad*," Lucy lies. "And you didn't dream it. We did drop Quinn, but her missing husband showed up, and she wanted to get out of there."

Madeline looks up. "What? Whose missing husband?" She looks at Quinn. "John?"

"It's a long story." Quinn sighs as Lucy puts the fresh mug in front of her and sits down at the table.

Madeline looks from Quinn to Lucy, back to Quinn. "Well, I'm certainly not in a rush."

Quinn leans back in her chair, looks down at her front, the soft cotton of her dress creased over her belly. It's time, she thinks.

Time to tell the story of her life.

She looks up at the two women in front of her and starts at the beginning.

She leaves out the part about her and Bent.

But everything else, she tells them. The miscarriage. The deployments. John's disappearance. The pregnancy.

When she finishes, an hour has passed.

The twins have gone upstairs to get dressed. A lone piece of bacon sits on a plate in the middle of the table, and Madeline picks it up, nibbles on it. Lost in thought, as though she's processing what Quinn's told her.

"Well, I feel like a jerk," Madeline blurts. "You come here every day and take care of my boys. My *children*! And I'm so self-absorbed that I had no idea your husband is missing. And I'm on you about feeding the boys more fiber!"

"It's not your fault—it was just easier to not talk about it," Quinn explains. "Really—it was nothing to do with you. I just wasn't ready to talk about it until I understood it. If that makes any sense."

Lucy nods. "She's right. There are subjects I avoid discussing for the same reason. Some things you just don't want to talk about until you're good and goddamn ready."

Quinn and Madeline wait for her to continue, but she just looks at them, sips her coffee.

"Well if there's anything you need, Quinn. Anything. I mean, for God's sake, we're family at this point. The boys . . . me . . . we'd be lost without you—what the hell!" she says, looking out the window over Quinn's shoulder. "Why is there a police car in my driveway?"

Lucy moves the curtain aside. "Oh, it's just Bent," she says, and Quinn feels her insides twist.

She brings her mug to the sink, busies herself with washing it, letting her hair hide her face while Madeline opens the door and Bent steps in.

She runs a dish towel over the mug, aware that she's concentrating on it more than necessary while Bent stands only a few feet away from her, making small talk with Lucy and Madeline.

She feels his eyes on her when she reaches up to the cabinet to put the mug away.

When she turns, he's looking at her, and she holds up her hand as a greeting, not trusting her voice.

"Can I talk to you, please?" he asks, and maybe it's the uniform he's wearing or the formal tone he uses, but she follows him out the door, as though declining isn't an option.

He walks to the driveway, leans against the police car, and waits for her to reach him. She stops a few feet from him, and he doesn't move closer, just stands across from her.

"I'm sorry to just show up here," he says. "But I need to talk to you."

She looks at the house behind her and back at him. "How did you even know I was here?"

"You didn't get my messages? I called last night."

"I haven't checked my phone—the battery's dead."

"Oh, well. Probably for the best—I was sort of rambling. Libby was late coming home, and I couldn't track her down. I called thinking you might know something, and then I called Lucy and she said you were here. She was going to wake you, but Libby walked in."

"Is she okay? What happened?"

"She's fine—that's not why I'm here. Look, I'm sorry about last night—all of it. And you were right—that's your home. I want you to feel safe there—no—I need you to feel safe there. When I found out you left, it just . . ." His voice trails off; he shakes his head. "John won't be back. Not until you're ready to see him. And I won't bother you. Last night was—it'll never happen again. I promise. Just come home."

She looks down at her feet, trying to find the right words. "Thank you," she says finally. "For asking John—"

"Quinn, don't thank me," he interrupts, his face pained. "Say anything you want to me, but don't say that."

She looks up at him, but he won't meet her eyes. He turns and walks to the car just as the back door opens and the twins pile out, racing to the police car. They swarm him, begging for a ride, and he tells them to go back inside and ask their mother, that it's fine with him.

Madeline is already on the porch, and she calls to him, asking if he's sure—maybe just a quick one around the block, and Bent holds his hand in the air, opens the back door, and the boys pile in.

"Seat belts," Bent says to them, and shuts the door.

Quinn walks to the porch and stands next to Madeline while Bent turns the police lights on, then the sirens. She sees the boys through the windshield, their fists in the air, cheering.

"The world needs more men like him," Madeline says wistfully before she turns and walks in the house.

Quinn stays on the porch, watches as the police car disappears down the street. She stays even after she can no longer see the flash of the lights through the trees.

Stays even after the lonely wail of the siren fades.

21

Libby

Bent is walking out the door at three in the afternoon for a double shift when he stops to say that today, Desiree is in charge of me.

I put down the book I'm reading and look at him, and he shrugs.

"Lucy's at work and I want someone here in case you get another migraine."

"It's been, like, six days. I can't stay locked in this house forever."

Bent sighs, stares at my forehead as though he's searching for some sort of clue.

It's the same argument we've been having every day since I came home late from Jimmy's. I'd lied and told him I was at Katie's. That she'd come home from the Cape for the night and we were watching TV when I felt a migraine coming on and then we'd both fallen asleep.

Now he's convinced the migraines I used to get when I was younger are back, even though it's the first one I've had in years.

Bent and I were upstairs earlier this week when Lucy launched into a lecture about migraines. How emotions manifest in the body and the importance of managing stress, which is why I had to spend the next few days telling Lucy, over and over, that no, I wasn't upset about anything, and yes, I'd tell her if something was bothering me.

"You'll talk to me, right?" she kept asking, until Desiree shouted from the kitchen, *Ask her again and she'll be talking to a dead body.*

Then Bent chimed in that all the arguing wasn't helping, and Desiree appeared in the doorway, glaring at me because I was the worst liar in the universe.

Later, she pulled me aside and hissed in my ear, "A migraine? I give you my car. I keep my mouth shut about who you were with. All you had to do was come up with a halfway decent lie. And that's what you come up with? A migraine? Happy *fucking* house arrest."

There was nothing to say because she had a point—I hadn't remembered how worried Bent was back then. Add Lucy's tendency to overreact and it's been the longest week of my life.

Bent crosses the room, kisses the top of my head. He's been working more than usual this week and using the back stairs instead of the front to come and go. It's obvious he's avoiding Quinn—which really isn't necessary, since she's barely been around either.

"I'm bored out of my mind," I say. One last-ditch effort before he leaves.

"Well, invite Katie over," he says. "Only this time tell her to stay awake."

Then he's gone, through the kitchen and out the door, the sound of his keys jangling while he walks making Rooster lift his head up, a hopeful look on his face.

"No rides today," I whisper, and he huffs, rests his chin on the arm of the couch, and shuts his eyes.

I listen to the sound of Bent's truck pulling out of the driveway, the rumble of the engine growing fainter until I can't hear it anymore.

A minute later, the front door whips open, and Desiree walks in, scans the room, and zeroes in on me.

"I heard the warden leave," she snaps. "Why are you still lying there?"

"I can't go out. He said only Katie could come over."

"Does this girl even exist? Or did you just make her up to cover your ass?"

"Of course she exists. You've met her, like, a million times. She's just down the Cape. Besides, who cares if I said I was with Katie or Jimmy—I *was* just sleeping. And I *did* have a migrai—"

"Honestly, don't even say that word! Don't even whisper it to me. Florence Nightingale upstairs won't shut up about it. Thinks you should be on suicide watch or something."

"Well, they are stress-induced," I mumble defensively.

"Excuse me?"

"Nothing. So you don't care if I go out?"

She sighs, walks to the front door, and puts a hand to her ear.

"Do you hear the sound of that?" she asks. "It's your goddamn freedom. Now get the hell up and *do something*."

The door slams behind her, and minutes later, I hear her footsteps on the porch stairs, and just like that, the house is empty for the first time in days.

I get off the couch and walk into the kitchen. My phone is on the counter, and there's a text from Jimmy, saying that he hopes I'm not climbing the walls.

We talked on the phone the morning after my migraine—he'd called me in a panic, saying he felt awful for falling asleep. But Bent knocked on my door, and I hung up quickly.

If I had a car, I'd drive over and see if everything's okay, but I want to see if Flynn's around. When Bent couldn't find me the other night, he showed up at Flynn's house, hoping I was there.

Apparently, Flynn was having a party out back, and Bent almost walked in on it. Now Flynn's mad at me, even though I've sent him a bunch of texts apologizing.

I press his name on my phone, and he answers after it rings almost a dozen times in a voice that's less than friendly.

"You're alive," he says. "Good to know."

"Look—I know you're mad. But I haven't been able to get out of the house since Sunday, and I didn't want to just keep texting back and forth. Come by and we can talk."

"Right—so your psycho father can rip into me again?"

"Flynn, he's not even home. Just come."

"Walk over here if you're so gung ho on talking," he says stubbornly.

"Fine, I will—" I start to say, but the phone goes dead.

I sigh and grab Rooster's leash and spend the next five minutes coaxing him off the couch, and we finally make it outside, turning right toward Flynn's house.

We make it three houses down the street before Rooster starts sniffing and circling a patch of grass between the sidewalk and the curb. I wait while he does his business, and when he's finished, I clean it up, tie the bag closed.

Sully steps out from behind the truck in his driveway, a garden hose in his hand. He stops the stream of water directed at the hood and grabs his chest like he's having a heart attack.

"Is that a ghost or the real Libby Winters?" he asks. "Thought you might have skipped town going missing like that the other night."

I roll my eyes at him. "Two hours past my curfew and the whole town knows about it."

"Not the whole town. Just the police force. You know—the entire bar at Sully's." He laughs as if he's joking, but I don't smile, because it's true.

"When is Desiree moving back in your house? She said the other day that she misses you," I lie.

Sully grins. "You're full of the stuff in that bag in your hand. Bent tried the same shtick. Is she driving you nuts?"

I shrug. "It's just weird . . . you guys not together."

"I'm a simple guy, Libby. I want simple things. A nice house. A happy wife. Maybe a couple of kids or a dog. Desiree? Who knows what she wants. One day it's this. The next day it's that. I can't keep up. She's—what's the word I'm looking for—cryptic."

That's about the last word I would use to describe Desiree.

"Do you mean complicated?" I ask.

He sighs. "You know what I want? Desiree. That's all. If we have kids—great. A dog—perfect. If we don't . . . we don't."

"You can borrow him whenever you want." I point at Rooster, who's lying on the ground, stretched out as though he's on our couch and not a filthy sidewalk.

"I said simple. Not dumb. Only a sucker like Bent would get a mutt who takes a dump the size of Texas." He points at the bag in my hand. "Keep walking. You're stinking up my lot."

He laughs at his own joke and sprays a stream of water at the soap suds dripping off the fender of his truck.

I wave goodbye, and tug on the leash, but it's another five minutes before Rooster gives up the staring contest with me and finally gets up.

Flynn's house is only the next street over, but Rooster stops every ten feet to rest, and when we reach the front porch, he leans against the railing, as though he can't be expected to climb the handful of steps to the door. I drop the leash, let him stay where he is, and ring the doorbell.

Flynn opens the door and steps out onto the porch. He has a

purple bruise under one eye, his hair matted as though he hasn't showered in days.

"What happened to your eye?" I ask.

"Your asshole father beat me up," he says stone-faced, then smirks. "I'm kidding. You should've seen your face, though." He turns his mouth down at the sides, sticks his bottom lip out. "Classic Plural."

I turn and walk down the stairs away from him, pick up Rooster's leash.

"Don't get all offended. I'm just kidding. I was messing around with some of the guys the other night, and things got a little rowdy."

"What guys?"

He shrugs and rattles off a few names. I squint at him, and he shakes his head.

"See. The look on your face. You don't even know them."

"Since when do you *know* them? Didn't one of them drop out of school last year and the other is in and out of juvie?"

"Walsh didn't drop out—he got suspended. A bogus illegal locker search, if you ask me. And yeah, Murph's had some shit go down. What are you? On your father's payroll or something?"

"Look—I just came by to say I was sorry. I was late getting home, and my father showed up here and you're mad about it—"

"Showed up? He walked around the side." He points to the backyard. "One o'clock in the morning and we're all sitting around the fire, booze and . . . shit . . . everywhere . . . and here comes Officer Plural. Looking for you!"

"Well, he didn't say anything to me about it—"

"Only because I met him in the driveway!" Flynn growls. "If he'd made it around back, I'd probably be in jail right now."

"He only came here because he couldn't find me, and you're my friend—he wasn't trying to catch you doing anything wrong—"

"And why couldn't he find you? Where, oh where, was Plural?" He glares at me. "What? Cat got your tongue?"

"If you stop talking for two seconds I can explain—"

"Oh, please—save it! But you're welcome for covering your ass—he asked me about Katie and Erin. I made up some story about how I lost my phone, so I didn't have their numbers. I didn't want him to find out neither one of them is back in town." He tilts his head, stares at me. "I also didn't tell him that if he wanted to find you, he should go looking for my fucking brother. You were with him, weren't you?"

"Flynn, nothing is going on. We're just friends—"

"And I asked you, as *my* friend, to stay away from *my* brother. What part didn't you get?"

He steps forward, standing over me and Rooster, his voice loud. He's above us on the porch, large and looming, and I smell it suddenly.

"Are you drunk?" I ask, waving at my nose. "You stink."

"I had a beer. It's probably just my shirt. We were doing shots the other night and the last one missed my mouth. Jesus, Plural . . . there you go, with that look."

"You had a beer? It's, like, four o'clock in the afternoon."

But he doesn't answer, just backs up, his hands in the air, a frightened look on his face.

"What the fuck is with Rooster—is he . . . growling at me!"

Rooster brushes against my leg, and when I look down, he's on all fours, the fur on the back of his neck standing up. He's leaning forward menacingly, a noise coming from him that I've never heard before, his eyes trained on Flynn.

"Rooster! Stop it!" I pull him back, but he doesn't move.

"I don't know what his deal is, but I'm not waiting for him to get his teeth into me." He backs up, steps inside, not taking his eyes off Rooster, who's making so much noise now, he sounds like a grizzly bear on the other end of the leash.

Rooster lunges suddenly, his body on the stairs between me and Flynn, the white of his teeth showing, and I know I can't hold him anymore.

"Shut the door!" I scream at Flynn, who gives me a panicked look and slams the heavy wooden door just as Rooster leaps up the steps, barking loudly until Flynn disappears from the glass window.

I call his name, yank his leash, and he looks back, his eyes wild, but he lets me pull him back to the sidewalk and away from the house.

Rooster stays with me, walking faster than I've ever seen him move, running almost, and when we're finally home, he noses the door and whimpers, as though he can't get in the house fast enough.

Upstairs, he jumps on the couch in his favorite spot, and when I sit down next to him, he climbs into my lap, panting.

I whisper that it's okay, but his body trembles uncontrollably under my hand. His ears are flattened to his head, his eyes searching my face, as though he has no idea what just happened.

I press my cheek against his head, listen to the sound of his heartbeat, trying not to picture Rooster's face when he growled at Flynn, teeth bared and eyes white, wild and feral.

His gentle heart tormented by something just outside of his reach.

22

Quinn

She sees him everywhere.

In the grocery line at the store, there's a man checking out in front of her, and the way he reaches behind him to pull his wallet from his back pocket stops her dead while she blinks him into focus.

It happens at the gas station. At the park with the twins. Sitting at a red light, catching the truck next to her out of the corner of her eye.

It's never him—just someone with the same build. Similar hair or clothes. Any number of things that remind her of him—and that's the thing—*everything* suddenly reminds her of Bent.

It hasn't helped that Madeline decided to use some of her vacation hours this week; Quinn suddenly has more free time than ever before.

It came as a surprise. Madeline never took time off—maybe a day or two in all of the years Quinn has worked for her. Then earlier in the week, she told Quinn she wanted to lighten her schedule with the pregnancy. She said it with a cheery smile until she saw Quinn's face.

"What's wrong?" Madeline asked. "You look panicked."

"Oh, no—it's just . . . I would need to find something part-time if my hours are cut. I'm not sure what's going to happen with John . . ." Her voice trailed off.

Madeline looked at her for a long moment, then sighed.

"See? This is what I mean. I'm completely out of touch. It's just been work for years—me counting on you for everything. And here you are with a whole life I don't know about. And you know why? Because I never asked . . . that's why!"

"Well, I didn't expect you to—"

"I'm just a jerk sometimes." Madeline cut her off. "A self-absorbed jerk!"

"That's not true—" Quinn interjected, but Madeline held up her hand.

"No, it's not your job to make me feel better right now. I told you, didn't I, Luce?" She pointed at Lucy, who looked up from her fabric book on the table.

"We were watching a show the other night, and this woman says to her husband: 'You know every time you do something wrong, you try to fix it by telling me that you're an asshole?' and I turn to Lucy and say—that's me! I do that! I'm the asshole husband!"

Lucy waved her hand dismissively, looked back at the book. "We all do that. Everyone's the asshole husband sometimes."

"You're not," Madeline countered. "Quinn's not." She paused. "I was going to say Desiree's not, but . . ."

Lucy looked up. "Desiree will tell you she's an asshole. She's just never sorry about it."

"Anyway. Quinn—don't even talk about another job. Consider yourself salaried. Lucy and I will be working on the house in the mornings this week, and I'll let you feed the boys lunch, but then go get some rest. Read a book. Relax. Take care of you."

Quinn didn't know what to say besides thank you—Madeline seemed a stranger to her lately. *Giddy* is the word that came to mind. And truthfully, she wasn't sure what to expect; the old Madeline was known to make promises she didn't keep.

Whether it was to the boys—*this week we'll see that movie—I'll come home early from work!*—or to Quinn—*I'll handle their Halloween costumes this year, I promise!*—Madeline's good intentions were inevitably lost in the mayhem of her overbooked schedule.

So Quinn was thrilled to find herself walking out of work on Monday, the entire afternoon spreading out in front of her.

She hadn't wanted to go home. Instead, she turned her car north on the highway and headed away from Paradise.

She did this all week. She stopped wherever she wanted on her afternoon trips. No schedule. No agenda. Not a single person in the world who knew where she was. At first the thought made her insides clench, her breath stutter in her throat.

But the more she thought about it—what had changed? Every day, she was alone.

She was a daughter to parents who were no longer alive. She had a job, but until recently, her boss didn't even know the details of her life. She was married, had the ring on her finger to prove it—but even when John was home, in his mind, he was somewhere else.

And somehow, ever since John's first deployment, she's let her days take on a relentless monotony. Weekdays, she went to work, ate dinner, went to bed. Saturday was the dump, the gym, cleaning the house. Sunday, she might grab coffee with a friend, but often, she'd grocery shop, do laundry, prepare for another week.

It occurred to her that over the years, she'd accumulated things to show her existence: a birth certificate, a marriage license, a college degree . . . but she'd never really thought about herself outside of these narrow margins—who was she after all? Especially now, with the hours stretching in front of her and nowhere to be?

By the end of the week, she learned a few things.

Nothing overly important: she liked to drive with the radio off, the quiet somehow more pleasing to her ear. Hiking wasn't her favorite, and she got restless sitting on the beach after two hours, even with a good book. She enjoyed walking into a dark movie theater in the middle of the day, and she liked to be home at dinnertime, regardless of whether she needed to be.

Now it's Friday, and she's on the road again, this time something specific in mind. Earlier, Madeline and Lucy returned from the design store sooner than expected and took the boys out to lunch, and Quinn got in her car, headed to the New Hampshire border.

She'd been building up the courage to do this all week—no, more like weeks and weeks. Ever since Bent had told her about the puppy.

She wanted to see it—needed to see it, really. The thought bouncing around in her head. Back and forth, in her mind, she toyed all week with the thought of going to see the now-adult dog—he would be four years old, if her math was correct.

No amount of reasoning made the desire to see it with her own eyes lessen. It was the opposite: the more she thought about, the more she rationalized that she had every *right* to want this.

The puppy had belonged to her—she had chosen him among a litter of a dozen of his siblings—and just like that . . . he was gone, sent away.

Then last night, lying in bed, she'd heard Bent's footsteps above, and she sent him a text before she lost her nerve.

Do you know the address of the family who have the puppy?

She waited, thinking of how she'd missed seeing Bent this week. He'd been a ghost around the house—even if she wanted to run into him, she wouldn't have—that's how infrequently he was home.

She felt a twinge inside, a sharp stab knowing he was avoiding her.

He answered her promptly with the address. Just what she asked for and nothing more—his response precise and short, and she returned with the same.

A simple *thank you*.

Now the ride is shorter than she expected, the map on her phone showing she's arrived even though she's surrounded by green fields as far as she can see on both sides.

She pulls the car over to the side of the road and looks at Bent's text again, makes sure she has the correct address.

The street is wide, but she hasn't passed another car for miles.

She hasn't really figured out what she'll do when she finds the house—it occurs to her now that in the best scenario that runs through her mind, the dog is merely sitting on the front porch inside a fenced yard on a neighborhood street where she could just park and watch for a few minutes—just long enough to put her eyes on him, to *see* him in the flesh. She remembers the white spot on his chest, the patch of fur bright and distinct on his black body.

But this isn't a neighborhood—it's farmland.

Across the street, a silo splits a field in two. Her eyes scan the road ahead of her, searching for a house, but there's only the flat paved road, the double yellow line stretching before her.

To her right, a dirt road runs between two fields and disappears out of sight. She shuts the engine and gets out of the car, her legs stiff. There's a white rail fence surrounding the field in front of her, and she leans against it, watches several horses grazing in the distance. The wood is warm under her hands, and she pulls her shoulders back, tilts her face to the sun.

Maybe it's for the best.

She wonders, in some way, if she isn't just stalling for time.

Her husband is home, after all. And she's the one avoiding him now. John hasn't been in touch—just as Bent assured her—but she knows he's waiting, somewhere, sometime, to talk to her.

The problem is, Quinn has no idea what to say to him. In some far-reaching place in her mind, she thought seeing the dog might help—that this slice of her past that she's just learned about might, in some way, help her understand what to do next.

But there is no next—nothing to do besides get back in the car and go home.

She waits until the stiffness in her legs fades before she turns to the car.

She's opening the door when a truck pulls up next to her, the window down. A man looks out at her from the driver's seat, a cup of coffee in his hand.

"Car trouble?" he asks in a way that suggests it's not the first time he's asked that question.

"Oh, no," she says. "I'm not broken-down. Just at the wrong address."

He looks up at the road, back at her. "Where are you trying to go?"

She reaches into her back pocket, pulls out her phone, and repeats the address Bent gave her.

"You're in the right place. We had a sign, but the storm last winter took it down. Haven't gotten around to putting it back up. You're here about a dog, right?"

She blinks at him. She didn't think Bent would tell them she was coming, and now she's flustered, a heat spreading up her neck.

He studies her for a moment, then tips his chin at the road in front of him. "I'll take you up. My wife's probably waiting for you."

She watches the truck pull down the dirt road in front of her.

She gets in the car and shuts the door, the keys heavy in her hand as she starts the engine.

Her mind is numb as she follows him—buzzing with the words she'll need to explain. She'll just be honest, she decides—just tell them who she is and maybe ask to see the dog, and then she'll go.

In another minute, the trees lining the road end abruptly, and a white farmhouse appears before her, so large and imposing it seems impossible she couldn't see it from the street. The truck veers to the right, over the grass, and parks in front of a small barn, but she stays on the circular driveway and stops in front of the house. She takes a deep breath before she opens the door and steps out.

It occurs to her after she's already out of the car that she's just followed a stranger to a house in the middle of nowhere, and when the man steps down from his truck and she sees the state trooper uniform—a statie is what Bent had called him, she remembers now—her body relaxes, and she feels the churning in her stomach ease a bit.

"She's likely outside," he calls, and motions for her to follow. He disappears around the side of the house, and when she walks behind him and turns the corner, he's standing in the doorway of a massive barn, next to a woman who smiles when Quinn joins them.

"I guess I have you to thank for getting him to finally fix the sign," she says, cutting her eyes at the man. "I'm Sally—good to finally meet you in person. I wasn't expecting you for another two hours, but this works—look . . . they're awake."

She steps into the barn and points to a stall, the door open. Quinn walks forward, peers inside.

The stall is clean and warm, sunlight streaming through the open window. On the floor is a jumble of moving fur, and it takes Quinn a minute to realize she's looking at a litter of puppies.

"You're a breeder?" Quinn blurts. Sally's forehead wrinkles and she frowns at her husband.

"She had the right address," he says defensively, and looks at Quinn as if she's tricked him in some way.

"I'm sorry," Quinn says quickly. "I just . . . you said dog, and I thought—I'm obviously not who you think I am."

"You're not from the veterinarian's office, I take it?" Sally asks. "The new tech?"

Quinn shakes her head. "My name is Quinn." She pauses. "Quinn Ellis. You met my husband, John . . . a long time ago. He asked you to take our puppy."

They're both silent, looking at Quinn blankly. A minute later, the man's expression changes.

"Ah," he says. "Lucky."

"Who?" Sally glances at him. "You mean the dog?"

Her husband tilts his head at her, waits.

"Oh! The *dog*," she breathes, her eyes wide when she looks at Quinn. "Well, my gosh—we've thought about you over the years. I mean, we've *talked* about you!" She looks at her husband, who nods in agreement. "I wanted Steve to keep in touch with your husband, but he didn't feel it was right."

"It wasn't right—he asked me not to. You have to respect someone's wishes, Sal. Even if you don't agree with them."

"A text now and again is all I meant," Sally says. "Sometimes that's all it takes in these cases. Just someone to say—Hey, there. I *see* you. I'm here."

"Okay, let's not assume anything." He gives Quinn an apologetic look. "My wife is a fixer. A very passionate fixer who sometimes meddles where she doesn't belong."

Sally raises an eyebrow at him. "And my husband is a combat veteran and a policeman." She looks back at Quinn. "And I breed and train service dogs for vets with PTSD. So let's just say, I'm damn good at recognizing trauma. And your husband—well—he had trauma written all over him. Heck, I'm not telling you anything you don't know. Spouses are on the front lines dealing with this stuff at home."

"I didn't know if you'd know my name. I wasn't sure what my husb—" She stops, clears her throat. "I wasn't sure what John told you when he asked you to take the puppy."

"He didn't tell us anything other than he was home from the war, and his wife surprised him with a puppy, and it just wasn't going to work," the man offers. "Then he found out what Sally does, and he was a little more forthcoming."

Sally makes a small noise. "*Forthcoming* is a stretch—he admitted not keeping the puppy was his fault," she explains. "He didn't want to talk about himself. But that's common with guys still serving. They think if they ask for help, they're jeopardizing their chances for advancement. Putting their careers at risk."

"I'm Steve, by the way." The man holds his hand out to Quinn. She shakes it, and they're silent for a moment.

"I like his name," Quinn tells them. "Lucky. We never even gave him one, and I always wondered . . ."

"We can't take credit for that. Our kids came up with it. I'd just started my company." Sally points to the puppies. "We had our one dog—and the kids were on me and on me to keep one of the puppies, and I flat-out refused. The last thing I needed was to take care of one more thing. Then Steve got a call from Bent. I was dead set against it, but then I met your husband, and I just . . . I couldn't say no. He was so desperate. Just kept repeating that this was the life the dog deserved. The kids couldn't believe I said yes—believe me, I couldn't either." She chuckles. "So, they came up with the name Lucky. That's what it was to them. Just great good luck—" She pauses, looks up. "I'm sorry . . . I'm blabbing on and . . . it was probably awful for you."

Quinn shakes her head. "No—I mean, yes. I never wanted to give him away. But it's nice to know he's in a good home. Bent told me he was, but . . ."

"But you wanted to see for yourself," Steve finishes for her. "Well, that we can do." He steps back, leans out the door, and whistles, a piercing sound that echoes in the barn.

A minute later, a dog appears in the doorway, wagging his tail and circling Steve's legs. He runs over to Quinn, and she feels his tongue on her wrist before he bounces over to Sally, a black blur between them.

Quinn watches him, grins. "I thought I'd be sad, but it's impossible when he's so . . . happy. He looks exactly the same. Just bigger."

"Tell me about it. He needs to lose a few, but he loves his snacks. And someone shares when he shouldn't." Sally slides her eyes over to Steve.

"Don't listen to her. You're perfect," he tells the dog.

He looks at Quinn. "So, I hope I'm not prying, but . . . why now? I told John you both could visit. I know he wasn't interested, but I'm surprised we never heard from you."

"He didn't tell me where he took him. I'm sure I could have pressed him, but I didn't really see the point. It would have been too hard to see him. Honestly, I don't even know why I'm here now. Things are a bit unsettled in my life at the moment." She shrugs. "I guess I wanted to close the loop on something."

Sally studies her. "I've thought about you often," she says. "We do a lot of work with vets because we struggled when Steve came home. But my husband was willing to do the work. I see so many guys like John—their wives bring them, and they don't want the help for one reason or another. But it's not them I lose sleep over."

Sally disappears into the stall. When she comes back, there's a puppy in her arms.

"This guy reminded me of Lucky right away. He's silly and happy and . . . just full of beans." She holds the dog out to Quinn, who takes him in her arms.

Sally looks at Quinn. "It's the wife I lose sleep over. It's you. The one fighting a war you didn't ask for." Sally reaches out and pets the dog, smiles when he burrows his head into Quinn's neck. "I think he's just found a new home," she tells Quinn.

Quinn doesn't answer because she's afraid to blink, as though she's in a dream, cradling him against her, the smell of his warm body finding a place in her memory. The tiny beat of his heart pulsing against her own.

23

Libby

It's dark by the time I hear Quinn's car pull in the driveway. I've been listening for her all afternoon, but I wait another fifteen minutes or so before I knock on her door.

"Can you come upstairs?" I ask when she opens the door. "It's Rooster."

She looks behind her nervously, as though someone's in the house with her. She steps in the hallway, closes the door carefully behind her.

"Is he okay?" she whispers. "Where's Bent?"

"He's working," I say quietly, and then frown at her. "Why are we whispering?"

I look at the closed door and feel my face flame. I hadn't heard anyone come in with her, but clearly, someone is inside.

"Sorry . . . I didn't mean to interrupt. It's not a big deal." I turn for the stairs, and she grabs my arm.

"Libby. Wait, oh, just come in. I can show you better than explain it."

I follow her into her house. She walks into the dining room, waves me over to where she's standing.

"Look." She points to the corner.

The light in the room is dim, and it takes me a minute to see what she's pointing at. There's a small crate on the floor. A blanket spills out of it, where a puppy is curled in a ball, sleeping.

I put my hand over my mouth and look at her, eyes wide.

"I know," she says. "Believe me. I know."

"Where? I mean how?"

She sighs. "That's a story for another day. But I'm not even sure I should keep him. It's sort of a trial run for the weekend."

"Can I?" I ask, and she nods.

"I actually tried to wake him up, but he's out cold. I think the trip did him in."

I sit on the floor next to him and gently pick him up, put him on my shoulder. He makes a small noise but doesn't wake up, and I put my nose against his fur, breathe in.

"You *need* to keep him—why wouldn't you!"

"Because I'm pregnant! And I have a full-time job! And my missing husband who's just magically reappeared gave away our last puppy. I haven't even talked to him since he's been back because I have *no* idea what I want to say," she blurts in one breath, and sighs. "It's not the best time to get a dog."

I'm watching her talk, and her eyes haven't left the puppy since I picked him up. Not once. I tell her that, and she sighs louder.

"I didn't even know you were looking for a dog."

"I wasn't—that was the last thing on my mind. It was a gift. And I could've said no—I could've! But I didn't want to. I *don't* want to." Quinn looks at me. "That's it. I mean, there you have it. Like it's that simple. Like I deserve everything I want."

"Well, maybe you do," I tell her, and she pulls her eyes away from the dog for the first time, a doubtful look on her face, as though I've just told her a flat-out lie.

"What happened with Rooster?" she asks suddenly.

I tell her how Rooster acted at Flynn's house, and how he's

upstairs, sleeping on his back with his legs in the air, as if nothing happened.

"I mean, he seems fine now," I tell her. "But it took him forever to calm down. I've never seen him act like that."

"What did Bent say about it?"

"I haven't told him."

She waits for me to continue. When I don't, she looks at me sideways. "And why haven't you told him?"

"He's weird about Flynn. And I can't tell him without mentioning that Flynn was being a jerk earlier—he smelled like he'd been drinking, and his voice was loud, and he was sort of standing above us, yelling. I just wonder if it triggered something in Rooster. Maybe because of what happened with his owner. Bent said the guy who killed her didn't even remember it because he was so drunk."

"The woman who gave me this little guy knows a lot about that type of stuff. I'll ask her. I'm more worried about why your friend was yelling at you. Drunk. In the middle of the day."

"Remember when you told me the dog was a story for another day? Well—same."

She studies me. "You'll come to me if you need to talk, right? Or just, you know, need anything."

"Yes—but do *not* let Desiree hear you say that anytime soon."

She gives me a puzzled look. "I'm serious, Libby. Whatever you need. Just ask."

I tilt my head at her. "In that case, any chance I can borrow your car tonight? I promise it will only be for, like, a half hour."

"Of course." She gets up and walks over to her pocketbook, brings back her keys. "But you don't need to be back that soon. I'm not going anywhere the rest of the night."

I place the puppy back on the blanket and stand up, decide it's probably best not to mention that Desiree said the next time I borrowed her car, hell would be frozen over.

I'm walking away when I hear her call my name. When I turn, she has a solemn expression on her face.

"I have to make a decision this weekend," she says. "I can't keep putting off talking to John, but if I don't keep the puppy . . . maybe you could come with me to bring him back?"

I nod, and she closes the door. But not before I see her eyes fill.

I get in the car and drive to Jimmy's—he finally answered one of my texts and said he needed to talk to me.

There's a chance Bent could come home and find me gone, but when I talked to him an hour ago, he got off the line quick because there was a pileup on the highway.

And Lucy had called to remind me my dinner was in the fridge upstairs. She asked if I wanted to join her and Maddie instead, and when there was a pause on the phone while I tried to figure out who Maddie was, Lucy said, "We would love it if you joined us, Libby."

Something about the way she said *we* made me take the phone away from my ear and squint at it. I told her I had plans, and it wasn't until Quinn pulled in the driveway that I remembered Desiree talking about how Lucy was never home anymore since she started hanging out with Quinn's boss.

Bent had raised an eyebrow, asked if Desiree was jealous that Madeline had taken away her only friend. I'd left the room when Desiree gave him the finger, sick to death of them arguing with being stuck in the house all week.

Now I turn onto Jimmy's street and park in front. The house is dark, and I text him that I'm walking around to the back, but the phone rings a second later, and it's him, telling me to wait—he'll be right down.

There's something in his voice that I've never heard before, and when he jogs down the back stairs, I can see by the way he's not looking at me that something is wrong.

He stands in front of me, his arms crossed.

"What's wrong?" I ask.

"Nothing," he says unconvincingly.

"Your text said you wanted to talk. Is everything okay?"

"Yeah, I mean I've got a lot of shit going on. I really just wanted to say goodbye. You know, I'm leaving, so—"

"Wait—you're leaving now? I thought you had until the beginning of September?"

He shifts his weight, an anxious look on his face. "No—it's . . . I'm leaving when I told you. It's just . . . I'm going to be busy with packing and getting ready."

I picture the military bag in the corner of his empty room. Packed and ready to go. "That's more than a week away—"

"I can't see you anymore," he says abruptly, glancing at me and then looking at his feet. "It's not that I don't want to. It's just for the best."

"Best for who?"

"Libby—I'm leaving for a year. And you're still in high school and your father doesn't even like me. . . ." His voice trails off.

I study his face. He refuses to look at me. "How about the real reason now? Let me guess—Flynn?"

He meets my eyes. "He's my brother, Libby."

"So just like that, he says you can't see me, and you say what? Fine? No problem?"

"I didn't say fine! He was upset—he knew you were here the other night. I told him nothing happened, but he doesn't believe me."

"It's none of his business—"

"Stop!" His eyes flash, and he puts his hand up. "I can't do this, Libby. It's not fair to you—and that's my fault. That's on me. He's my brother and he's asking me to step away. Look, he doesn't really believe I'm going to stay sober. And hell, I deserve that—I do. I can't fix that I made my house a shitty place to live when he was growing up. I can't go back and fix it. But I *have* to do this. Do you understand? I have to try to make it right between us."

"And not seeing me . . . that makes it right?"

He tilts his head at me. "He's just trying to protect you. That's how much of an asshole my brother thinks I am."

"He was drunk today. Well, drinking. Did he tell you that? Maybe ask him what he has to say about walking in your footsteps?"

He puts his hands in his pockets, breathes out. "That's part of it. We made a deal. I leave you alone, and he knocks it off with the booze and whatever else."

"Well, happy to be your bargaining chip," I tell him, and he winces.

"Libby—this isn't what I want—" he starts, then stops. "I'm sorry," he tells me in a quiet voice, and then he's gone, climbing the stairs and disappearing inside the house.

The light in his bedroom turns off, as though he wants to make sure I know I'm not welcome anymore.

I cross the backyard toward the path alongside the house. Out of the corner of my eye, an orange glow lights up the dark.

"Trouble in paradise?" a voice says.

I look past the big elm in the middle of the backyard. Quinn's husband is sitting in a lawn chair behind it, only a few feet away from me, invisible if not for the light from the cigarette in his hand.

"That's creepy," I tell him. "Do you eavesdrop all the time?"

"No," he says simply, as though it's an honest question. "Only when it's more awkward to tell someone I'm here than to pretend I'm not."

"Why are you here? I thought you came home to be with Quinn, and you're here, like, every time I come over."

He raises his eyebrows. "Is that what she wants? To be with me?"

I snort. "Why don't you ask her? I mean, she's your *wife*."

"She doesn't want to be with me," he says, ignoring my question. "She thinks she does, but she doesn't." He pulls a bottle from between his legs and takes a sip. "She wants the house, the kids, the white picket fence. The American dream." He laughs. "The American fucking dream . . ." he slurs and takes another sip.

"So? What's wrong with that?"

He looks over at me, surprised. "Nothing wrong with it. It's just there's two sides to that dream—the ones who live it, right here. And the ones who go out and fight for it. Maybe some people know how to do both. But I don't."

"Is that what you came home to tell her? That you're leaving?"

"I was always leaving. I've been training in special ops since I left. I told her I was going back. We had some . . . words . . . before I left. Thought we could both use some time to cool off."

"Quinn didn't know that. She thought you were missing."

"Yeah? Well, missing's a state of mind, I guess. She knew I was reenlisting. I'm not the one making the choice here." He takes a puff of his cigarette.

I don't want to ask the question, but it sits heavy in my throat, threatening to crush my lungs if I don't get it out.

"And Bent? He knew?"

"He was the first call I made when I left that night. Drove straight through to the base and called your father. Told him to keep an eye out for her. That I wasn't going to be reachable until I came back."

"Why didn't you just tell Quinn where you were?"

"Because she doesn't want me to go. Thinks I need to get some sort of mental help. That's not exactly the type of thing you want going around. I didn't want her tracking me down, talking to my superiors about how I should stay home, when home is the last place I want to be."

"So why come back?"

He takes a drag of his cigarette, blows it out. "Because I took a vow. And I'm not going to desert her. I'm not going to get some shitty desk job and put on a tie every day, but I'll stay if she wants me to."

"Stay in Paradise? Like in our house?"

"I'm shipping out for a fifteen-month deployment." He cuts his eyes at me. "I meant stay her husband." He puts the bottle to his lips, tilts it back.

The cigarette between his fingers is burning so low it's touching his skin, and I know he must feel the heat from it.

It must be starting to hurt. To burn. Maybe it's even unbearable.

But he doesn't move. Just sits in the chair, as though he can't feel anything at all.

~ 24 ~

Quinn

She was worried with the puppy sleeping so much in the day that it might be a long night—and turns out, she was right.

Quinn had put him in the crate after Libby left and brought him into her bedroom. He was still sleeping when she closed her eyes, but he woke hours later, whimpering at first, and then high-pitched barking that seemed impossibly loud coming from his tiny body.

Which is how they're in the backyard after midnight—the puppy on a leash that Sally lent her, prancing around the backyard with Quinn following along.

She brought a flashlight, not wanting to wake anyone by turning on the outside light, and she tries to keep the beam on the puppy as he darts between bushes and tumbles in the grass. He stops every so often to look up at her, almost tipping over backward once, making her smile even though it's the middle of the night and she wants nothing more than to be asleep in her bed.

The ground is wet under her feet, the smell of freshly cut grass strong. She follows the puppy to the dim corner under the oak tree, and when she turns toward the house, she sucks in her breath, the silhouette of a man appearing from the darkness.

She points the flashlight at him just as a beam of light blinds her. She shrieks and nearly drops the flashlight on the ground.

"Quinn? Is that you?" she hears Bent say.

"Yes! Can you turn that thing off—I can't see!" she hisses, aware that the yell she let out has probably woken up the entire neighborhood. She squeezes her eyes shut, white spots dotting her vision.

When she opens her eyes, Bent is standing next to her.

"You scared the crap out of me," she says, and he twists his face at her.

"Me? I'm just driving by, checking that the street's quiet, and there's someone sneaking around in my backyard with a flash-light!"

"I wasn't sneaking around—"

"Quinn, I didn't know it was *you*. What are you doing out here? What the hell is that?" He points the light at the lawn.

"Isn't he the cutest?" Libby interrupts, suddenly appearing next to them, as if it were the middle of the afternoon. "Did some-body yell? I heard something and looked out the back window and saw you guys."

She picks up the puppy, kisses it on the head, and holds it out to Bent.

"Come on," she teases. "You know you want to hold him."

"Where did you get him?" He takes the puppy from Libby, turns him on his back, and scratches his belly before placing him on the ground.

"From the address you gave me," Quinn says. "I didn't know she was a breeder."

"I didn't either. I used to see Steve at this charity golf event, but he stopped playing. Too busy with the kids probably. He texts me dirty jokes sometimes. We keep saying we want to get together, but you know how it goes."

"Well, you were right, they're really great."

"Who's great?" Libby asks.

"Old friends of mine. So . . . this?" He gestures to the puppy.

"A gift," Quinn says. "I told them I needed to think about it. And check with the landlord, of course."

Libby lets out a snort. "The landlord is the biggest softie around."

"Lucy's no pushover," Bent replies.

"I meant you. You think she should keep him, don't you?"

He doesn't answer, but Quinn feels his eyes on her, and when she looks over, he's watching her, waiting for her to look at him.

"I think Quinn needs to do what's best for her," he says.

They're all quiet until Quinn says she needs to get some sleep before the dog wakes her up again. Libby hands her the leash and makes Quinn promise to call her later in the day so she can see the puppy—maybe take him for a walk.

Quinn goes inside, puts the puppy back in the crate, her eyes closing before her head is even on her pillow.

When she opens her eyes next, it's almost ten in the morning and the puppy is still asleep. She has a cup of tea and showers and at noon, Libby is at the door.

She lets the two of them play while she cleans the house. They spend the next hours blocking doorways with empty moving boxes to contain the puppy to the one room without a rug.

He chews on the lamp cord and licks the electrical outlet. At one point, Libby looks over at Quinn after they childproof the room and says in an offhand way that it's good preparation, eyeing Quinn's middle, and Quinn feels her stomach flip—the mention of the baby reminding her that she's been avoiding John.

In her mind, she's tried all week to sort out her emotions, but in the end, the entire process amounts to her feeling as though she's wandering through a dense maze. Each step twirls her in a direction she isn't sure she wants to go, leading her to an opening here and a dead end there until she's paralyzed, unable to move.

Finally, she decides, it's time.

So, while Libby sits across from her on the floor, her back against the wall on the other side of the room, the puppy rolling over her outstretched legs, Quinn texts Bent.

Can you tell John I'm ready to talk? Tonight at 9?

Three gray bubbles appear on the screen and disappear. Seconds later, they reappear, and she thinks he must be typing a long response, but when his message shows on her screen, it's simply *yes.*

Quinn picks the late hour for two reasons: the puppy will be asleep if he follows the pattern from the previous night, and she's sure he will, as they've kept him busy all day.

More importantly, she wants to see what sort of shape John is in at that time of night. Before he disappeared, she couldn't remember the last time he was sober past dinnertime.

Now it's nighttime again, and Quinn is sitting on the front steps, waiting for John, flinching every time a car passes, her body tense.

It's the same way she used to feel when she was young and a nor'easter threatened to take out the power lines and damage houses and flood the streets, the ocean rising over the sea wall. Her parents would stock up on milk and bread and candles, and they'd all wait—her mother saying how much she *loved* storms.

Quinn would nod and smile, but inside, her heart raced, the palms of her hands cold from the storm that might make her world go dark. The wind threatening to make her house shake and tremble and moan.

Bent's truck isn't in the driveway, but she knows he's home—

earlier they borrowed Quinn's car so Libby could follow Bent to the repair shop. Something about a leaky radiator.

When they returned, both Bent and Libby disappeared upstairs.

The light from the full moon gives the darkness a hazy glow, and she listens to the crickets sing instead of concentrating on the minutes ticking past nine, then nine thirty, then ten o'clock.

She's about to call Bent to double-check that John said he'd be here, even though Bent had texted back *all set* hours ago, when she hears a door open inside and footsteps on the stairs.

Libby steps out onto the porch. She walks down the stairs and stands on the front lawn, leaning against the railing, looking down at Quinn.

"I probably should pretend I don't know your husband was supposed to be here an hour ago, but Bent's been pacing the living room, and I finally got it out of him."

Quinn smiles. "It wasn't a secret. I didn't say anything because I'm sure you've had enough of my annoying drama as it is."

Libby shrugs. "I think of annoying drama and Desiree comes to mind. Not you."

Quinn's happy to have some company. She's about to tell Libby how the puppy didn't even fuss when she put him in his crate when a black truck careens around the corner, the windows open and the radio blaring.

It passes them and stops several houses down, the rumble of the engine loud as the truck sits motionless on the street.

The rear lights turn white, and Libby glances at Quinn as the truck reverses until it's in front of them, the cab high off the pavement from the massive oversize tires holding it up.

"Plural!" a man's voice yells from inside the truck, and Libby takes a step forward.

"Libby," Quinn says softly, reaching her arm out, something in his voice making her heart speed up.

"It's just Flynn," Libby tells her.

But Quinn stands up and follows Libby to the curb, stands right next to her.

The passenger door swings open to show three guys packed into the bench seat. Flynn, sitting in the middle, climbs clumsily over the passenger seat, elbowing his friend in the face, who shoves him out of the car, both howling and swearing as he tumbles to the street, the smell of alcohol surrounding them.

He gets up slowly, his eyes slits, and steadies himself by grabbing onto the mirror on the door.

He blinks at Libby and stumbles onto the sidewalk next to her, and Quinn takes a step closer.

"Plural—I was just thinking about you, and here you are—what the hell are you doing?" he slurs.

"I live here, Flynn," Libby says. "Remember?"

He covers his mouth with his hand and laughs as if someone has just told him a hilarious joke.

Libby sighs. "Go home, Flynn. You're wasted."

He looks as though he might get back in the truck, but his expression changes when he glances past them to the driveway.

"Wait a second—where's Officer Winters? Maybe he wants to come out and harass me some more."

Libby scowls at him. "Oh, will you get over it? Stop acting like such a victim. You can't even give your own brother a break without being a crybaby about us hanging out together."

"A crybaby—she just called me a crybaby," he shouts to his friends, who don't seem to be paying any attention to them until a beer bottle comes flying out the window and smashes on the sidewalk behind Flynn.

He stumbles, almost bumping into Quinn. Quinn grabs Libby's arm and tries to pull her away, but Libby won't budge.

"You're just mad because I took Prince Charming away from you. Well, you can thank me later. You have no idea what a fuckup he is."

"Well, at least he's trying, Flynn. At least he's doing something. Look at you—you're just a stupid drunk," Libby yells.

Quinn pulls Libby's arm again, trying to get her in the house, when there's a whoosh past her head.

Bent appears before Flynn realizes someone is next to him, and suddenly Flynn's arm is behind his back, and he's wincing, standing on his tiptoes, Bent's arm around his neck.

"Listen carefully," Bent growls. "Sit on that curb and put your hands behind your head, or I'm going to beat the living shit out of you."

Flynn makes a gurgling noise, and Bent slams him to the ground, where his body lands in a sitting position, a stunned look on his face.

"Hands up!" Bent says, and Flynn obeys, his eyes wide.

"Get out of the truck," Bent barks, walking over to the passenger door.

The two in the truck turn to look at him, and it's clear they have no idea what's just happened. The one in the passenger seat jumps back when Bent reaches through the window, his eyes wild.

The massive tires squeal as the truck lurches forward, the engine screaming as the driver guns it, the smell of diesel fuel filling the air.

Bent pulls his arm back just as the truck peels away from the curb and races down the street.

He pulls his phone out and gives it to Libby.

"Call the station and tell them to send a cruiser to the house."

"Wait—"

"Do it!" he barks, and she stares at him for a minute before she looks down at the phone, presses the screen, and puts it to her ear.

"You're going to fucking arrest me?" Flynn slurs, trying to arrange his legs underneath him to stand. "I'm going to sue you for police brutality. You have no right to keep me here."

Bent looks down at him. "You're on my property. And you have my kid, who never raises her voice, yelling at you. And you see that dog?" He points to the window upstairs.

They all turn and look up at the second-floor window. The top half of Rooster's body is looming in the window, his teeth bared, a series of ferocious barks making their way down to them.

"That dog wants to eat you alive, and he only does that when someone acts like an asshole to the people he loves. So, your best bet is to shut your mouth until you sober up and be happy I came down here instead of him."

Flynn shakes his head. "I only came by to say hello—Libby was standing outside. I was on the sidewalk until you laid me out on your property. And she's the one who started it. But you don't know that, either, right? Because you don't know anything. Ask your perfect angel daughter about my brother. You know, the one she was sleeping with the other night while you were busting my nuts."

Bent's expression doesn't change—Quinn wonders if he's even heard what Flynn said, but she knows he had to—he's standing right next to her, his hand still on Flynn's shoulder.

"Go upstairs," Bent tells Libby in a quiet voice.

Libby glares at Flynn, and he must feel her eyes on him because he looks up, slumping over drunkenly with the movement.

"I hate you," Libby whispers, and Flynn's head jerks back, as though he's been slapped.

"Libby—" Bent chides, but she's gone, up the porch stairs, slamming the door behind her just as the police cruiser pulls up.

An officer gets out of the car and walks over to them.

"What's up?" she asks.

"Give me your cuffs," Bent says, and she takes them off her belt, hands them over.

"Get up." Bent pulls Flynn up by his arm. "Hands behind your back."

"Come on, Mr. Winters," he says, crying now. "Please."

Bent doesn't speak, just clicks the cuffs on his hands. He leads Flynn to the car, puts him in the back of the cruiser, and walks back over to them.

"Got a pen?" he asks the officer.

She takes a pen out of her chest pocket and hands it to him. He pulls a scrap of paper out of his pocket, holds the cap between his teeth while he writes, and hands the paper to her.

"Get out an APB on this plate. Black Chevy. Left taillight out. I think it was the Walsh kid in the passenger seat, but I didn't recognize the driver. We'll get a name out of Flynn at the station. I'm going to grab a ride with you. Just give me a minute," he says, and she nods and walks back to the cruiser.

Quinn remembers the bottle smashing on the sidewalk and bends to pick up some of the glass, but she feels his hand on her arm and straightens.

"Leave it, Quinn. I'll clean it when I get back."

"No—it's okay. Go. I'll check on Libby when I'm done. Make sure she's okay." She pauses. "What's going to happen to him?" She looks at the cruiser.

"Flynn? Nothing. I'll put him in a holding room. Let him sober up. He's a good kid hanging out with the wrong crowd. I just want to scare him." He turns and pauses, looks back at her. "Do me a favor and stay inside. At least until I'm home."

"Are you worried about the guys in the truck? That they'll come back?"

His eyes slide past her to the street, to where the truck sped off, but he doesn't answer. "I'll just feel better if I know you and Libby are inside together," he says finally, and walks to the car.

She watches as they drive down the street, disappear around the corner.

She leans down and fills her hand with glass from the broken bottle and rushes to the side of the house to the trash barrels, where she empties her hand quickly, making sure all the tiny slivers are gone, thinking of her hand running through the puppy's fur. Even though she's hurrying, it's several minutes before she's putting the lid on the barrel.

Her heart is racing—her hands shaky. The night suddenly seems darker than usual, the smell of beer and diesel fuel thick in the humid air. Rooster's barking still ringing in her ears from his spot in the window above and the hollow sound of Flynn's body smacking the ground.

She hurries across the front lawn, heading for the porch stairs, when she hears her name. She jumps, blinking into the night, stepping away from the voice until the bushes lining the front of the house brush the back of her legs.

John is standing on the sidewalk, his truck idling behind him, the driver door still open, jutting into the empty street.

Quinn crosses her arms, stays where she is, and he walks forward, stops in front of her.

"I didn't know if you'd still be awake. I meant to come earlier, but it got late."

"Why?" she asks.

He lifts his eyebrows. “Bent called and said you wanted to talk—”

“No. I mean why are you late?”

He studies her, looks at the ground, the small movement making him sway slightly on his feet.

“You’ve been drinking,” she says quietly.

“I’ve been *thinking*.” He smirks. “And yes, that required a bit of fortification.”

“Well, come back tomorrow. I’m going inside.” She moves to turn, but he grabs her arm.

“I won’t be here tomorrow,” he tells her, and pauses, as though waiting for her reaction.

In the silence, she hears the low rumble of an engine. Over John’s shoulder, the black truck from earlier turns onto the street. It speeds up, then comes to a screeching halt in front of the house, only inches from where John is parked.

Someone in the truck yells out to them, a torrent of insults, the word *Pig* making its way to her ears over the engine and loud music.

John whips around and takes a step toward the voice, but she grabs him.

“John—stop! They think you’re Bent! Just ignore them, it has nothing to do with you.”

He rips his arm away from her so forcefully she stumbles forward.

“Nothing to do with me? They call him that—might as well call me it too.” He points at the truck, strides forward. “Get out and say it to my face, punk,” he shouts at them.

The driver lays on the horn, presses it several times, hoots and laughter coming from inside before they peel off down the street, the truck zigzagging, a stream of smoke spurting from the exhaust pipe.

John is on the curb now, as if he might follow them, his eyes blazing, the veins in his neck bulging.

She steps closer, trying to get him to focus on her face. "Let them go, please. Come inside. If we're not standing out here, they'll just go away."

She touches his arm again, but he sneers at her, a look of disgust on his face, and bats her hand away.

"You want me to go inside and *hide*? You think I'm hiding from these punks? Fuckers don't know who they're messing with." He walks over to his truck, yanks open the passenger door, and reaches into the glove compartment. When he shuts the door and faces her, he's holding a gun.

She can't breathe suddenly, unable to pull her eyes away, the shock of it turning her numb.

John is breathing heavily, as though they were in the middle of a battle instead of being harassed by teenagers, and she forces herself to speak.

"John. Look at me. Look at my face." He glances at her, but it's as though he doesn't know who she is, his eyes looking through her, his pupils large and empty. "You need to go home. Those are just kids in that truck. Teenagers!"

"Don't give me that shit. Boys half their age have tried to blow my fucking head off."

"We're not in the Middle East—we're not at *war*! Go home, right now. I don't want that thing near me." She points to the gun, but he ignores her, his eyes glazed over.

She hears the truck before she sees it. Hears the thunder from the engine, loud as a tank, minutes before she sees it turn the corner onto the street.

Then it's slowly pulling up in front of the house. Or maybe everything around her is moving in slow motion—the guy in the passenger seat sticking his head out; John raising his arm; the look of shock, then terror on the guy's face, followed by the deafening roar as the truck lurches forward to escape the pointing barrel of a gun.

John's truck is still idling where he parked it—too far into the street—the driver's-side door ajar.

The truck surges forward with such force that it fishtails and plows into John's door, ripping it from the hinges and sending it sailing through the air, where it slams to the ground.

She hears a scream and looks at John, but he's no longer standing next to her. He's shoving the damaged door aside, moving it out of the way. His truck is dented, sideways in the street from the impact. But he climbs inside the driver's seat, disappearing inside the gaping hole where the door once was.

And she realizes it's her voice that's screaming as she watches him tear away from the curb, speeding after the truck up the street.

She doesn't pause for a moment. She turns and runs, slams into the house, and races up the steps. Hurrying to reach Libby, rushing to the phone, trying to get help.

She's on the stairs when she hears it.

Car horns wail and tires screech. The raw sickening scrape of twisting metal. Then a thunderous *BOOM* so loud it seems the entire world hears it. The noise brings her to her knees. She stops breathing, squeezes her eyes shut.

Then there is nothing.

A silence so bottomless, so empty, she holds on to the railing to keep it from swallowing her whole.

25

Libby

The noise shakes the house, shifts the ground underneath me, knocks the pictures off the walls, and blows out the windows.

That's what it feels like, at least.

Even Rooster startles and gets to his feet from his spot on my bed, looks at my closed door and back at me accusingly, like everything I've just whispered to him about how *he's okay* is just one huge fat lie.

It took me forever to coax him away from the front window. Away from barking and growling at Flynn and my father down below.

And now, the sound of whatever just exploded outside has him standing up, barking again. I tell him to stay and close the door behind me.

The house is empty, and I'm hurrying to the window to see where the noise came from, when the front door opens so hard it bangs against the back wall, the glass threatening to shatter.

Quinn rushes in, her eyes wild, the puppy pressed tight to her chest, a panicked look on her face, as though the loud noise she heard outside is a physical thing that's coming to get her.

"He has a gun!" she hisses, and rushes past me to the window, cranes her neck to see up the street. I look over her shoulder, but there's nothing but trees and sky.

"Who? Bent? What was that noise?" I ask, but she runs back to the door, locks it, looking through the glass frantically before ducking underneath it.

"Quinn. Calm down—"

"What if he comes back here? Whatever that noise was—it's right there!" She points up the street. "He's drunk, and he has a gun!" she says again. "We need to call the police—your father! I ran down to get the puppy, but I can't find my phone, and I wanted to get out of the apartment!"

She pats her pockets, even though she's wearing a sundress, and goose bumps run down my arms, the terror on her face making the room grow cold.

And suddenly I know she's talking about her husband. He must have shown up after all. Drunk. With a gun.

Bent always says domestic disputes are the most dangerous calls. How they can turn deadly in the blink of an eye. And I've never doubted it—we have Rooster to prove it.

I don't stop to think now, just grab Quinn's arm and rush through the house, shutting lights off as I go.

"Where are we going?" she blurts, but I don't answer, just push open my bedroom door and yell at Rooster to *come*, and thankfully, for once, he listens, jumps off the bed and runs past us.

I open the back door and look out in the hallway. It's pitch-black, but I don't turn the light on.

"Up to Lucy's," I whisper to Quinn, and she grabs Rooster by the collar and hurries him up the stairs. I close the door behind me and follow them. Upstairs, I find the spare key and let us in.

The kitchen is dark, only the small light on under the microwave, and we file quietly into the living room. Quinn moves to the window, shielding herself behind the curtain. She peers out and looks back at me anxiously.

"I can't see anything. There's flashing lights, though. The police are there."

"Don't worry," I whisper, trying to keep my voice calm. "He doesn't know Bent's sisters live here. If he comes back, he won't come up here."

I slip my phone out of my back pocket and call Bent, but it goes right to voice mail. I send him a text that we're at Lucy's and to call me ASAP.

Quinn is still staring out the window, and I tell her to sit, gesturing to the couch. She ignores me until I point out that all the stress isn't good for the baby. She sighs, and I hold my arms out for the dog. She hands him over and sits on the couch, but on the edge, as though she's ready to run.

The puppy squirms frantically in my arms, and I look down to see Rooster sniffing at him, his tail wagging. I look at Quinn and she shrugs, nods. I put him on the floor, and he launches his body at Rooster, who sinks to a crouch, his head the size of the puppy's entire body, and rolls on his back. The puppy takes this as an invitation to jump on Rooster's neck and disappears over him, tumbling in a heap.

We're quiet, watching them play as the sound of sirens fills the street.

"What happened?" I ask, and she picks up from where I left my father and Flynn on the street.

When she finishes, I get up and look out the window again.

"Maybe we should go out there? I mean, find out what happened?"

"No, you didn't see him. The look on his face—he wasn't there anymore. Like something flipped, and he just was somewhere else. And the rage in his eyes. I've never seen that before. Like he wanted to . . ." She pauses, looks at me.

"Wanted to what?"

"Hurt someone," she says softly, and glances at the window, a fearful look in her eye, as though afraid that someone might be her.

I leave her alone for a minute. Walk to the kitchen and fill a small bowl with water and grab the newspaper from the table.

In the living room, I put the bowl on the floor, and the puppy trots over and laps at it, while Rooster catches his breath and watches him. I spread out the paper in the corner and bring the puppy over, and it's only a second before he makes a small circle in the center. I crumple it and leave the rest of the paper on the floor in case he needs to go again. When I come back from throwing it out in the kitchen, Quinn is watching me.

"What?" I ask, and she shrugs, shakes her head, and a tear rolls down her cheek. She wipes it away, sniffs.

"Ever since I've moved in here, you and your dad, you've just . . . been so great. And here I have you hiding up here like some sort of prisoner. You must wish I never moved in."

I wave her away. "That's not true. I like having you here."

"Yeah, I bet," she says sarcastically. "You didn't at first. And you know what they say about intuition."

"Okay, I admit—I wasn't crazy about you moving in." I smile weakly. "But I didn't even know you then . . . and it was more about having another person moving in here. We used to have our own house, and after my mother died, I pretty much had Bent to myself. But . . . it's been kind of nice these past months. You know, coming home to people who like to be here."

I glance up, not sure if she'll understand, but she nods, looks me in the eye.

"Your mother?" she asks. "Is that who you mean?"

"She wanted a different life. And she made us believe we were stopping her from getting it. And then she got sick and died." I sigh, shrug at Quinn. "All before I had the guts to tell her how I felt. That we never seemed to be enough."

Quinn studies me. "Maybe her wanting to leave had nothing to do with you and everything to do with her. The hard part is figuring out how to not take it personally."

I pause, consider this. "And how do you not take it personally?" I ask finally.

"I'm still working on that one," Quinn says, and laughs. "But I think coming home to people who are happy to see you is a good start."

A door slams downstairs, and we both jump. Quinn stands up quickly and puts her back to me, between me and the door, her arms out, shielding me, it seems, from whatever might come through the door.

"Quinn, it might just be—"

"Shh!" she hisses, and we listen as footsteps climb the stairs until they're just outside Lucy's door. Quinn reaches behind her and grabs my wrist, pulling me close to her, her hands cold, and I feel her body relax when we hear a key in the lock.

Bent steps in and looks over at us, his eyes finding Quinn, his face pale, his shirt covered in blood.

"There was an accident," he says. Rooster rolls off his back and stands up, the puppy between his legs, and whines at Bent, as though he knows the meaning of the word.

"Are you okay?" Quinn asks, but he doesn't answer her.

He clears his throat, a deep sound that rumbles through the quiet hallway.

"You need to come with me," he says. "It's John. He's at the hospital."

She looks at him and nods, bends down and picks up the puppy.

"I'll put him in his crate and meet you out front," she says, and walks out.

Bent hurries past me, downstairs to our apartment. I call Rooster over to me and shut Lucy's door behind me. Bent glances over at me when I walk through the door, but his face is blank.

"What happened?" I ask, but he turns and walks away. I follow him to his bedroom. He pulls off his T-shirt, throws it in the small wastebasket in the corner.

"Why is your shirt covered in blood?"

"There was an accident," he says again, walking past me to the bathroom and shutting the door. I hear water running and when the door opens, he won't look at me.

"What happened?"

"Libby. Just—" He turns and puts his hand up. "Look, I need to go to the hospital—"

"I'm coming," I say.

"No, it's going to be a long night."

"I wasn't asking," I tell him, and grab my sweatshirt off the coat rack and walk out the door before he even has a chance to argue with me.

Quinn is on the porch, and there's a police cruiser waiting for us out front.

Bent opens the passenger door for Quinn, but she slips into the back seat with me. The officer who's driving pulls away from the curb and turns to Bent to say something, but Bent catches her eye and shakes his head. She looks back at the road, and we drive to the hospital in silence.

In the waiting room, Bent disappears for a moment, and when he returns, he pulls me aside.

"I'm going to have Lucy come get you. Quinn's filling out paperwork, and I have to find—"

"I'm not leaving," I interrupt. "I'll just sit here. I'm fine." I point to a row of empty seats, and he frowns at me but kisses my forehead and walks away.

I settle into the seat, glance around. The room is empty besides an older couple in the corner gazing blankly at the TV mounted on the wall.

I close my eyes, make a pillow out of my sweatshirt, and rest my head against it, trying not to picture Bent's shirt covered in blood.

Hours pass. I fall asleep and wake up, stretch my legs, and sit down again, my eyelids heavy.

Then Bent is shaking me awake, asking me if I want to go home. I ask if Quinn's leaving, and he says no, and I shake my head, and he sighs, stares at me. He tells me he has to leave for a minute to go to the station, but he'll be right back.

I find the cafeteria and buy an orange juice and a muffin and sit at a table while I eat. Then I take the elevator back to the waiting room and see Bent standing at the nurses' station. He glances up and motions for me to come over.

"The truck Flynn was in earlier was involved in this. The two morons weren't hurt more than a couple of stitches and a broken arm, but they're in a lot of trouble—possession, DUI . . ." He pauses, looks at me. "I went to the station to tell Flynn, and when he found out you were here, he asked me to bring him." He points to the row of seats against the wall. "You might not want to see him, but I thought you could both use a friend right now."

I look over at where Bent pointed and see Flynn, his head against the wall, his eyes closed.

When I walk over and sit in the chair next to him, he looks over at me and blinks. His forehead creases, and he leans forward, puts his face in his hands.

He doesn't make a sound, but his shoulders tremble. I grab a handful of tissues from the nurses' station. He shakes his head when I sit down and hold one out to him. A second later, he sniffs, wipes his eyes, and sits up, looking over at me, his eyes red rimmed and swollen.

"Crybaby," I say, and he makes a noise that's somewhere between a sob and a snort and puts his arm around my shoulder, pulls my head toward him. I wait for his knuckles on the top of my head, but I feel his breath in my ear.

"I'm such an asshole," he chokes out.

"You really are," I whisper, and his arm tightens on my shoulders before he lets go of me.

"I wish I could say I was too drunk to remember any of it. But I remember everything. Every fucking awful minute of it." He sighs, a sob threatening to slip out again.

"Seriously, stop crying. You're embarrassing."

He smirks, shakes his head. "I can always count on you to set me straight, Plural." He studies me. "Still hate me?"

"Yup." I nod. "Always."

He looks over at Bent. "Be serious for a second. How much trouble did I get you in? You know, talking about Jimmy."

I shrug again. "It's Bent. He doesn't stay mad. Plus, he's got other things on his mind."

"He told me if I thanked him one more time, he was going to kick my teeth in."

"You thanked him for arresting you?"

"He didn't arrest me. They just put me in a room, and your father showed up and told me he wasn't going to let me go anywhere until I sobered up, and I should put my head down and sleep it off. So I did. Next thing I know, he's shaking me awake—telling me what happened and that he wants to take me home, but I made him drop me off here." He breathes out, a ragged, wet sound. "I would've been in that truck, Libby. You know they're probably going to jail? I would've lost everything—"

"I don't want to think about that. So, tell me things change. Because you're a different person when you drink. And I don't want to be sitting in this room someday and you're the one back there." I point to the emergency room.

He nods. "Jimmy's on his way over. I called him . . . you know, to ask for his help. He was really great about it." He looks over at me. "I'm sorry about all that with him. It was just shit between him and me. He let me down a lot before he got sober. Made promises he didn't keep. Lied. Stole. There isn't a lot he didn't do—let me put it that way. I didn't want him near you—not that you can't take care of yourself, so don't look at me like that. Anyway. It didn't occur to me until I woke up sitting in the fucking police station that I was Jimmy. On the way to becoming him, at least."

Bent is on the other side of the room on his cell phone, and he glances over at me, and I point to the sign that says no cell phone use, but he's doesn't seem to notice me, and when he hangs up, his face is white, colorless. And then he turns, and someone is hugging him, her arms are around his waist, her face pressed into his chest, crying, it seems.

And when she lifts her head, it takes me a second to realize, the woman sobbing in my father's arms is Quinn.

26

Quinn

The official cause of death is severe brain injury—not suicide, as Quinn suspects. She doesn't know if that's accurate. Perhaps he lost control of the car. And perhaps he only meant to numb his mind for the night, to silence the demons that spoke to him when it was too quiet, but the truck he was driving hit the tree at the top of the street. The scrape of metal she heard was the two trucks colliding, but the thundering blast was John's truck careening off into an enormous cherry tree, nearly slicing it in two.

The last medical evaluation of John only proved to Quinn that he lied to the doctor—negative for any symptoms of post-traumatic stress syndrome. On paper, John was fit and ready to serve—not even a trace of the alcohol and painkillers in his blood the night his life ended.

But that doesn't surprise her—even the handful of soldiers she spoke with who'd been with John the past several weeks in training said he seemed happy; *focused*, *alert*, *intense* were some of the words used to describe him. She knew they were telling the truth—he only struggled when he was home. In civilian life.

Where there were no orders to follow or battles to win or brothers who would die for you.

Madeline had offered her house as a gathering spot after the burial, and now Quinn is busying herself putting finger sandwiches on a platter to avoid John's mother.

Susan sits in one of the folding chairs in the living room, sniffing and dabbing a tissue to her eyes, slumped against her husband while he talks animatedly at Bent, who's nodding absentmindedly and clearing his throat every several minutes.

"He's not listening to a word that guy's saying," Libby mutters to Quinn.

"What's with the wife's lips?" Desiree whispers, turning in her seat so only they can see her face, pursing her lips so they're absurdly pronounced, and Libby snorts, covers her face with her hand.

"Those are his parents!" Lucy hisses from behind the island where she's slicing a ham. "I'm sorry, Quinn." She cuts her eyes at Desiree.

Madeline is standing next to her, and she leans forward, peering into the living room at Susan and sliding her eyes over to Desiree in agreement behind Lucy's back.

"No—it's fine. John's probably laughing somewhere up there hearing you say that. He hated all the stuff she did to her face."

"Does she know?" Madeline blurts, pointing at Quinn's middle. She looks over at Lucy, who closes her eyes briefly.

"Damn it. Sorry, Luce—that's none of my business, Quinn."

"I don't see anything wrong with the question," Desiree says. "I mean, you're not showing yet, but that clock is ticking, and pretty soon, BAM!" She puffs her cheeks out and puts her hands far out in front of her flat stomach.

Lucy scowls. "Pregnancy is a magical time for most women. Don't listen to her, Quinn—she has issues."

"I hated it," Madeline offers. "Felt like an enormous elephant."

"I don't have any issues—not every woman has to buy into the whole marriage and kids equals everlasting bliss bullshit, Lucy."

"Oh, stop it," Lucy hisses. "The only one who has a problem with you not wanting to get married and have kids is you. It's not an issue that you don't want to—it's an issue that you talk about it incessantly. Everyone is sick and tired of hearing about it. Get married or don't. Have kids or don't—but please, shut up about it!"

Desiree pretends she doesn't hear Lucy and looks at Quinn.

"So . . . does she know or not?"

Quinn shakes her head. "It hasn't really seemed real. But I'm starting to show. I put on a skirt today that I've had forever, and I couldn't button the top." She looks up at them. "So . . . it's really real."

Out of the corner of her eye, she sees Madeline poke Lucy's arm. Lucy looks at her and gives a small, almost imperceptible shake of her head.

"What are you two making faces about?" Desiree asks accusingly.

"Let's show her. Come on, Luce—I can't wait anymore," Madeline pleads.

"There's a roomful of people out there—"

Madeline waves her off. "If we go through the den, nobody will even know. Come on, you guys," she says, and disappears with Lucy following closely behind.

Quinn looks at Libby, who shrugs and stands up, and they traipse single file through the den and up the carpeted staircase to the wide hallway on the second floor.

Madeline is waiting in front of the guest room, and she pushes open the door dramatically and sweeps her arm forward, motioning for Quinn to follow her.

Inside, Madeline moves to the corner next to Lucy, both looking at Quinn with hopeful expressions.

The room has been transformed into a nursery—a pale soothing sage on the walls, the once-dark walnut floor covered wall to wall with a soft, plush rug that Quinn's feet sink into. There's a crib against the wall, a mobile above it, and blankets folded neatly on the sheet-covered mattress. A changing table sits next to it, the shelves on the bottom stocked with diapers, wipes, and an assortment of baby-related products.

In the corner is a bed so inviting she has the urge to walk over and lie down, a pillow in the center embroidered with a *Q*.

Libby walks over to the glider on the far side of the room and sits down in it, rocking slowly back and forth.

"Impressive," she says, studying the room.

Quinn can't speak, a sob forming in her throat. She wipes a tear from her face, lets her fingers graze over the family of stuffed animals arranged on the small bench next to her leg.

"Are you surprised?" Madeline asks, clapping her hands. "I was so nervous you were going to catch us doing this last week!"

"Wait—I'm confused." Desiree looks from Madeline to Quinn. "Are you moving in here?"

Quinn is startled by the question and pauses, looking from Madeline to Lucy.

"She's not moving," Libby scoffs. "Right, Quinn? I mean, that's crazy."

Madeline steps forward. "I'm not suggesting anything, Quinn—Lucy and I started this room before John . . ." She pauses. "I know you told me you wanted to keep working after, and I wanted you to have a room if you decided to bring the baby with you instead of having to find alternate care. But if you want to move in here—with what's happened—I would love to have you. Lucy and I talked about it—and you know the boys would love it too. And I could help with the baby . . ."

"She already has a home," Libby blurts, her voice loud in the small room.

"Why did the two of you talk about it?" Desiree asks, looking from Madeline to Lucy. She squints at them, and her eyes go wide. "Wait . . . are you guys, like . . . together? As in, like, a couple?"

There's a long moment when nobody speaks, and suddenly Quinn's aware that someone is standing behind her.

She turns and sees Bent standing next to the changing table holding a stuffed bunny with long arms and legs, *Thumper* stitched on its chest.

He looks at the crib, a line forming between his eyes. Libby storms past him, brushing his shoulder as she walks out the door, her footsteps heavy on the stairs.

"Libs?" he calls and walks to the door and looks out and turns back to them. "There's some sort of beeping in the kitchen, and I didn't know what it was—"

"Oh—the rolls!" Madeline throws up her hands and hurries out of the room.

Lucy shifts her eyes to Quinn. "We'll be downstairs," she says, and lifts her chin at Desiree, who follows Lucy out of the room.

They stand in the room across from each other. In the silence, Quinn hears the clock shaped like a moon on the wall, ticking away time. Bent looks over at her.

"Is your boss having a baby?" he asks.

Quinn takes a deep breath and lets it out. "I'm pregnant."

He blinks, leans forward like he doesn't understand.

"Bent?"

"Yeah—I heard you." His face is blank, stunned.

"It's not . . ." Her face flames. The word *yours* refusing to pass her lips. "I didn't find out until after John disappeared," she says quietly.

He rubs his forehead. "But he's been gone for months. When did you find out—I mean . . . how did they do all this?"

"I've known for a while. I just needed time to process it."

He shakes his head. "Wait, were you when we . . ." He stops. "The night we were together, you knew?"

"Bent, it's complicated—"

"No." His face turns hard. "It's a simple question. Did you know?"

"Yes, but it's not like I decided—"

"Jesus! You didn't think I might have wanted to know that?"

"It just happened. It's not like I planned—"

"Oh—I'm aware it just happened, Quinn. Believe me. Every fucking day I'm aware it happened. He was my friend . . ." He bends over, puts his hands on his knees.

"I'm sorry. I should have told you. I was having feelings for you, and then we were dancing and—"

He straightens, a look on his face that makes her stop talking, as though something's just occurred to him.

"What? Wait a second, here. This whole time I've been thinking this was all my fault. You had *feelings* for me? So . . . what was I, then—your backup plan? Just in case John didn't come back?"

He's shouting now, and the words slam into her, push her back against the wall.

It takes her a minute to hear what he's said. Even then, she doesn't believe it.

"You didn't just say that to me. Tell me you didn't just say that to me."

"What did you tell John the night he showed up? Huh? That you had feelings for me, but hey, welcome home. Let's play house again!"

"That's not fair. He was my husband—and I wanted time to think before I talked to him. Let's not pretend you didn't know how to get in touch with him. I knew that you could find him—"

"And I would have called him! I would have told him to come home!"

"I didn't want him to come home!" she shouts, the words slipping out. The minute she says it, she's knows it's true. And suddenly she can't stop herself from talking. All the words she couldn't find these past months pouring out of her.

"That day you showed up at my house after he left—I was terrified. Lost. And you know why? Because I had no idea what *I* wanted. Not John—*me*! Because I didn't know who I was outside of *us*—this couple that we had been since high school. Along the way, John and I grew up. But we didn't grow together. We wanted different things. Different lives. What you said that night—that he was a good soldier, just not a good husband—I didn't allow myself to feel that until it was out there. To really take the time to think about what I wanted. To think about what I *want*."

She looks at him, waits until he meets her eyes.

"I was going to tell John about the baby. But we were over. I'm sorry I didn't tell you I was pregnant. But I'm not sorry about that night we were together."

He looks as though he might say something, but he's silent. He stares at her until he turns, tosses the stuffed animal on the bench, where it bounces and falls to the floor.

She's left standing in the nursery alone, the bunny at her feet, one arm flopped over his face, covering his eyes, as though he can't bear to watch.

27

Libby

The guy in the passenger seat of the truck isn't doing jail time, and the driver got a hefty fine, but he's sent to rehab instead of prison, and this seems to be the only thing comforting Flynn—he's told me at least a dozen times in the ten minutes I've been in the car with him.

"I should've been in that truck. It was my idea to drive by your street!" he says again, and I look over at him.

"What's that look for?" he asks.

"I'm not saying it isn't awful—but it's not like it was your fault. You were at the police station when it happened."

"Only because of your father! You know I could've kissed any scholarships goodbye. And Walsh's arm is in pieces—they put a steel rod in it. I mean, I might've never played basketball again if your father hadn't made me stay out of the truck—"

"Flynn—stop! You've said it, like, a million times. I can't listen to you gush about Bent every time we're together. Where are we going anyway?"

When Flynn picked me up, he said he had an errand to run, and he needed me to come with him, and now we're crossing the tracks on the other side of town, where there's only the abandoned warehouses and the commuter rail station.

He ignores me and pulls into the train station parking lot and over to the drop-off area. Outside my window, clusters of people are standing on the outdoor platform, waiting for the train. He puts the car in park, points to something outside my window.

I follow his finger to a guy in a camouflage uniform sitting on the bench, his face turned away from us, looking down the tracks, a canvas military bag upright between his legs.

"Hurry up," Flynn says. "Train's coming."

I look at him. "Flynn, I'm fine—you don't need to—"

"I'm not doing it for you," he says, and leans forward, looking past me to his brother. "I'm doing it for him. Go—I'll wait here."

I get out of the truck and shut the door. The noise makes Jimmy turn, and when he sees me, he stands up, pulls the hat off his head, and holds it between his hands while I walk over to him.

When I reach him, he looks over his shoulder at the train coming to a halt, the doors opening.

"I wasn't sure if you got my messages," he says.

"I did. All five of them. The texts too."

He blushes, looks down at his feet. "Sorry about that. I don't want any doubt in your mind that I know I acted like a jerk."

"Well, you weren't alone in that." I glance over at Flynn's car.

"I wish I could make it up to you—"

"Come home," I interrupt. "Come home in one piece and tell me everything that happened. Every single thing. That's how you can make it up to me."

The train horn sounds, and he grabs his bag, puts his free arm around my shoulders and kisses my cheek, his breath whistling past my ear, and then he's jogging toward the open door, disappearing inside the train.

I wait until it pulls away from the station and walk back to the car.

Flynn watches me while I buckle my seat belt, looks at my face, and shakes his head. He sighs, puts the car in drive.

"Oh, Plural," he says. "You've got it bad."

I don't answer him, just look out the window as the train grows smaller and smaller, until finally, it's gone.

On the way back to my house, Flynn launches into a story about his girlfriend—ex now—and I'm not really paying attention until he tells me that he's done with women for the foreseeable future.

"Yeah, right," I say.

"I'm serious, Plural. I need some serious me time—no distractions. You know, figure out some shit. Self-improvement 101. So, until further notice—you're the only girl who gets my attention."

"Lucky me," I say as he pulls in my driveway, shuts the car off. "Are you coming to the cookout?"

Lucy had invited almost the entire neighborhood to a Labor Day cookout in the backyard, and Bent had been upset. He told her with all the awful stuff that had happened in the past week, he didn't think it was the right time to have friends over. But Lucy had looked up from cleaning the grill and said she couldn't think of a better time, actually.

Now there are cars parked up and down the street, and music drifting out to us from the backyard.

"Is Desiree going to be there?" Flynn asks, and laughs. I slam the door behind me.

"Libs—it was a joke. Come on." He punches my shoulder playfully, and we walk toward the backyard.

Rooster is lying on the grass next to the porch, and he gets up lazily when he sees us, and Flynn stops and drops to one knee, waits for Rooster to walk over to him.

"See, he still loves me," he says as Rooster nudges his hand with his head to get him to pet him.

"You've brought him a bone every day this week. You're just buying his affection," I tell him.

"Whatever it takes, Plural." He looks at me and winks. "Whatever it takes."

Bent is standing in front of the grill, flipping hamburgers, and when he sees me, he puts down the spatula and walks over to us. He says hello to Flynn, who shakes his hand so eagerly that Bent frowns and slaps him on the back, tells him to go make himself useful and make sure the hot dogs don't burn.

"He's growing on me," Bent says, watching Flynn hurry toward the grill.

"Welcome to my life," I tell him, and he looks at me, gestures for me to follow him to the side of the house.

"That's the most you've spoken to me all week," he says when we're alone, his voice low. "Not mad at me anymore?"

"I was never mad—I just think you could've been nicer to Quinn. I mean, she hasn't been home at all, and it doesn't take a genius to figure out that it's because of you."

"Me? Why me?"

I scowl at him. "You stormed out of Madeline's house when you found out she was pregnant!"

"First of all—I didn't storm—and yes, it was sort of a shock—"

"Well, how do you think Quinn felt when she found out? Believe me, she's been stressed about it too."

He squints at me. "You knew?"

"Pretty much everyone knew. Except you."

He sighs, looks down at his feet and back at me. "Anyway—she's here. I stopped by Madeline's earlier and asked her to come . . . so . . ." He tilts his head at me. "Let's just go back to normal, okay? Cut your old man some slack." He puts his arm around me, leads me into the backyard, and squeezes my shoulder before he walks over to the grill.

Quinn is standing next to Lucy and Madeline, hovering over Desiree on the ground with the puppy. She's cooing and blowing kisses at him, a delirious look on her face.

"Libby—have you ever seen anything as cute as this!" Desiree gushes, and I shake my head, speechless. I catch Sully's eye and he shrugs, as though he has no idea what's happening.

Desiree slept over at his house the last two nights. Apparently, they've shelved talking about kids since Desiree got the yoga retreat gig on that island. She told Sully he could tag along, and now he's taking surfing lessons and talking about how he's fine being a kept man, following his girlfriend around the islands while she trains her wealthy clients.

"I've never seen her like this," Lucy whispers to me. "I actually didn't think she was capable of it."

Desiree looks up at Sully, squeezes the puppy to her chest. "Maybe when we get back, we can get a dog?" she says, a hopeful expression on her face.

Sully shrugs again. "We can do that."

Desiree grins and holds the puppy in front of her, their faces only inches apart. "I'm going to get one just like you! Yes, I am! I'm going to be a mommy to a sweet little boy just like you," she tells him in a voice that makes Lucy turn to Libby with a blank look on her face.

"Well, I'll be," Lucy says, taking Madeline's hand.

Madeline wraps her arm around Lucy's waist, and Libby watches them wander over to the table covered with trays of food.

Quinn is standing next to her, gazing at them as well.

"Are they like . . . together?" I ask.

Quinn turns, a faraway look on her face. “Funny you should ask. Madeline asked me this morning if I thought it was weird that they spend so much time together. I didn’t know what to say—I couldn’t tell if she was hinting at something. Then she said that she just loves Lucy—everything about her.”

“What did you say?” I ask.

Quinn looks at me and shrugs. “I told her you love who you love.”

I feel something wet on the back of my leg and look down to see Rooster standing next to me, an enormous bone in his mouth, his tail wagging back and forth.

Across the yard, Flynn catches my eye, points to me and Rooster, and lays his hand over his heart, lets it rest there, determined it seems, to fix what was broken.

Epilogue

She names her son John Luke, a combination, in her mind, of the best parts of his father.

The first few months after he was born were a blur—she wouldn't have survived without all the help.

Lucy kept her refrigerator stocked with meals, and either Libby or Bent stopped in every day to visit or do a load of laundry or walk the dog. Even Desiree surprised her, taking the baby outside in the stroller or bringing him upstairs so Quinn could nap.

Madeline insisted on paid maternity leave, but Quinn didn't use it all—the twins are in kindergarten full-time now, and the nursery at Madeline's house is much nicer than the one at her house anyway.

Plus, she finds the baby sleeps through the night on the days he's with the twins—the trips to the park or playing in the backyard more entertaining than when they're alone, just the two of them.

He turns six months next week, and Quinn still can't believe he belongs to her.

She finds herself standing over his crib sometimes, just watching him sleep. Which is what she's doing now. There are piles of laundry to do and the house is a mess and it's already two o'clock in the afternoon and she still hasn't taken the dog for a walk, but she'd rather stand here, gazing down at her son.

She hears a knock on the door and tiptoes out of his room, walks to the front door. When she opens it, Bent is in front of her in the hallway, standing with his hands shoved in the pockets of his jeans.

"Hi," he says. "I hope it's not a bad time."

"It's not. Come on in." She opens the door wider, but he doesn't move.

"No—that's okay. I, ah, just wanted to ask you something."

She looks at him, waits. He pulls his hands out of his pockets, studies his palms.

"What?" she asks finally.

He looks up at her. "Well . . . I wanted to see if maybe . . . I don't know . . . you wanted to grab a bite to eat tonight. Maybe see a movie?"

She raises an eyebrow. "Like a date? Are you asking me on a date?"

"I remember you said you'd never been on a date before. I've been wanting to ask you but, you know, with the baby . . ." He stops, meets her eye. "So yeah. A date. Would you like to go on a date with me?"

"Yes," she tells him. "I'd love to go on a date with you."

He smiles, nods.

"But maybe we could just do dinner here," she says. "I don't have a babysitter."

"Oh—stupid me. Libby said she'd babysit. If that's okay."

"Of course, it is—he loves Libby. It's just . . . I don't want her to feel like she has to—"

He shakes his head. "It was her idea. She said if I didn't stop pining away and ask you out, she was going to murder me."

"Pining, huh?" She smiles, and he shrugs, nods.

She leaves him standing in the hallway after they say goodbye.

She shuts the door but a moment later, when she moves the curtain covering the glass, he's still standing where she left him, looking at her, with that tilt of his head. That look. She waves him away, and he winks at her, finally turns to the stairs.

She walks to the nursery and stands over the crib. On the table next to her are several pictures.

One of her favorites of John, smiling at the camera, a football between his hands. Another of John and Bent in their uniforms.

A larger frame sits on the corner of the table. The picture of John's father, her son's grandfather. The man John knew nothing about.

She's already writing down memories before she forgets them. Stories she can pass on to her son; details that can't be forgotten; a life that must be remembered.

She looks down at her child sleeping in the crib. Drinks in his features, his lips already so much like John's. She will tell her son about his father.

She will tell him all of it.

Acknowledgments

My deepest gratitude and thanks to: My editor, Kaitlin Olson, for her intelligence, insight, and dedication to this story. The book is better for it.

The entire team at Atria for their enthusiasm and hard work.

My agent, Danielle Burby, for her unflagging guidance, generous spirit, and brilliant mind. I could wish for no better advocate and friend.

Kristy Barrett (A Novel Bee), Stacey Armand (Prose and Palate), Kate Olson (kate.olson.reads), Chandra Claypool (wherethereadergrows), Kourtney Dyson (kourtneysbookshelf), Laurie Baron (booksandchinooks), and the many other bookstagrammers and bloggers who spend countless hours helping authors get our books into the hands of future readers, simply for the love of the written word.

Ged Driscoll, Ben Dexter, and Jim Vachon for their military expertise and patience answering questions.

(Former) Staff Sergeant Alexis Hilgert (USAF) and Major John Hilgert (USA) for offering their wise counsel. From correcting errors to reading drafts, they helped with details large and small, and the novel would not have been the same without them.

Pam Loring, founder of the Salty Quill Writers Retreat, along with Deb Boles, Melanie Winklosky, Jill Butler, and Lisa Greggo. All talented writers and women with incredibly generous spirits who enriched my days and nights on McGee Island during the early stages of this book.

Fellow writer and cherished friend Lisa Roe for her good humor, huge heart, and remarkable wit.

My mother, Peg Hamilton, for her inexhaustible faith, and all my family and friends for their continued enthusiasm and support. In particular, Chris and Tina Hamilton, Julie Spence, Jen Roopenian, Nancy Schofield, and Jen Tuzik.

Lauren Wheble and Mitch Miller, Heidi Wheble and Scott Hosker, Hutton and Alyssa Collin. My beloved fam squad, for the love, laughter, and friendship they bring to my life.

Sam, Matt, and Mia. For the gift of you.

And most of all, my husband, Tom Wheble. For everything.

About the Author

Lisa Duffy is the author of *The Salt House*, named by *Real Simple* as a Best Book of the Month upon its release in June 2017, one of *Bustle*'s Best Debut Novels by Women in 2017, and one of Refinery 29's Best Beach Reads of 2017, as well as a She Reads Book Club selection.

Lisa received her MFA in creative writing from the University of Massachusetts. Her short fiction has been nominated for a Pushcart Prize, and her writing can be found in numerous publications, including *Writer's Digest*. She is the founding editor of *Roar*, a literary journal supporting women in the arts. She lives in the Boston area with her husband and three children.

This Is Home

Lisa Duffy

This reading group guide for This Is Home *includes an introduction, discussion questions, ideas for enhancing your book club, and a Q&A with author Lisa Duffy. The suggested questions are intended to help your reading group find new and interesting angles and topics for discussion. We hope that these ideas will enrich your conversation and increase your enjoyment of the book.*

Introduction

Sixteen-year-old Libby Winters lives in Paradise, a seaside town north of Boston that rarely lives up to its name. After the death of her mother, she lives with her father, Bent, in the middle apartment of their triple-decker house. Bent's two sisters, Lucy and Desiree, live on the top floor. A former soldier turned policeman, Bent often works nights, leaving Libby in her aunts' care. Shuffling back and forth between apartments—and the wildly different personalities of her family—has Libby wishing for nothing more than a home of her very own.

Quinn Ellis is at a crossroads. When her husband, John, who is back home after serving two tours in Iraq, goes missing, suffering from PTSD that he refuses to address, Quinn finds herself living in the first-floor apartment of the Winterses' house. Bent had served as her husband's former platoon leader—John refers to Bent as his brother—and, despite Bent's efforts to make her feel welcome, Quinn has yet to unpack a single box.

For Libby, the new tenant downstairs is an unwelcome guest, another body filling up her already crowded house. But, soon enough, an unlikely friendship begins to blossom as Libby and Quinn grow a little more flexible and begin to redefine their understanding of family and home.

With gorgeous prose and a cast of characters who feel wholly real and lovably flawed, *This Is Home* is a nuanced and moving novel of finding where we belong.

Topics and Questions for Discussion

1. For the novel's epigraph, Lisa Duffy chooses a quotation by the poet Muriel Rukeyser: "My lifetime / listens to yours." Why do you think she picked this particular line to embody the novel? Discuss how you think it relates to the themes and characters of *This Is Home*.

2. The novel alternates between Libby and Quinn's points of view in every chapter. Do you think this was an effective storytelling technique? Also, why do you think Libby's chapters are narrated in the first-person point of view, while Quinn's chapters are written in the third person? What overall effect did this have on your reading experience?

3. Libby begins her side of the story with a story about her father, Bent: "The year I turned ten, my father shot the aboveground pool in our backyard with his police-issued pistol" (3). Why do you think she begins with this particular anecdote? What does it tell us about both Libby and Bent?

4. Rooster Cogburn, the ninety-seven-pound shelter mutt, is just as much of a character in the story as his human coun-

terparts. Discuss Rooster's role in the story: How does he bring the characters together, and how does he stand as another symbol for family?

5. "Paradise is like that, though; everything stuffed in tight" (5). While Libby may be speaking literally of her town in this statement, consider the sentence with "paradise" taking a more figurative meaning. Do you agree? In what ways might the setting of *This Is Home* constitute a kind of paradise for its inhabitants?

6. *This Is Home* shows a wide range of different types of families: Libby, Bent, Desiree, and Lucy; Madeline, her twins, and Quinn; Quinn and John; Flynn and Jimmy; Madeline and Lucy. What defining traits do all of these families share? Discuss any other nontraditional families in the book that you can think of.

7. "And in my mind, I'd think, dying isn't the only way someone disappears" (29). Consider this statement of Libby's. What do you think she means? Do you agree?

8. From relationships between veterans and their wives to Desiree's resisting a life as a mother, how do the characters in *This Is Home* respond to—and resist—traditional gender roles?

9. "I said John is a good soldier. Doesn't mean he was a good husband" (132). Consider this statement of Bent's. How do you think we change in the many different roles we embody in a lifetime? Discuss.

10. Compare Quinn's attraction to Bent to Libby's attraction to Jimmy. In what ways are they similar?

11. Photographs carry great sentimental value to the characters in *This Is Home*, especially Quinn. Why do you think photos mean so much to her?

12. Jimmy reads some sections of Tim O'Brien's novel *The Things They Carried* aloud to Libby. Consider this particular passage: *"You feel an intense, out-of-the-skin awareness of your living self—your truest self, the human being you want to be and then become by the force of wanting it. In the midst of evil, you want to be a good man"* (204). How might this passage relate to Bent, Jimmy, and John?

13. Why do you think it's so important for Quinn to see the puppy that John gave away? What does her willingness to finally go look at him signal about her character development?

14. Consider the meaning of "home" as it relates to the novel. How does the meaning shift from character to character? Discuss how "home" can carry both positive and negative connotations for the characters of *This Is Home*.

Enhance Your Book Club

1. Consider reading Lisa Duffy's first novel, *The Salt House*, with your book club. Do you find any themes that are similar to those in *This Is Home*?

2. Tim O'Brien's short story collection *The Things They Carried* is an important book for Jimmy. Consider reading with your book club; how might its stories of war remind you of the characters in *This Is Home*?

3. Visit the author's website at LisaDuffyWriter.com to learn more about her and to read some of her short fiction, essays, and interviews.

4. What is your own definition of home? Consider making a photo album, scrapbook, collage, or other art project that shows your personal definition of home, and then sharing it with your book club.

A Conversation with Lisa Duffy

What inspired you to write *This Is Home*? How did you visualize the vivid and wide cast of characters?

The inspiration for this story wasn't one specific thing. It was a couple of things that stuck with me over a period of time. I had read an article in the newspaper about a Massachusetts National Guard unit deploying to Iraq for a third tour. It spoke about the challenges of the multiple deployments from different perspectives—the soldiers going overseas and the spouses and children at home. Several years later, my daughter graduated from high school and some of her friends decided to join the service. Kids who had plenty of other options, but who wanted to serve. For me, the story began there, with a desire to explore the sacrifices and challenges of having to say goodbye to someone who is going to war, perhaps for long stretches of time.

As far as visualizing my characters, I tend to discover them as I write. Word by word, line by line. It's never a process of visualizing the cast of characters first, and then writing. It's finding them by writing the story.

Besides writing your own stories, you also help others write their own. What have you learned about yourself as a writer from your experiences teaching?

I've learned through teaching that writers typically have a brutal internal voice. One that can often silence that great sense of intuition that every writer has when it comes to crafting their own unique story. Teaching has taught me to be patient with my own process. To be kind with myself when I'm struggling. Sometimes the best thing I can do is to get up from my desk and just leave the story alone for a bit. Come back to it a day or two later with fresh eyes and a renewed hope for what's on the page.

You live in the Boston area, where the novel takes place, and you render the area's atmosphere so strongly and lovingly throughout the novel. Can you talk about why you chose coastal Massachusetts for the setting of *This Is Home*?

The novel is fiction, but I borrowed some pieces from my own life and went home to my roots for this book. I grew up in the middle apartment of a triple-decker twelve miles outside of Boston. My father was a policeman in town, and we had relatives living in the apartment below us for many years.

One of the things I love about people from this area is their allegiance to the town they grew up in. There's always such a sense of pride, of identity and belonging. With an edge to it sometimes as well. A sort of "I can say anything I want about my hometown, but don't you dare criticize" attitude. It doesn't matter if the town is wealthy and idyllic or income diverse and crowded. Paradise, the fictional town in the novel, is both of these at the same time. Which is true of many towns in Massachusetts, both inland and up and down the coastline. It was true of where I grew up.

I tried to develop a tangible sense of place in the novel because I think most people feel strongly and deeply about where they come from. I think it's true of how the characters in the novel feel about Paradise. I know it's how I feel about my hometown. I guess this book is my best attempt at a love story to my childhood, my house, the old neighborhood.

In your guest post for She Reads, you mention that you went back to school for writing at age thirty-four. Can you talk more about that experience and what drove you to pursue your dreams?

I always wanted to be a writer. I attempted my first novel when I was nineteen. I got the chicken pox and had to stay inside for two weeks so I wrote every day. Then, about ninety pages in, I realized it was awful. I kept writing, but it was always something I did in my spare time. And even then, it was sporadic. Then suddenly I was thirty-four and my third child started preschool, and I sort of looked up from life and realized that I wasn't ever going to be a writer in the sense that I wanted to be if I didn't put my energy in that direction.

I had an unfinished bachelor's degree, so I went back to school part-time. I took some creative writing classes and when I completed my BA, I was accepted into the MFA program as a fiction candidate.

My kids were school age by then and I was working, so the whole process took me about six years, from my first day on campus to my last, but I enjoyed it. It was a gift, really, to be in that learning environment. I'd do it over again in a heartbeat.

You are the founding editor of *ROAR*, a literary magazine supporting women in the arts. What inspired you to found *ROAR*? How has it helped you to connect the larger writing community—and, in turn, how do you think that has helped you?

ROAR magazine started in a publishing class at UMass Boston. I was working as a grad assistant, living an hour away from campus, raising my three children when I took the class. On a personal level, I was very aware of protecting my creative time while trying to balance the other roles in my life.

ROAR was a response to that. A desire to create a physical space where emerging women writers could publish their work. *VIDA* had just come out with their count, and the conversation about gender and publishing informed that decision.

The experience was really valuable within the context of the literary community as *ROAR* was really a team effort—a labor of love for our group of editors. It allowed me the opportunity to work with some extremely talented and inspiring people. We published four issues that we were very proud of, as well as an online component.

It was also enormously helpful to be on the other side of that table. I wasn't a writer in that role but an editor working within a team of editors, having to accept or reject the work of other writers. I learned how subjective the selection process is and how editors really need to fall in love with a story to get behind it. Sometimes there's nothing wrong with a story, it's just not a good fit. That was helpful to keep in mind when I was sending out my own work and piling up a stack of rejections.

How do you deal with writer's block? What drives you to keep going when you figuratively "hit a wall" while writing?
I try not to think of it as writer's block. That's such a negative phrase. Words are important, especially the ones we tell ourselves. So that's not something that's in my vocabulary. When I'm at a difficult point in the writing process—say, starting a new story, which is always tough for me—I try to just show up every day and see what I can do. It's too easy to let the demons of the blank page get in your head. Part of the job is to accept all parts of the

creative process. Some days I'm going to write easily, and other days I might need to do a little digging. The trick is to just keep going. Stay the course.

What are some of your favorite novels or authors? If you had to pick one that you think has inspired you the most, who or what would it be?

If I had to pick one, I'd say Anne Tyler. *Breathing Lessons* is a novel I've read over and over and I still go back to it to see how it's put together, how it moves through time. Even as I'm writing this I'm thinking of a handful of favorites that I reference often. But in terms of a favorite author with a body of work that I cherish, absolutely Anne Tyler.

What do you like to do in your spare time other than writing?

I tend to be a homebody, so I'm fortunate that my home is my favorite place. We spend a lot of our spare time at home, with family and friends. My husband and I have six kids, from teenagers to adults. The older ones have spouses. We have a tidal river in the backyard, a gorgeous view. There's always something going on. Boating and cookouts in the summer. Dinners and game nights. Everyone loves to cook and eat. We call it the last frontier because everyone brings their dogs and we have two labs, so it gets noisy and crowded and pretty chaotic, but we love it.

Are you working on anything now that you'd like to share with us?

I'm working on a novel set on an island off the coast of New England about people who are brought together after an accident leaves a young girl orphaned. It explores the concept of insiders and outsiders and how these labels are formed and perpetuated.

What do you most want readers to take away from *This Is Home*? What emotion do you hope lingers when they close the book?

I hope readers take away from it that they were happy to spend time with these characters and in this story. That's the most I could ever hope for as an author.

And, of course, what does *home* mean to you?

Home to me is the place where I'm most comfortable in my own skin. Where I can just *be*, and that's enough.